YOU CAN'T MAKE THIS $#!+ UP!

Retail: Politics like you've never seen it before!

MIKE TRIGGS

 FriesenPress

One Printers Way
Altona, MB R0G 0B0
Canada

www.friesenpress.com

ISBN
978-1-03-915453-7 (Hardcover)
978-1-03-915452-0 (Paperback)
978-1-03-915454-4 (eBook)

1. FICTION, BIOGRAPHICAL

Distributed to the trade by The Ingram Book Company

This book is dedicated to Kent Patet, (1966-2009) my retail mentor and friend.

I remember Kent telling me on my first day on the sales floor that if I wanted to be a successful retail professional, I would have to do far more than just stand behind a counter and ring up sales. He taught me how to engage my customers, share a story and not let him or her leave the store without a shopping bag in their hand and a smile on their face.

Kent also showed me that I could have a rewarding life after politics if I would just venture out of my deep dark closet and allow my true self to shine through.

Little buddy, you were taken from this world way too soon! May you rest in peace my friend!

Table of Contents

Note From the Author

By all accounts, I was the best little boy in the world. But like most little boys, it didn't take long before a few a few naughty words started to creep into my vocabulary. And naughty words were something that were not tolerated at the Triggs household.

I vividly remember one evening we had just sat down at the kitchen table and started to eat when the doorbell rang. I got up to answer it, and when I returned to the table my dad asked who was at the door.

"Oh, it was just "poopie" Mary Ann. I told her we were eating dinner."

The instant my dad heard that naughty word, he grabbed me by the collar and took me to the bathroom and brushed my teeth with soap.

In retrospect, the word was just "borderline" naughty, but to this day every time I even think of swearing, I remember the taste of that pumice powered, heavy duty, Lava hand soap in my mouth. For that reason, I have chosen to use a *Grawlix*, a string of typographical symbols, used to represent the naughty word on the cover and others that appear throughout the book.

Prologue

I was deep in slumber when my ear-splitting alarm clock went off.

While tempted to hit the snooze button, I just couldn't chance over-sleeping and being late for this morning's finance committee at the Governor's Mansion.

So reluctantly, I jumped out of bed, quickly showered, shaved, warmed up some leftover coffee in the microwave and took one last glance at the presentation I would be giving in a little over an hour.

Even though I felt good about what I had stayed up most of the night preparing, I couldn't help but be on edge as I pulled out of my driveway. To calm my nerves on route to the mansion, I began listening to my favorite Pavoratti CD.

While my Italian isn't the best, I was singing along with Pavoratti's Nessun Dorma when I turned onto Cambridge Road and was about to belt out the aria's dramatic finale – *"Dilegua,o notte! Tramontate, stelle! Tramontate, stelle! All'alba vincerò! Vincerò! Vincerò!* –w*hen it happened my front right tire blew out!

I looked at my watch and it was obvious I had no time to change the tire. So, I pulled my car off to the side of the road and sprinted in pouring rain the six blocks to the mansion.

When I arrived everyone at the dining room table could see I was dripping wet. Everyone except for Governor Hanson, who snarled, "Triggs, you do know that breakfast was at six!"

I attempted to apologize, but all I could get out was, "I'm sorry but I had a...."

That's when Hanson snapped. "I don't want to hear about it. Shut up and sit down."

That's how my day started, like a Puccini tragedy. Only it was going to be all downhill from there.

When it came time for my presentation, I realized the ten copies of our strategic political plan were sitting in my brief case in my car six blocks away. Without the notes or handouts, I had no choice but to wing my speech as best I could. And I felt pretty good about how I pulled it off.

That was until at the close of the meeting, when the governor cornered me near the fireplace and pointed his finger in my face, saying, "You little wet bastard! Don't you ever, ever, EVER arrive for one of these meetings late again! And another thing, what the hell were thinking dripping all over the hardwood floors and priceless antique furniture?"

I was about to say "I had a %^<#ing flat tire" but before I could utter a word, he had spun on his heels and was bounding up the staircase to the second floor.

Tears were starting to flow down my cheek when State Senator Jordon Hillsbury pulled me into the kitchen, out of site of the other committee members.

"Mike, Ing Hanson is an asshole! We all know he's an asshole. But set your feelings aside. He's "our asshole" and it's your job as his campaign manager to get him re-elected!"

I was about to thank him when he pulled me into a long embrace and whispered in my ear, "It's going to be okay."

Little did he know my worst day ever wasn't over yet.

Senator Hillsbury gave me a ride back to my car and asked if I needed any help changing the tire.

"Thanks for the kind offer, senator, but I'm already soaked. There's no reason for both of us to be wet."

By the time I got back to the campaign headquarters, my administrative assistant Helen told me someone was waiting in my office. It was Chip Peters, the political reporter for the Madison State Journal.

"Chip, sorry about my soggy appearance. I had to change a tire after a breakfast meeting at the mansion. What brings you out on this damp morning?"

"I'm here about the list," he said.

"What list?" I inquired.

"Well, if you haven't seen it yet, it's probably best you close the door and sit down before I show it to you."

As I scanned the sheet of paper he handed me I read the title: "Twenty-five Gays and Lesbians Who are Close to Governor Hanson." There were twenty-five names listed and mine was number one on the list.

I jumped to my feet and said, "What the hell?"

Before I could say anything else, Chip interrupted. "Mike, it's something Orville Quisling is shopping around to the press hoping someone takes his bait. But trust me, we think it's sleazy and we're not going to give your primary opponent the satisfaction of printing it. And quite frankly, I could care less who you are sleeping with."

I pounded my fist on the desk and said, "Damn it Chip, I'm not sleeping with anyone!"

"Hey, settle down!" Chip said. "Quisling is a loser. His campaign is going nowhere. He's grasping at anything to get on the front page and the ten o'clock news. For obvious reasons we have no plans to use it, but just in case some other news outlet does, we're going to need a quote from you."

"Seriously?" I pointed to the door. "Get the hell out!"

As he was leaving, he said, "I'm really sorry Mike. You can keep the list."

"Gee, thanks!" I slammed my office door and continued scanning the paper more closely.

Oh my God this is going to destroy people's lives.

In addition to me, two of my seven staffers were mentioned, as was a prominent doctor, the CEO of Milwaukee's biggest bank, a state senator, the dean of the UW law school, and the governor's recently announced nominee for the Wisconsin Supreme Court. And that was just the first eight names.

There was a knock at the door and when I opened it, a quivering Helen said, "I'm sorry to bother you Mike, but Bill Maurer from the Milwaukee Tribune is holding for you on line one, and you have messages to call Ruth Ann Hainsworth from the Associated Press and Jason Rodgers from Channel 11."

"Tell them I am tied up in meetings all morning, I'll get back to them this afternoon."

Behind the closed door I flipped the Rolodex on my desk to the letter Q. I knew that there was a reason I had kept Orville Quisling's business card. I picked up the phone and dialed his number.

After a couple of rings, I heard the smarmy little turd say, "Hello this is Orville Quisling".

"Quisling this is Mike Triggs! If that %^<#ing list of yours ever shows up in print or on the news you better hope to hell you have some very good proof because I will be seeing you in court with a libel suit!"

I could hear him chuckling on the other end of the line.

"Oh, Mike, I've got plenty of proof. All anyone needs to do is look at you and see that you are a snappy dresser. Those snazzy bow ties, shiny black wingtips, and $50 haircuts are all the proof anyone would need to know you are obviously a gay boy!"

I am speechless. There are just no words.

After a brief pause Quisling continued. "We all know that you're in your thirties, not married, and the only woman you are ever seen with is that fat Helen from your campaign headquarters. My wife Juliette tells me Helen is a graduate of the College of Saint Anne, which I've heard is a hotbed of lesbianism."

I couldn't believe what he was saying. But he continued.

"Plus, I've been told from a really reputable source that you do needlepoint!"

"Snappy dresser, shiny shoes, bow ties, the fact I've never married and do needlepoint! If that's your proof I'm guilty on all counts. And what the %^<# do you care what I pay for a haircut?"

He simply laughed and I continued my tirade.

"As a matter of fact, my parents raised me to care about how I look in public. I may be single, but for all intents and purposes I've always been married to my job. Late at night when most married men are in bed with their wives or someone else's wife, I'm at our campaign headquarters figuring out how we're going to whip your ass so bad your kids are going to be embarrassed to go to school the day after the primary.

"And as for my needlepoint hobby, are you $#!"+ting me, Quisling? Maybe you haven't heard that NFL great Rosie Grier did needlepoint! Are you telling me that made him gay?"

He simply responded with, "Well, you never know..."

"When I get home at night my needlepoint is the one thing that I can do to totally take my mind off politics and stupid $#!+heads like you. You might also want to know I've won blue ribbons at the Iowa and North Dakota State Fairs for my needlepoint. Add that to your %^<#ing proof!"

With that, I slammed down the phone.

I assume he got my message.

* * *

For the next three weeks calls continued to come in from reporters around the state. Like Chip Peters, every reporter was critical of Quisling's salacious interest in people's sex lives. In fact, Beau Johnson, the political reporter from Madison's ABC affiliate WKOW, said, "The only thing anyone in the Capitol press room could remember about Quisling's time in the Wisconsin Assembly was his late night 'fact-finding' tour of a State Street adult bookstore and his bill to outlaw the sale of dildos and artificial sex organs."

Eventually when it became apparent the press wasn't going to take his bait, Quisling made sure his list was passed around political circles and of course it was all Republican and Democrat insiders were talking about.

In the meantime, I had dropped 27 pounds, was taking pills to go to sleep at night, and drinking massive amounts of coffee or energy drinks to function during the day. Not even my needlepoint could take my mind off the that frick'n list.

The final shoe dropped when W. K. Ashley, the governor's campaign chair, stopped by the office one morning and announced, "This whole thing with Quisling's list has kind of become a distraction for the campaign and the governor thinks that it would probably be best that you 'take one for the team' and resign."

He looked like he was waiting for me to say something, but when no words formed on my tongue he continued. "Mike, with your talent and abilities you'll have no trouble getting another job. In fact, it might just be a chance to totally reinvent yourself."

Ashley then handed me a check for five thousand dollars and said, "This little token of our appreciation should help tide you over until you get another opportunity."

He stood up, reached over the desk, shook my hand, and said, "We'd like you to have your desk cleaned out by noon so your replacement can hit the ground running this afternoon. And don't worry about it pal, we'll tell people that you left the campaign for health reasons."

Chapter 1

I Will Survive

It has been three months now since I left the campaign. That $5,000 severance check from the Hanson campaign didn't go far, so I sold my house in Madison, put most of my stuff in storage, and moved temporarily to my parent's cabin on Wood Lake near Sheboygan. There I've spent the last couple of weeks sending out resumes, only to receive one rejection letter after another.

It was soon apparent that the Republican Party and its candidates had no interest in hiring someone who had been branded a homosexual, especially in lieu of the salacious rumors that AIDS was the "health reason" why I had exited the governor's campaign.

This morning I woke up crying. Here I was, 39 years old, and fired from the job I loved. It was the career I had trained for and for the first time in my life I was unemployed with no prospects of a position on the horizon.

While I knew I was a survivor, there just didn't appear to be a path forward, at least not immediately.

Then it hit me. I could lie in bed feeling sorry for myself all day or I could get out of these damn sweatpants I've been living in, get showered, shave off that stubble and put on a suit, just like I had done every day of my professional career!

As I finished tying my bow tie it occurred to me that now I was dressed, I really had no place to go and nothing to do.

Then an idea came to me. How about getting a shoeshine?

One of my pet peeves has always been scuffed-up shoes, and since there was nothing really wrong with me but a scuffed-up ego, maybe getting my shoes buffed would be just the ticket for moving on with my life.

Off I went to the Von Oostrom department store for a quick visit to their shoeshine stand. I knew for at least for fifteen minutes I could sit back, relax, and let Leonard Jackson polish, buff, and brush my Allen Edmunds wingtips.

When Leonard inquired how my job was going, I instinctively responded, "Oh okay."

He gave me a skeptical look. "That didn't sound very convincing Mike. What's up buddy?"

I told him I got fired and that I didn't have any ideas for what I was going to do next. Leonard's concerned face suddenly brightened up with a suggestion.

"It's probably not up to your pay grade, but Von Oostrom is always hiring. In fact, if you go up to the Human Resources Office and ask to speak to Devin Krayfisch, tell him I recommended you."

"Crayfish? You mean like a crawdad?" I asked.

Leonard slapped his thigh laughing loudly. "More of a douchebag than a crawdad, but he's the guy you need to see."

I hesitated. "I don't know...." It would be quite a step down to take a job in retail.

"Hey," he continued, "those guys on the selling floor get a commission and you can make good money. With your personality and that wardrobe, you should be hired with no problems."

I still wasn't sure how to react. Then he continued.

"That is unless you can't pass the pee test!"

That sounded like a challenge to me!

After we finished laughing, he said, "The Human Resources Department is on the third floor. Now go up and fill out an application."

So, I did.

He was right about Mr. Krayfisch. The man was every bit as slippery, slimy, and ass-kissing as a douchebag could be. I'm guessing he was in his late twenties, maybe early thirties. A short, skinny little guy, perfect teeth, not a hair out of place, limp handshake and pasted-on fake smile. He kind of reminded me of a grown-up Mormon missionary in an Armani suit.

He walked me across the hall and introduced me to the store manager, Nettie L'Amour. She was a pear shaped, frumpy woman. I'm guessing in her late fifties, wearing an ill-fitting plaid jumper that looked like something a

Catholic school girl might wear. And unlike Mr. Krayfisch's perfectly-styled hair, it looked like she might have cut her own with a steak knife. Not at all what I expected the manager of a classy department store to look like.

After a few pleasantries and a short interview, the two hired me on the spot. They didn't even do a background check or make me pee in a cup!

Even though I had bad vibes about Ms. L'Amour and Mr. Douchebag, I needed the job and Von Oostrom had a stellar reputation in the community. If it didn't work out, at least the paychecks could tide me over until I found something else.

After filling out some paperwork I was told to report for my orientation next Monday at 8 a.m.

So, I was once again gainfully employed, only this time not knowing what I was getting myself into. It certainly couldn't be worse than working for a powerful ingrate who viewed me as nothing more than a political whore who could be tossed aside when his service was no longer needed. No job could possibly be worse than that. Could it?

Chapter 2

Capisce?

Monday, 7:45AM

They told me to park on the third floor of the parking ramp. That was the easy part of my first day on the job.

Since customers always come into Von Oostrom on the ground floor, I just assumed that was how employees would enter the store as well. I took the elevator down, but that was an incorrect assumption, The doors were locked and I took the elevator back up to the third floor.

Had I been paying attention I would have seen the sign that said "Von Oostrom Employees Only."

Unlike the chichi department store where I had often shopped, the inner sanctions of V. O. were kind of dingy. When I walked through the door there was a cage that looked like it was made of chicken wire, I was greeted by what I assumed to be a security guard who snarled, "What do you want?"

I told him I was here for my orientation and he grunted something, pointing to the door on my left.

On the other side I was greeted by Mr. Krayfisch who told me I was the last of the four in the orientation class to arrive and we proceeded to a small training room. There I saw an older (really older) woman with a hair style that reminded me of the Bride of Frankenstein, as well as a young perky blond thing that looked like she may have been a cheerleader, and a beefy redheaded gal with an underbite similar to my neighbor's English Bulldog.

Oddly enough, no one said anything for five minutes, when suddenly a buzzer went off at exactly 8 a.m.

Krayfisch turned off the buzzer and announced, "Well it looks like no one was 'tardy'. You will soon find out that tardiness is not tolerated at Von

Oostrom! Whether you are five minutes or one second late for work you will be counted tardy. Does everyone understand that?"

Everyone nodded yes. But just as we were about to move on, the chubby redhead said, "But what if you oversleep?"

Douchey responded with a blunt, "TARDY!"

The Bride of Frankenstein's hand shot up. "What if it's snowing really hard?"

Perky started to ask, "What if y…."

Before she could even get her question out, the man I was now thinking should be called The Douche snapped, "TARDY."

He seemed to be waiting for me to have an ignorant question as well.

I smiled. "Tardy is tardy, five minutes or one second. If you are late, you are…," then in my douchiest voice said, "TARDY!"

"Okay, people. Now that we understand that simple thing you will notice there is a clear plastic purse in front of you," he continued. "You are to carry it every day in lieu of your regular purse. This is where you will put your car keys, cell phone, sunglasses, and lady things like lipstick, nail files or tampons. Then you check it with Junior, who will be sitting in the cage. You should have met Junior when you came in a few minutes ago. At the end of your shift, you will be able to retrieve your bag after checking out."

We all stared silently at his rambling.

"Capisce?" he asked abruptly.

I rolled my eyes.

Seriously, I thought to myself, *when was the last time anyone said the word Capisce? Does he think he's a New Jersey wise guy or is he just a smart aleck?*

Miss Perky was furiously trying to take notes when she looked up from her notebook and fervently asked, "Is that spelled with a K or a C?" Douchie ignored her question.

Another eye roll.

I know this is going to be a long day.

Mr. Krayfisch cracked his knuckles, saying, "Now that we have that little bit of housekeeping out of the way…"

My hand shot up, "What if you don't carry a purse or don't own any girl stuff?"

"You've got car keys, don't you?" he said disgustingly. He then went back to repeat, "Now that we have that little bit of housekeeping out of the way"

I again interrupted, "What if you ride your bike to work?"

I can tell I'm starting to really get under his skin, and I enjoy it!

"Do you plan to ride your bike to work?"

"I don't own a bike," I responded with a smile.

"Then why the hell did you ask the question?" His upper lip was starting to quiver and I could see his teeth grinding.

I wanted in the worst way to ask him what a tampon is!

But I decided not to push him to his boiling point. It was obvious he was getting close to losing it.

He started over on his "housekeeping" spiel and when finished the little weasel said, "We probably should have introduced ourselves at the beginning of this orientation but I was so anxious to go over our expectations for arriving to work on time I guess I forgot."

He went first, telling us that his name is Homer Krayfisch the third, but he prefers to be called Devin. He was from Heber, Utah and had been a Mormon missionary in Bolivia before becoming a BYU graduate. For fun he said he likes show tunes, aerobics, and putting together jigsaw puzzles.

I knew it! The minute I laid eyes on this guy I knew he was a Mormon. Everything about him screamed Mormon Missionary! The dark suit, the skinny tie, the white shirt, the sober look. The only thing missing was the cheesy smile.

Homer/Devin then pointed to The Bride. She told us her name is Tonette and that she has been doing hair for 34 years. She said she likes to play Yahtzee with her grandkids and would be working in the Evening Gown Department.

Tonette?! What the hell kind of name is Tonette? I thought a tonette was a plastic flute that I learned to play in elementary school. And that hairstyle might have been popular 34 years ago but you don't see anyone wearing it today for cripes sake.

The chubby redhead told us her name is June LaFarge and said she was recently divorced after her husband had taken off with a younger model.

She said "she's not bitter" but I'm dubious.

June told us she spends her newfound spare time emailing a guy from Aruba. She enthusiastically told us that her fourteen years at the Panty World

Outlet store in Cedarburg has prepared her for her new job as the manager of Von Oostrom's Intimate Things & Stuff Department.

Intimate Things! Intimate Things! What the hell do they sell in Intimate Things & Stuff? Edible Underpants, dildos, maybe handcuffs? I'll bet she'll have all kinds of things to write about to her pal in Aruba!

Since I could see that Perky was chomping at the bit to talk, I asked if she'd like to go next.

"My name is Roxanne Dubbert. I'm a recent graduate of the University of Wisconsin in fashion merchandising. My cousin Bart is Devin's boyfriend and he recommended me for the job."

I could see Devin was grinding his teeth again. He interrupted, "I think I need to clear something up. Bart is not, I repeat, not my boyfriend! He rents a room in my basement, but he is not my boyfriend. Is that clear? I am 100% heterosexual and have a girlfriend back in Utah."

Oh brother, a girlfriend back home. You mean one that you probably haven't seen in six years?

Roxanne looked a little stunned but continued. "I almost forgot to say I was a cheerleader for girl's lacrosse team. Go Badgers! I can't wait to start in the Activewear Department."

I knew it. Miss Perky was right out of cheerleader central casting. But who knew they had cheerleaders for lacrosse?

Finally, it was my turn to talk. "My name is Mike Triggs and I was Elizabeth Taylor's chauffeur. I'll be working in the Men's Furnishings Department."

The group didn't know whether to laugh or act surprised, so they just stared at me.

Then Homer/Devin gleefully added, "Mike failed to mention that he had a distinguished career working in politics for President Bush, as well as a Senator from one of the Dakotas, and was recently fired as the campaign manager for our own Governor Ing Hanson's re-election."

That was a part of my background I didn't want others to know about. Jeeez, I know I'm going to hate this guy!

Krayfisch looked at his watch. "I think this is a good time for us to take a little tinkle break."

I shook my head and thought to myself, did he just say "tinkle break?"

As I was about to leave the room, out of the corner of my eye I saw Mr. Douchebag pointing his finger at Miss Perky and screaming, "He is not my %^<#ing boyfriend, CAPISCE!"

The rest of our morning was taken up by a walk through the various departments in the store and watching a two-hour documentary on the history of Von Oostrom. The video could have been edited down to fifteen minutes. I mean hey we are not talking the Kennedys or Rockefellers.

I tried to keep from dozing as we learned about young Einar Oostrom coming to America from Sweden to make his fortune in the Great Wisconsin Cheese Rush.

While Einar would try his best as a cheese monger in Milwaukee, Kewaskum, and Green Lake, his Colby, Swiss, and Cheddar just couldn't "cut the cheese" when it came to the refined tastes of Wisconsin's cheese-loving population.

Ultimately, he went to work in the Allen Edmonds Shoe Factory putting laces into shoes. While there he met and married another Swedish immigrant by the name of Jennie Youngquist. They eventually moved to Sheboygan where they opened a dry goods store.

After a couple of unfortunate bankruptcies, Einar and Jennie recovered financially and added a "Von" to their last name which gave the family a baronial *"je ne sais quoi"* as they moved up the Sheboygan social strata.

The Von Oostrom's had three sons Floyd, Lloyd, and Boyd. Young Boyd was kidnapped as a child and then died in a boating accident on Lake Michigan at the age of 17. Floyd and Lloyd would follow in their daddy's shoes in 11 states. and they expanded the Von Oostrom family business to 37 stores

Mrs. Von Oostrom was an accomplished pianist and would often be seen performing on the Steinway Grand Piano on ground floor of the flagship store on the corner of New York Avenue and North Fifth Streets. Her favorite tunes included "Rock'n Robin," "New York, New York," and "Do You Know the Way to San Jose," which was odd since they had no California stores.

She also served as President of the Board of the Sheboygan Metropolitan Opera Guild (SMOG).

At the end of the two-hour docu-drama I almost spit my coffee across the room when on the screen a 97-year-old hunched-over Einar Von Oostrom looked up from his wheelchair and said, "No sale is ever final here, because I'm Einar Von Oostrom and I own the damn store."

I asked if Einar was still living and Mr. Douchebag said, "Just in the Von Oostrom family minds. And with that ladies and gentleman we are going to adjourn for lunch. You can either eat in the mall food court or if you brought your lunch, we have a break room on first floor near the women's public restrooms on the south side of the store."

I groaned when I heard him say "And don't even think of changing the TV channel in the break room or the cosmetics girls will rip your heart out. Be back in the training room at by 1:00 and DO NOT BE TARDY."

I wouldn't even think of it.

All four of us newbies arrived back in the training facility where we saw Mr. Krayfisch sitting at the front of the room, hands folded, staring at the timer. Sure enough, at exactly 1:00 the buzzer went off.

"Good, no one was tardy. Apparently, everyone understands the rules," Krayfisch exclaimed gleefully. "We do not tolerate employees who arrive late to work.

"Having said that, sometimes things happen. And when it does Von Oostrom graciously gives our new hires six opportunities to be tardy in your first four months on the job. However, should you be tardy a seventh time, you will immediately be terminated. Capisce?"

All four heads nodded.

"Okay, when you arrived this morning, in addition to your plastic Von Oostrom purse you were given a folder of information and on it you'll find a number paper clipped to the outside. Please unclip that number now. This six-digit number will be your employee number for your entire career at V. O. Please take two minutes to memorize that number."

Of course, we saw Douchie set his timer.

194853. How the hell am I going to remember that number?

I thought and thought about the combination of numbers and tried to put them in terms of historical events.

19 - Richard Nixon's birthday was January 19th:

48 - Arizona was the 48th State to enter the Union.

53 - Oh my god, that's easy. I was born in 1953.

I yelled out, "BINGO – 194853. I've got mine memorized!"

Everyone gave me a funny look.

They are probably thinking I'm a nerd! I guess that's better than being a douchebag.

When the buzzer went off, Krayfisch said, "Okay people come with me and I will show you where the two timeclocks are located."

We walked around the corner to the door we had entered earlier this morning. To the left of the cage, just inside the door, we saw the first time-clock. Junior grunted something, but I couldn't make it out.

We then proceeded to the customer service desk where we met the Customer Service Manager, Nancy Sedaka.

Mr. Krayfisch said, "Nancy's uncle is Neil Sedaka, so we kind of think of her as a celebrity around here."

Since when does having an uncle who is a D-List Celebrity make "her" a celebrity?

We weren't there long.

I'm guessing breaking up isn't very hard to do for Nancy Sedaka.

Then we proceeded down the escalator to first floor to the employee lunchroom where the second time clock was hanging on the wall. Homer/Devin told us that just to be safe, we should plan to punching in seven minutes before the start of our shift so as to not be tardy.

We were shocked to hear him say that we would not be paid for those seven minutes, "V. O. likes eager beavers who are in their department ready to work when your shift starts."

Eager beavers? Is this guy for real?

We trekked back up to third floor where Krayfisch told us to please take the employee handbook out of our folder. I was kind of expecting to find a book or at the very least a booklet, but what I found was an 8 ½" x 11" piece of cardstock imprinted in big block letters "Von Oostrom Employee Handbook" on the front.

When I was about to flip the "Handbook" over Homer snapped, "Do not turn the handbook over!"

We sat there for what seemed like a couple minutes. I guess he wanted us to read or memorize the cover of the handbook. Finally, he said, "You may now turn the Handbook over and read the handbook."

Maybe I'm wrong but I have always assumed that if a book has a cover, something would be found inside that cover. But in this case, all that was printed on the 'back cover' was: "Rule #1 – No sale is ever final here; Rule #2 – There are no other rules."

"Does everyone understand the Handbook?" he asked.

Most of us looked dazed.

"The Von Oostrom family has long thought that the best advertising is the word of mouth we get from a happy customer. So, like you heard Einar say in the video, no sale is ever final here!"

When he didn't get a response, he barked.

"Capisce?"

June's hand shot up. "But what if the item has been worn by the customer?"

"It doesn't matter!" Homer said. "Accept the return!"

The Bride asked, "But what if they don't have a receipt?"

"Doesn't matter. Take it back cheerfully! Give them their money back."

Miss Perky had a puzzled look on her face and clearly didn't get the concept. "But what if they say they paid in cash?"

"Open your cash register and give them cash. If you do not have enough cash in the drawer, call the Customer Service Department and someone will bring you a cash advance to cover the return."

He turned to me and said, "How about you Mike? Do you have any questions?"

I gave him a thumbs up and said, "Nope, I got it. It's not our money. Make the customer happy!"

He seemed pleased for once.

The rest of the afternoon was taken up role playing a couple of sales and return vignettes, learning how to use the cash register and going over company expectations. Do's, don'ts, and dress codes.

All of them seem to be "rules" but I guess if the Von Oostrom family wants to call them expectations it's not worth quibbling over semantics.

We were also each given our own Personal Customer Notebook to keep track of our clientele. We were told that our notebook should be used to cultivate relationships, keep track of purchases, sizes, likes, tract contacts and give us the ability to notify our "Personal Customers" when new collections arrive.

At the end of the orientation Homer awarded the three ladies with a monogrammed V. O. charm, which I presumed was to be worn on a bracelet, and I received a V. O. tie tack.

Who the hell wears charm bracelets anymore and how am I going to wear a tie tack on a bow tie?

Then one final warning from Mr. Douchebag: "Tomorrow is a very important day for you, you'll be released to the sales floor. I expect you to arrive early, stay late, and smile the entire time!"

When he saw that none of us were even close to smiling, he yelled.

"Capisce?"

We nodded.

As I walked past Junior on leaving the store, I thought about being thrown to the wolves on the sales floor the next day.

When I walked out the door clutching my plastic purse and notes from orientation, I couldn't help but wonder, "What just happened?"

So, I went home and wrote it all down and decided that I would start to keep a journal and write about the day's events every night before going to bed.

"Who knows," I thought, "maybe one day I'll turn my journal into a book. Because after all, you just can't make this $#!+ up!"

had raised her hand in a clenched fist, and it looked like Kent was scratching his back, or maybe he was just scratching his butt.

Confused by their signals, I quickly approached the sock customer with my friendliest, "Hi!"

I wasn't prepared for the reaction I got.

"Back off asshole! I'm just looking for black socks and don't need help from you or anyone! Do you understand? I don't need help!"

I started to say, "Sorry, I was just trying to be friendly," but he cut me off mid-sentence.

"Shut your pie hole, buster. I told you I don't need your help and I mean it."

I got as far away as I could and opted to let one of my co-workers get the tiny commission from the $10 sock sale.

I've decided the next time I see Nettie L'Amour I'm going to suggest we come up with uniform hand signals for V. O. associates to communicate with each other.

We could clasp our hands together to signify a needy shopper who wants way too much hand holding and attention; zip our lips to signal the customer is a chatty bitch; put our hand around our throat for the person who talks too much and wastes our time; twist our hands like you're wringing out a wet rag when you have a real cheap skate; and fold hands in prayer for that customer only God can help.

Then there are the shoppers who have said they are just looking, but it is obvious from overheard remarks that they are clearly in the wrong section of the store. Most would prefer to wander aimlessly on their mission, only to leave the department saying, "I can never find what I'm looking for in this store."

The customers who are on cellphones the entire time they are shopping really get my goat. You end up communicating with little waves, smiles, pointing, more smiles, and thumbs up signs as you hand them their receipt with the boxed merchandise.

Today a guy was blabbing away on his phone as I boxed three dress shirts. His buddy on the other end of the line was so loud I could hear both sides of the conversation all too well.

I listened to the faceless voice say, "We need to do lunch someday."

My customer responded, "Sounds like a great idea. Are you up for today?"

"Sure," I heard from the phone, "I'll meet you in twenty minutes at the Titty Bar."

Who knew they had food at a Titty Bar? I wonder if I could get a tossed salad?

I probably should have asked, but of course the customer was on the phone and I didn't want to disturb such a titillating conversation.

Chapter 11

Byron

Thursday, 9-6 Shift

Every day at lunch I have noticed a deathly pale and emaciated guy with protruding, brilliant blue eyes that is eating alone. His lunch never varies - a can of sardines, saltine crackers, a boiled egg, and a carton of strawberry yogurt. I've observed he is always wearing a Green Bay Packers hat with headphones plugged into to his Sony Walkman and doing a crossword puzzle.

Today I decided I was going to ask to join him and I was so glad I did. His name is Byron and he told me the most tragic story. He has AIDS and had recently returned from Florida to say goodbye to his sister there because he fears he doesn't have much longer to live.

He had driven all the way to Sarasota and when he got there his sister was so afraid of contacting the disease, she had refused to let him come in to see his niece and nephew. She spoke to him for less than two minutes through the closed screen door before asking him to leave.

After telling me that horrible story he must have noticed that my eyes teared up, so he asked if I needed a hug. Hugging is probably prohibited for the workplace, but I felt like he's the one who needed an embrace.

As we hugged, I couldn't help but notice a couple of girls from the cosmetics counter giggling at the sight of two grown men holding each other in the middle of the lunchroom as the tears flowed freely down both our faces.

I'm so looking forward to getting to know Byron better. I really sense he needs a friend.

And come to think of it, I could use a real friend at this place as well.

Friday - 7-4 Shift

I worked with Kent this morning and told him about my lunch yesterday with Byron. He said that he knew Byron was one of the three "out" gay employees at V. O. but he hadn't heard that Byron was HIV+.

I knew that Kent had lost a couple of college classmates to AIDS and that he had walked in Sheboygan's AIDS Walk last fall, so I knew he would want to reach out to Byron.

I couldn't wait for lunchtime to come because I wanted to get to know Byron better as he was the first person, I have personally known to have the disease and wanted to be supportive.

Byron's eyes lit up when I sat down beside him. He immediately took off his headphones.

"I don't want to interrupt anything," I said. But secretly did.

"No problem. I was just listening to an ABBA cassette that I've heard hundreds of times."

I found out that we were the same age and our high schools were in the same athletic conference, although neither of us had been athletes.

Just like Kent, Byron had a twin sister. However, unlike Kent's sister who was very close to her gay brother, Byron's sister had mostly shut him out of her life because of his sexuality. Once he had been diagnosed with AIDS, she had cut him off entirely.

When I asked about his parents, Byron somberly said they were both dead. Apparently, he and his mother had always been close but he felt he had always been a disappointment to his father. By the anger in his voice, it was obvious there was more to his story but I decided to save those questions for another lunch.

As we talked, I couldn't help but notice the big diamond ring on his bony, withered hand. I asked if he had a partner.

"I did for almost eleven years but I lost him to cancer five years ago next month. Dick and I always hoped to one day get married, but that's something that will obviously never happen in this country," he said with tears rolling down his cheeks. "I bought the ring after his death with some of his life insurance money to remind me of the life we shared together."

I put my hand on his. "Byron, one day you and Dick will be reunited in heaven where you will get to spend all eternity together. Love is love and I'm sure they will have same sex marriages in heaven." He smiled. His half-hour lunch break was coming to a quick end so we would hopefully finish the conversation on Monday.

Back on the sales floor I finished putting out the rest of the new stock Kent and I had unpacked this morning. I am so glad that I decided not to open a Von Oostrom credit account when I started here. There is always something new I'd like to buy and I can only imagine what kind of a credit payment I would have to make. When I know it's a cash sale it is much harder to part with the money in my wallet.

I had just finished with the stock and who walks into the department but our store manager, better known as General L'Amour.

She snapped at me immediately. "If you don't have anything better to do than stand with your thumb up your butt, then grab a rag and start dusting."

I despise that bitch! For someone with a name that means "love" (albeit in French) she sure is filled with hate.

But then I thought about Byron and how hatred of anyone will never result in love, so I decided to turn the other cheek, pick up a rag, put a smile on my face, and see if I could prove to my boss that my name could be the one that really means love.

Saturday, 9:45-6

I saw Petites Department Manager Judy Conniver this morning while waiting to punch in for my shift. "I sure have enjoyed getting to know your stock guy Byron," I said, making conversation.

She put both arms up in alarm, "I'd be careful if I were you. He has AIDS you know!"

There it was again—more subtle hatred.

"Thanks Judy, I know. But you can't catch AIDS from talking to someone or just being nice to a person who is HIV positive."

"That might be true," she said, "but I can tell you he creeps me out and all the girls on my team resent having to use disinfectants to wipe down everything he touches. We shouldn't have to work with someone like that."

I was incredulous and didn't know how to react to such an ignorant statement. But she continued.

"If our Von Oostrom customers knew we had someone like that working here they would shop elsewhere. I shouldn't have to lose commissions because store management doesn't have the courage to fire a walking time bomb that could explode all over us."

I decided to be blunt with her. "Judy, you of all people should know better. Your husband is a heart surgeon for crying out loud! I don't think your loss of a couple hundred dollars in commissions would ever make a dent in your family budget!"

She just turned and huffed off. I normally try to be loving person, but it's difficult when supposedly intelligent people spew such hate.

Tuesday, 7-4 Shift

This early morning shift is the least favorite of all I work. Spending my first hour vacuuming the department sure isn't my idea of a fun time. I can hardly get motivated to vacuum at home!

Fortunately, Kent and Queen came in at 8:00 and the three of us spent the next couple hours unpacking two big boxes of silk pajamas and put dozens of fill-ins in the Ray-Ban sunglasses display case.

I had lunch with Byron again. He looked like death warmed over, but considering he just had another round of chemo he seemed to be in really good spirits.

He said he was looking forward to a Wisconsin Nude Dudes party this weekend in Port Washington.

"Nude Dudes? I didn't know you were into that!"

"Oh, for crying out loud Mike, don't be such a prude. It's just an all-male nudist group who get together for monthly events, usually in members' homes. We've got bi, gay, and straight guys who are members."

I kind of winced when he was telling me about it.

"Don't be so pinched up buddy," he said. "There's nothing sexual about it. We even have some Republicans, so you would feel right at home if you'd ever want to come along with me to check it out."

"I don't know. That's just a little out of my comfort zone."

"Listen I know you've been nude in the locker room at your health club and probably even sat nude in the sauna. And I'm going to guess that you have even probably gone skinny dipping in some Wisconsin lake at some point in your life."

We both chuckled. He got me. "I guess I'm guilty on all counts. But just the same, I think I'll pass."

"You'll be sorry. We always have great potlucks. Sometimes we go hiking, have pool parties, go bowling after-hours, and one of my favorite events every summer is canuding."

I must have looked puzzled.

"Oh, that's canoeing nude." he explained.

"Well, I'll think about it," I said. "But this weekend I need to trim the brush on the shoreline up at my parent's cabin. It's getting so overgrown mom says it's hard for them to see the lake."

I don't know if I ever could go naked in front of a group of guys or go canoeing nude. But if I ever did, I know that I would have to trim my own overgrown bush first!

Wednesday, Day off

Who could possibly be calling at 8:25 in the morning on my day off?

I thought of not answering and going back to sleep but the damn phone just kept ringing and ringing, so I forced myself out of bed and picked up the phone.

It was Kent and from the sound of his voice he was crying. He said that shortly after he got to the store this morning, he heard a blood curdling scream that appeared to be coming from the second floor. Then he saw Judy Conniver running out of her stockroom yelling, "He's dead, he's dead!"

Kent was crying uncontrollably. Finally, he spit out, "Mike, it's Byron. Judy found him in their stockroom. There is blood all over the place and the police are just arriving. At this point no one knows for sure if he was murdered, or what happened."

I sat there absolutely stunned. Byron and I had lunch together the day before and everything was fine. We laughed, we joked, and now he was dead.

He said he'd call me back when they knew something more. About 11:30 I got another call from Kent and he said that the police had ruled out murder and speculated that Byron had been dead for at least fifteen hours. The medical examiner had said Byron most likely had fallen and experienced a major head wound. It appeared Byron had fallen multiple times slipping on his own blood and ultimately bleeding out. Which probably explained why the back room looked like a crime scene.

There were so many questions running through my mind. Why hadn't someone heard his calls for help? Why didn't anyone find him yesterday when the store was open? How could this happen?

I tried calling back several times for more details. No one knew anything new but Queen did say that Nettie L'Amour had showed some real leadership and delayed the store opening until noon. Apparently, the Petite girls had been sent home as their department was cordoned off with yellow crime scene tape.

I'm just sick. We all knew he was dying but why now? Why this way? And could I have done anything to help him?

Thursday, Day off

After all that happened yesterday, I'm so glad I had two days off in a row. I'm not sure how I could have gone to work, put on a smile, and acted like everything was normal. It's not. Not yet.

Friday, Noon-9 Shift

I didn't want to go to work but I'm so glad I did. I needed the outpouring of support I received from my co-workers who knew that Byron and I had become friends. Our customers had also heard about the accident at the store and seemed to genuinely care how all of us were doing.

I'm not sure I could have been up for the typical drama that comes with a Friday night shift, and fortunately I didn't have to work with either Debbie or Frenchie. That would have pushed me right over the edge.

At one point in the afternoon a little girl looked up and said, "You look sad, mister."

I said, "I am sad. I lost a friend this week."

The sweet little thing intuitively said, "Can I give you a hug?"

"Of course, you can," I answered. "Of course, you can."

I just wish I could have given Byron one last hug too.

Chapter 12

Byron's Family

I usually wouldn't have much good to say about a funeral, but Byron's this morning brightened my day like nothing I could have ever imagined.

While both Von Oostrom management and the Petites Department staff sent beautiful floral bouquets, neither Nettie L'Amour, Devin Krayfisch, Judy Conniver, or any of the Petites team could see it in their hearts to be there. Kent, Nancy Sedaka and I were Byron's only co-workers to attend.

Byron had told me that he was never a religious person, so I wasn't surprised when I heard that his memorial service was being held at the Northwest Funeral home's private chapel.

When we got to the place, inside the entry we found pictures of Byron and friends on three large poster boards on easels that apparently, he had put together himself, anticipating his death. Nancy remarked how happy he looked in all of the pictures. And she was right.

The photos showed him as a child, with his beloved pets, having fun in bars, partying with drag queens, at backyard barbecues, on boats, riding bikes, marching in Pride parades, and at the AIDS walk.

One of the poster boards was devoted to his Nude Dudes. While all of the pictures had been appropriately cropped for the occasion, we couldn't help but notice one of the pictures had a little flap of pink construction paper attached to it. Masking tape on the flap was like an invitation to lift it up to see what was under it.

Of course, I was the one who had to lift it up. Underneath he had drawn a smiley face and written, "I knew you would look." That was so typical of Byron's sense of humor.

When we entered the chapel, we were introduced to his twin sister and her husband, who had flown in from Florida for the service. We expressed our condolences but neither of them showed any interest in what we had to say.

It was also quite noticeable that there were two sides of Byron's life represented at the funeral. While the three of us, the sister, and her husband were all dressed up, the right-hand side of the room were men of all ages dressed casually in rainbow-colored assortment of shorts and t-shirts. And considering where we were, they appeared to be a raucous fun-loving group.

Before we took our seats on the wild side of the room, we walked up to the casket to pay our respects. Byron was wearing his Green Bay Packers ball cap and a purple AIDS Walk polo shirt. Placed beside him were a couple dozen of his favorite cassettes, his Sony Walkman, and his headphones. Standing guard at both ends of the casket were two giant flamingos, whose heads and bodies were Mylar balloons connected with a crape paper necks and legs attached to cardboard feet.

At the beginning of the service the funeral director announced that Byron had known that he was dying and had planned out his service several months ago. He had specifically requested that there be no traditional organ music or eulogy. In fact, the music he had selected were Sister Sludge's "We Are Family," The Village People's "YMCA," and Donna Summer's "Last Dance," all of which were favorites from the disco era that he had loved so much.

At the end of "We Are Family," the funeral director said Byron had told him that family isn't always blood. It's the people in your life who want you in theirs, the ones who accept you for who you are. Your real family are those who would do anything to see you smile and who love you no matter what.

Ironically, as if on cue, Byron's twin sister and brother-in-law got up and exited the chapel never shedding a tear.

The director continued, "Byron also told me that it is virtuously impossible to listen to the next song while sitting. So, he encouraged you to stand, sing along, and spell out the letters."

And we did. The song was performed by those in attendance just as Byron would have wanted. What Byron could not have anticipated was half way through the Village People anthem, the air-conditioning kicked in, causing the two flamingo's heads to start bobbing up and down to the beat. At the end of the tune, they both turned simultaneously and actually started walking down the center aisle.

Kent and I, sitting in the back row, picked up the flamingos and returned them to their posts at the ends of the casket where they never moved again.

We laughed, we cried, we laughed some more.

As we caught our breath the funeral director said that Byron had also told him that there is only one thing that is certain in life and that is death. It was Byron's last request that his friends and any family there to approach the remainder of our lives as if it were our last dance, to cherish and embrace every moment of it.

There were no dry eyes when Donna Summer sang her last note.

At that point the funeral director walked over to a boombox, put in a cassette, and pushed play. What we heard shocked us.

"Hello everyone."

It was Byron's voice.

"Everyone who knows me knows that I always get the last word. And today is no exception. I want you to know how much I love each and every one of you. You are my family. Thank you for coming today. But before you leave, I want you each to think of a cause that is worth working for and work for it. Dedicate your life to finding what is good in this world and enjoy this dance as if it were your last."

As Byron finished speaking the funeral director walked to the casket, placed the headphones on Byron's ears and pushed play on the Walkman. As he returned to his seat, we heard the cassette deck play Judy Garland singing the words, "Somewhere, over the rainbow...."

And when that song finished, there was a short pause before we heard Louis Armstrong's voice. His classic song ended with, "And I think to myself what a wonderful world."

As they closed the casket at the end of the song, I thought to myself how blessed I was to have known Byron. If only for a few short weeks.

We mingled afterward and met Byron's rowdy friends. In the back of my mind, I had to wonder who among them were part of his Nude Dudes group. I'm sure he would have found it funny that I was trying to picture his funeral friends without their clothes on.

As we left the chapel, I told the funeral director how moved I was by the service and how sad I was that Byron's sister and her husband left before it ended.

He held my hand and said, "Don't be sad, they were only here for Byron's ring and could not believe that he had left his entire estate, including the ring that she so coveted, to the AIDS Resource Center of Wisconsin."

In the end Byron knew who his real family was, those who loved him no matter what.

Chapter 13

Homecoming Dance

Thursday, 7-4 Shift

Last week Ruth Ann Clements and her "Little Darlin" son Bobbie Jr. were shopping for a suit for his first homecoming dance.

The kid looked like he was about fourteen. Pimply-faced, with braces on his teeth, a skinny thing that probably should have been shopping in the boy's department but after quite a bit of work we finally managed to get him into a navy 36 Short suit.

Ruth Ann filled me in on the family's whole story while her "Little Darlin" was in the dressing room. For some reason she thought I needed to know that her husband, Bobbie Sr. owned the Clements BMW/Mercedes dealership. They live out at Wood Lake Estates, are members of the prestigious Whistling Straits Golf Club, and she is the President of the Sheboygan Junior League.

Actually, I don't need to know any of that...or care, for that matter.

The whole time we spent together picking out the suit, shirt, tie, and shoes she gushed over how her "Little Darlin" was on the Junior Varsity Football team and that her "Little Darlin" was on the Honor Roll at Trinity Academy Christian School.

So, who comes in first thing this morning returning everything they had purchased last week? Ruth Ann Clements, although this time her "Little Darlin" wasn't with her.

Her story today was that the kids just grow so quickly at that age, they decided Bobbie Jr. would just wear his older brother's suit, shirt, tie and shoes to Homecoming.

Of course, I cheerfully completed the return. But before giving her the receipt, I asked, "Did your 'Little Darlin' have a good time at the dance?"

That was all it took. "I'm so glad you asked. You've got to see the pictures!" *I have to try to feign interest, even if I did just lose a commission!*

She squealed with delight as she showed me Polaroid pictures of the couple with their corsage and boutonniere posing by the Clements' massive faux Tuscan-style fireplace.

"You know, my 'Little Darlin' said he and his date had such a fun time Friday night. Don't you think they made a cute couple?"

I nodded politely. The girl really was a little hottie.

But then I noticed something.

I was tempted to say, "What a coincidence that your son is wearing the exact same navy suit, shirt, tie, and shoes that you are returning this morning."

Instead, I thought I'd just zip it, and smiled politely as she left.

Previously worn items can't be placed back in the rack, they have to be marked out of stock. I guess Von Oostrom just cuts it's losses on those returns. I got busy so wasn't able to process them right away, but I had quite a surprise when I finally got around to taking care of her returned clothes.

It appeared that mama's "Little Darlin" got lucky on Friday night. I found a condom wrapper in the suit's jacket pocket. And daddy would be so proud knowing that his "talk" with his son before the dance about using protection had sunk in.

Isn't that the way it always goes? The people with the most money are always the cheapest SOBs on the planet. I guess that's why they have the mansion at Wood Lake Estates and I'm here at the V. O. counter marking their previously worn returns out of stock.

Ironically, about ten days ago I had another Trinity Academy Christian School freshman named Zach that was also in shopping for clothes for the upcoming homecoming dance. I asked if he had a nice date.

He replied kind of reluctantly, "Well, she's my mom's best friend's daughter. My mom nixed the girl I wanted to ask to the dance because she was too slutty."

I have to wonder if the hottie the Clements kid took to homecoming might have been Zach's first choice? Hopefully in a couple years Zach will be able to make his own dating choices.

Chapter 14

Surprises

Tuesday, 7-4 Shift

There was lots of stock to put out again today. Pajamas, underpants, socks, ties . . . you name it, we got it all.

As usual Frenchie wasn't much help, but fortunately a couple of the ladies from the Alterations Department came to help us get everything unpacked before the store opened.

Kent and I always joke that the Alterations ladies are Von Oostrom's International House of Pancakes. We've got seamstresses from Bosnia, Vietnam, Russia, Pakistan, and Kazakhstan.

Had Natasha Pavlov not told us her story, we would have never known she had been a former KGB agent in the former Soviet Union. Our short little babushka with a headscarf tied under her chin and layer after layer of sweaters is nothing like the sexy Natasha Fatale from the animated Rocky and Bullwinkle cartoons that I had loved as a kid.

I just couldn't wrap my head around the fact that this nice little old lady with the thick Russian accent had been a bad-ass Soviet spy. But after the fall of the Soviet Union, she and her husband Boris had immigrated to Wisconsin. And from her stories, there is obviously no love lost on her old nemesis, Vladimir Putin.

"Don't eva tvust dat man!" she said, although she sang the praises of Nikita Khrushchev and her brother-in-law Valentin Pavlov, who had spent a couple of months as prime minister under Gorbachev.

While Natasha was quite the talker, it was a little harder to get to know Bahija Hasni, who had immigrated with her husband from Kazakhstan. Bahija's English is excellent and it's difficult to notice any accent at all. She is a very devout Muslim and always wears the most beautiful ankle length dresses and the hijab which covers her head.

Bahija is without a doubt the best seamstress on our staff and would be the one I would call if I needed alterations of my own.

It's amazing what you can get to know about people when you work with them closely for a couple of hours. They always seem to be full of surprises.

For instance, this afternoon Kent brought in his new dachshund puppy named Hank for us to meet.

Suzanna said, "Oh a little Kielbasa doggie." She let Hank give her dog kisses as she squeezed him tightly. I would have never guessed her to be a dog person.

"I've always wanted a dog, but I just couldn't get one at this point in my life. So, until that day comes, I'll have to be content to be Hank's "doggie uncle".

In the early afternoon I had the cutest little old man come in. He had a WWII hat on, so I'm guessing he had to be at least 90 years old.

He was looking at Tommy Bahama Hawaiian shirts, so I asked him if he had a trip to Hawaiian Islands coming up.

"No, I've just always wanted to have a Hawaiian shirt and this one here has kind of caught my fancy."

"Well, if you have always wanted one, and you've found one you like, it sounds like you better get it," I said in my best salesman voice.

He happily agreed. And as I handed him his shopping bag, I couldn't help but think he had to be the most satisfied customer I had ever helped. I just wish he had tried it on so I could have seen him in it.

Unfortunately, about an hour later a wrinkled up old female prune marched up to my counter and before I could greet her appropriately, she said, "I'm returning this. There is NO WAY I'm allowing my husband to wear a shirt with NUDIE GIRLS on it!"

"I'm sorry ma'am, but those aren't exactly 'nudie girls.' If you look closely, you can see they are wearing grass hula skirts and coconut shell tops. And besides they can't be more than a half inch tall."

She gave me a pinched-up look and said, "Well, I know what they have on underneath!"

I wanted in the worst way to say, "The same thing you have under your bra and panties!" But of course, I didn't and cheerfully returned the shirt to her husband's account.

As she left, I felt sorry for the old guy. All his life he has wanted a Hawaiian shirt and that old bat had to throw cold water on his dream. It was apparent who calls the shots in that family.

It's interesting there are so many guys who can't make a decision about buying clothing without "talking to the boss." I guess the old guy who wanted the Hawaiian shirt isn't the only one that has an old battle ax at home ready to critique his every move.

My final surprise came in the middle of the afternoon when I was in the department alone. The ladies in my department had told me about a creepy guy who comes in shopping for shaving cream in a tub and he showed up on my shift for the first time.

He looked normal enough when he brought the tub of "The Art of Shaving" cream up to the counter. But then he unscrewed the lid and said he wanted me to test how fresh it was by sticking my finger in it and giving it a stir.

Ewwwwww. Who does something like that? It's just gross!

"I'm not doing it!" I said indignantly.

"Well how am I going to tell if it's fresh? The girls always do it for me."

"I'm sorry," I said. "I guess you're just going to have to come back when one of the girls is here."

He stormed off and I didn't really care that I had missed a fifty-dollar sale. I'm not sticking my finger in a shaving cream tub for a fifty-cent commission!

Chapter 15

Workout Sweat

Thursday, 8-5 Shift

I hope there is an especially warm corner of hell for the inventor of women's plus size yoga pants.

This morning an extremely large woman came in the department wearing a jogging-bra and tight-fitting yoga pants. It was obvious from the sweat dripping from her face that she had just come from an aerobics or Pilates class or some kind of workout.

She dripped her way through the department in search for the perfect necktie. At one point I looked down and noticed a pool of water forming around her shoes. I thought perhaps she was pregnant and her water had broken, but then decided she just hadn't taken enough time for an appropriate cool-down or shower before leaving the club.

I wasn't prepared for what happened next. When we got up to my cash register to pay for the tie, she reached down the front of her yoga pants and pulled out a sopping wet $100 bill.

Ewwwwww! Do I touch it? Of course, I have to touch it…it has to go in the register!

Like a consummate professional, I smiled nicely, picked up the moist bill, gave her the change, closed the register as quickly as possible, and thanked her for the pleasure helping her with her purchase.

Then I squirted about a pound of sanitizer on my hand.

A little later when I was telling Kent the story he asked, "What did she do with the change?"

"I couldn't look. I had already seen way more than I needed to see. Way more!"

Oh, if I could see Debby's face tonight when she closes the register and finds that still-wet, stinky hundred-dollar bill.

Speaking of sweaty, I stopped for a workout of my own after my shift.

After doing twenty minutes on the treadmill, I was sitting in the sauna with another old guy, and in walks a nice-looking guy who was in his mid-twenties. He took off his towel, spread it out on the bench and sat proudly in his birthday suit. Most guys would have wrapped themselves in a towel on or worn a swimming suit, but this guy was apparently very comfortable in his skin.

I couldn't help but notice that not only did he have more tattoos than I could count, but that both of his nipples were pierced and were about to get mighty hot in a few minutes.

There seemed to be a theme going on with his tats. Virtually all of them were cartoon caricatures. He had Roadrunner and Coyote on one arm, Popeye and Olive Oil on the other, the Tasmanian Devil on his butt cheek, and what looked like the upper half of Pinocchio's head under his belly button.

I kept thinking, "Please, oh please, I hope he doesn't tell any lies while we're sitting here."

Finally, I worked up the courage and said, "I can't help but notice that there is hardly an inch of your body that isn't covered by tattoos."

The guy proudly smiled. "Yah, I am thinking of shaving my head and having a tat of a bulldog with his leg up taking a piss tattooed on the side of my head."

Trying to think of a quick comeback I said, "Well, if you decide you don't like it you can always grow your hair out."

Then the old guy who was with me in the sauna piped up, "On the other hand, when you get to be my age you might not have any hair. What are you going to do then?"

I laughed and said, "When I was your age, I thought about getting an Izod alligator tattooed over my left breast. But I'd look pretty foolish now that I have all this hair on my chest. It would look like an alligator in a forest."

We all had a good laugh.

I'm serious hoping the kid comes to his senses. I love dogs but who needs to see a pissing bulldog on a man's bald head.

Chapter 16

The Unexpected Trip
to Milwaukee

Friday, Day off

Yesterday afternoon Kent said that he noticed that neither of us have to work today and he wondered if I would like to ride with him to Milwaukee. He said he was doing a "hand carry" that he'd be dropping off at the Pfister Hotel and coming back tonight.

"What the hell is a 'hand carry?'" I asked.

"Well, I sold a Hickey Freeman suit to the CEO of the Kohler Corporation and we had a problem with the alteration. He wasn't able to pick it up before he left for a weekend conference in Milwaukee. In this case, since it was our fault, I am going to be delivering the suit to the front desk of his hotel."

I thought the kid was going out of his way to provide customer service.

"The good thing," he continued, "Von Oostrom pays me 45 cents a mile for doing the hand carry. So, I get my base pay for the hour down and back, $54.00 in mileage, and usually the customer is so wowed by the service that he writes a letter which means I get another $10 in 'Kudo Cash' from Nettie L'Amour. I make out like a bandit."

I didn't have any plans today so I thought, "Why not?" And I always have a fun time hanging out with Kent.

The Pfister Hotel was built in the 1890's and is one of Milwaukee's magnificent landmarks. I always enjoy looking at its art collection that rivals any hotel in the world. After he delivered the suit, I suggested we have a cocktail in the hotel's lounge before heading back. But Kent said he had a better idea - the La Cage Dance Club.

"Why not? It's Friday night and we can sleep in tomorrow."

When he first mentioned the La Cage Dance Club I commented, "It's French. Ooh La La! I sure hope we won't run into Nettie L'Amour or Frenchie!"

"Oh, I guarantee we won't," Kent chortled.

The minute we walked in the club's door I knew we weren't in Sheboygan anymore. The music was loud, thumping, and there were cute guys and lots of young women everywhere you looked.

"For a minute there I thought you had taken me to a gay bar," I laughed. "But when I saw all the women, I knew that couldn't be."

"Oh, you're right, it is a gay bar. The gals are probably here for a bachelorette party or to ogle the go-go boys. Sometimes it seems like there are more women than men in the place. But that's okay, everybody is just here to dance, drink, and have a good time."

Almost immediately a couple of girls asked me if I wanted to dance. I decided to let loose. Kent was shocked. "You were quite the John Travolta out there on dancing to 'Stayin' Alive.'"

"It was fun. I guess I didn't know what to expect."

"Oh, you were probably thinking someone was going to hit on you. Sorry to break it to you Mike, but you're probably too old for getting propositioned but not old enough for someone to pick you to be their Sugar Daddy."

"Hey, I thought you were a friend," I objected. "Too old? So where do the old guys like me hang out?" I asked with a wink.

"How about we go to the Drag Show upstairs and catch the strippers once the bachelorette girls clear out?"

Oh, if my Republican friends could see me now.

I looked around and fortunately didn't see anyone I knew. That is until we ran into our co-worker's Debby's ex-husband, Stan. He introduced us to his new Filipino boyfriend Gabriel, who looked way younger than either of Stan and Debbby's sons.

We both promised to not tell Debby, but he said, "At this point I don't care."

I laughed my ass off during the drag show. We saw drag queens named Miranda Wrights, Pat McCrotch, Cookie Crumbles, and Penny Foryathots. They lip synced to Cher, Tina Turner, Dianna Ross, and other divas' greatest hits. But the performer who really stood out was Clorox Bleachman. She/he was hilarious and bleach blond, of course. She was just a tiny feminine thing but had a surprisingly deep bass voice that sounded almost like James Earl Jones.

After lip syncing and dancing her way through "Proud Mary," she walked over to a customer's table and opened her purse. Then she pulled out a little battery powered fan, aiming it up her mini skirt. "These panties are moist!" she joked.

You just knew they had to be!

"Every single one of the drag queens looked so good you would never know some of them they were men. Their costumes were totally over the top. The makeup could have been done by one of our girls at the Lancôme counter.

And, how do I say this, but ... everything was very "tucked in."

"Listen buddy," Kent said, "you should hear the screams when they pull off the duct tape!"

What a hoot! I'd pay to see that!

I looked at my watch and said, "Oh my gawd, it's 12:30 in the morning!"

"Well, it isn't like you have a pumpkin carriage to catch Cinderella."

This was way past my bedtime, and we had a long drive home, but believe it or not, I was having a great time. That was, until I glanced to my right and saw one of the strippers out of the corner of my eye. He looked familiar.

It was Damon, the part-time kid from our Young Men's Department. Damon, my female department manager's live-in boyfriend. When he isn't feathering their love nest, lifting weights at the gym, or studying to be a physician's assistant, he apparently has another gig on the side.

Damon had told me he works nights, but who knew he was stripping. And from the number of the fives, tens, and twenties he had stuffed into his lumberjack plaid G-sting he was making quite the haul tonight. Probably way more than Kent would pocket from his hand carry.

Kent ribbed me and said, "Don't worry about Macy. She knows! But when you have a body like Damon you can make big bucks on a Friday or Saturday night. Especially if there are five or six bachelorette parties. Those drunk girls are big tippers. And at this place they never strip all the way."

That lowered my blood pressure knowing that I had seen all there was to see. We ended up staying until Donna Summer's "Last Dance," which reminded me of how much Byron had loved that song. It put me in a melancholy mood for the long drive home.

All in all, it was quite the night. I bet Kent had been thinking up a way to get me to Milwaukee for a long time.

I was also glad Kent asked me to drive his car since he had way too many vodka tonics and he knew I had been drinking Pepsi all night. He may have hand carried the suit down to Milwaukee, but after a wildly unexpected night I had to practically hand carry him into his apartment when we got back to Sheboygan.

Chapter 17

Brats and Sausage

Monday, Noon-9 Shift

The funniest thing happened this evening and I'm still laughing about it.

Who comes in the store but Enid Furbusch. I see Enid in church nearly every Sunday, where she sits alone in the front pew on the left-hand side of the church right in front of Pastor Holbrook. No one and I mean no one, is allowed to sit in that pew other than Enid.

I found out the hard way one Sunday when I came in late and the only seats left in church were in her pew. She told me very loudly, "This is the Furbusch pew! My family has sat in this pew since the church was built and no one but a Furbusch will ever sit here." I saw the pastor snicker as I searched for another seat.

The late Mr. Furbusch had been dead for over twenty years so I was kind of surprised to see her in the men's department tonight. The poor thing has a bad case of osteoporosis and it looks like she has a hard time getting around. But here she was shuffling through the men's underwear in her full-length fur coat and swinging a huge Louis Vuitton handbag.

I greeted her with a big smile, "Well, Mrs. Furbusch, what a pleasant surprise to see you tonight. And may I say, what a beautiful fur coat! What kind of fur is it?"

She is so hunched over, she had to turn her head sideways to say, "It's a shaved beaver."

I was at loss for words as a big smile crept across my face. I wondered if I had heard her right.

As she rubbed her face on her arm, she looked up again and said, "There is nothing quite like a shaved beaver." Then she reached out her arm and said,

"Go ahead, honey, put your face on it." Then she asked, "Is this the first time you've touched a shaved beaver?"

I was so freaking embarrassed that it was all I could do to keep from laughing. Of course, she meant "sheered beaver" but I kept my cool and responded, "Yes, yes as a matter of fact, is my first shaved beaver."

She seemed oblivious to the fun I was having with her. I eventually sold her a package of Irish linen handkerchiefs. She volunteered she always likes to blow her nose on men's linen hankies.

But her exact words were, "I prefer blowing on your men's packages."

I tried to recover but it was too much and I turned away to laugh out loud. Between her beaver and my package, this conversation had suddenly become very uncomfortable.

Tuesday, 10-7 Shift

Shortly after opening this morning, a mother came in with seven kids. The oldest couldn't have been more than twelve. I said, "Hi kids, no school today?"

The oldest girl snapped back, "We don't go to school, we're home schooled." She then scolded me saying, "And we're little children, not kids. Kids are baby goats and the goat is a sign of the devil."

I can just imagine that home schooling lesson. "Listen up kids, today we're going to learn about the sign of the devil!"

A guy walked by later and asked if my bow tie was a clip-on. Obviously, he has never met a true bow tie aficionado. I quickly untied and retied it in front of him.

"Wow!" he said. "You make it look so easy. I wish I could do that."

"It actually is easy," I said. "If you can tie your shoes, you can tie a bow tie. It's the exact same knot."

He looked skeptical and responded, "But I don't usually tie my shoes up near my neck." I had to roll my eyes.

Just before my shift ended, I told one of my customers that I was looking forward to my weekend off and he gave me two free tickets to the Brat Eating World Championships that is held right here in Sheboygan. Maybe Joey Chestnut will be there—he recently won the Nathan's Hot Dog Eating Championship for the ninth time, eating 72 hot dogs and buns.

Then a thought hit me, I wonder if I should check with HR to see if I can accept the tickets. We're not allowed to accept tips, but tickets might be allowed. Maybe I'll just keep my mouth shut! What would Nettie L'Amour do if she found out?

Thursday, 7-4 Shift

Someone must have tattled about my Brat Fest tickets!

This morning during her morning announcements, Nancy L'Amour said, "It has been reported to me that an associate in the Men's Department was given tickets by a customer to this weekend's Brat Eating World Championship. I must remind you that accepting anything of value is a violation of V. O. Rules and Regulations, and is grounds for immediate termination."

Bitch! I hate her!

I also hate working the 7 a.m. But on the bright side, I did get to meet the sweet new blond girl in Men's Sportswear this morning. Her name is Kimber Lay, however, I think I'll be calling her Crème Brulee because her hair is a buttery yellow color with brown highlights, just like my favorite dessert. I'm just hoping she'll take a little more time styling her hair it in the morning. That twist on the top of her head is so unbecoming! Of course, every gay guy thinks he's a stylist!

Friday, Noon-9 shift

A guy walks up to my counter and said "I bought this Louis Vuitton purse for my wife and I'd like to have it wrapped."

Immediately alarms went off in my head.

Do we even sell Louis Vuitton? If so, why didn't he have it wrapped by the people in the Handbags Department? Since there wasn't a receipt, was it even paid for? Wouldn't something that fancy come in a box? Do I even have a box big enough to wrap it?

Then the guy says, "Be sure to wrap it in your gold foil wrap with the Von Oostrom coat of arms."

I assured him that V. O.'s high standards will only allow me to wrap it in our custom wrapping paper topped off with a beautiful handmade bow.

When I handed him the wrapped box he said, "How am I ever going to thank you." He gets out his wallet, starts digging through it and finally says, "Do you like breakfast sausage?"

Ummm.....

Then he hands me a dollar off coupon for Jimmy Dean Breakfast Sausage that looked like he had chewed it out of the Sunday newspaper.

For the longest time I had no words. Then finally I said, "Well thank you."

When I told Granny Snatch the story, she informed me that the handbag was obviously a knockoff and he wanted his wife to think it was real since it was wrapped on V. O. wrap.

I thought about turning over the coupon to HR, since it technically was a "thing of value" I wasn't allowed to accept, but since I saw it was expiring in five days, I decided not to tell them about the "gift."

I don't really like Jimmy Dean sausage anyway, so maybe I will just keep it in my wallet to bring out in the future when I retell the story. And trust me, I plan on retelling the story every chance I get!

Chapter 18

Pianists

Monday, Noon-9 Shift

One of the traditions that customers seem to really like at Von Oostrom is the grand piano located at the center of each store. From the time every store opens until the time it closes a pianist will be tickling the ivories, only taking short breaks throughout the entire day.

Our V. O. stores use a number of pianists in regular rotation. In ours, Jill Norman was professionally trained at the Julliard School. Her versions of "Clair de Lune" and Beethoven's "Moonlight Sonata" are guaranteed to attract a crowd and bring a tear to my eye.

Unlike Jill, who is a professionally trained pianist, Brian 'Boots' Kooter, plays by ear and has more of a boozy piano bar style. For years he and his Boots Kooter Trio played in Supper Clubs in the Appleton, Fond du Lac, Green Bay, and Sheboygan area. As he aged Brian wanted to stop traveling, so he agreed to share his music with our shoppers.

Whenever I come down the escalator, Boots will frequently ask, "Mark, do you have a favorite?"

For some reason he calls me Mark instead of Mike. I just smile and call out the first tune that comes to mind. Sometimes a puzzled look comes across his face and he says, "Can you hum a few bars for me." And I'll be damned if he can't play it like it had always been part of his repertoire.

Then there is Mrs. Joanna Kerplunkette, whom we all affectionately call Mittens. If you had to describe her musical style the only word that comes to mind is "bad." No, not just bad. "REALLY BAD."

She can't play a single line without at least five wrong notes. Key change? What's that? She keeps right on playing. If she gets bored with what she is playing, she simply switches songs without missing a beat.

The sad thing is she acts like every shift is a concert at Carnegie Hall. There have been times when I have wanted to go over and pull out the fall board (a board that pulls out to cover the keys when not in use) and crush her fat little fingers.

The other day I almost got Mittens fired. I saw her coming in for her shift and asked, "Hey Joanna, did you bring your 'Chorus Line' book with you today?"

She smiled, nodded, and asked if I had any favorite songs from the show. I said," Oh, I have always loved 'One! Singular Sensation' and 'Tits and Ass.'"

Halfway through her rendition of T&A I heard my arch-nemesis manager Nettie L'Amour's stern voice over the public address system, "Will Mrs. Kerplunkette please stop playing that song and come immediately to the store manager's office!"

Someone's in trouble now! And it's my fault!

I avoided Mittens the rest of the day.

I had a quirky customer this morning. He was a little short guy with the bushiest eyebrows I have ever seen. His Scottish accent was so heavy I had to pay attention to every word he said.

When I asked him what he did for a living he handed me his business card which read: Gervice MacKerbin, Registered Piano Technician, Vacuum Cleaner and Vibrator Repair.

The first two I understood but vibrator repair? I decided it was probably best to hold my questions for another day.

I felt so tall next to him as I had the difficult task of helping him find shirts that were small enough for him or that could be easily altered. He told me he would look around on his own, and as I left him, I heard Mittens start playing a medley from "The Wizard of Oz." "Somewhere Over the Rainbow" is one of my favorites.

But just as she was transitioning into playing the Munchkin song, I heard a voice near the tie case say, "Excuse me, excuse me, sir."

I looked down at what appeared to be the top of a child's head above the case with his fingers on the top of it. Thinking it was Kent Patet playing another practical joke on me I started singing to the music.

"We welcome you to Munchkinland, Tra-la-la-la-la-la, Tra-la-la-la-la-la-la."

I went around the corner, looking down expecting to see Kent. But to my surprise it was an honest to God "Little Person." An adult male that had the medical condition called dwarfism.

I was mortified by my insensitivity and began apologizing profusely. Fortunately, the short-statured customer thought it was hilarious. After sharing a good laugh, I sold him a necktie and had our alterations department come to shorten it for him.

As Mittens finished her Oz medley, I could only hope that something similar might happen with my manager Nettie L'Amour. She should show up just as "Ding Dong the Witch Is Dead" is being played.

Chapter 19

Purple and Red

Thursday, 8-5 shift

I had a pretty dull morning and had just come back from lunch when a woman came up to me and asked, "Excuse me, but do you think my husband would like silk boxers?"

Seriously, who asks a complete stranger a question like that? But I tried to approach her question with confidence by saying: "Well, of course he would! Let me show you what I have in stock."

She didn't seem very impressed with the boxer options and said, "It's for our anniversary, maybe you have some sexy silk pajamas."

As we walked to our pajama section I said "We always carry a basic black silk pajama, but I think I might have some bright red and purple silk PJs on the shelf."

Her eyes lit up and she squealed with glee. "I sure hope you have the purple ones in my husband's size."

When I inquired what size he wore, she exclaimed, "He's a Triple Extra Large!"

"Triple Extra Large!" I gasped. "In purple PJs he'd look like Barney!"

I knew immediately that came out very, very wrong. But seriously, I was having a hard time imagining that big of guy in sexy purple silk pajamas!

Fortunately, the lady thought it was hilarious. After we stopped laughing, I sold her a Coach wallet. Much safer. And something that Barney would never wear.

Friday, Noon-9 Shift

I hate working this shift because Friday nights at the mall are so darn boring. And to make matters worse, I got sent to cover the Children's Department from 6:30-9:00!

About half way into my gig in the kids section a four-year-old little boy had a complete meltdown. Not your everyday meltdown, it was more like the "Mother of all Meltdowns." The little brat was punching his pregnant mother and kicking his dad. Hard to believe the parents just kept shopping as if nothing was happening.

It got so bad other shoppers were really getting uncomfortable. I suggested the father might want to take the boy back to the dressing room. Dad didn't seem very happy about the suggestion but he picked the kid up and headed to one of the small changing rooms.

Only now instead of making things better the meltdown grew even worse. When I went back to check on them the kid he was flailing around and crying so hard that he had gotten a nose bleed. There was blood on the wallpaper, the carpet, the ceiling, and even running down the slats on the dressing room doors. It looked like a scene from a Freddy Krueger movie.

Finally, the mother emerged and gave the kid a package of Milk Duds. It was if she had waved a magic wand. The little brat became an instant angel.

Of course, someone needed to clean up the mess after the customers left. And I was the only person working the department.

I had Housekeeping paged, but was told it was after 8:00 p.m. and they had left for the night. I was about to have a meltdown of my own when Janice, the manager in charge, came to my rescue and sent me to the break room to get control of myself. She called Mall Security to put some yellow crime scene tape across the door and decided that we were going to just leave it that way for the night.

She told me that because of the amount of blood involved we would have to call in a company that removes hazardous materials. The carpets would have to be replaced, wallpaper removed, and the entire dressing room professionally repainted.

I can just imagine the look on the face of the Children's Department manager when she comes in tomorrow. I won't be the only one seeing red!

Chapter 20

Take Aim at Trigsey Day

Saturday, 9:45-6 Shift

I had the weirdest thing happen today. When I came back from lunch, I found a Sharper Image shopping bag on my counter. I didn't even look inside. Assuming some customer must have walked off without their package, I took it immediately to Customer Service and gave it to Nancy Sedaka.

By the time I got back to the department the phone was ringing. Nancy was on the other end, saying that apparently there was a gift in the shopping bag and an envelope attached to the box had my name on it.

I wondered who could possibly have left me a gift? I rushed right back to customer service to pick it up.

Had I been following the V. O. rules, I probably should have checked the package with Junior and picked it up on the way out the store. But my curiosity had the best of me so I thought I would go ahead and find out what it was. After all, it isn't every day someone leaves a special gift for their favorite salesperson!

When I got back to my department, I opened the little envelope and a note inside said: "Thinking of you!"

"Who's it from?" Queen asked.

"Well, I'm not sure. The note just says, 'Thinking of you.'"

"That is weird," Kent said. "It's an odd shaped box, I wonder what's in it?"

I carefully removed the beautiful wrapping paper and the words "Batteries Not Included" were the first thing I saw. I was excited that it might be some type of expensive electronics.

But the smile on my face quickly turned to shock as I opened the box and saw it was a Sharper Image electronic nose hair trimmer.

I was mortified! "Who the hell gives a nose hair trimmer for a gift?" I asked them. "This is just sick!"

Kent started chuckling. This had to be one of my co-workers pulling a practical joke on me.

Queen started teasing me. "Looks like Mikey's got a secret admirer!"

I accused them of insulting me with such an insensitive gift, but they both swore up and down that it wasn't them.

"Well, Trigsey, someone obviously thought you needed it," Kent said laughing even harder. "You'll just have to go pick up some batteries and come back tomorrow to show us your trimmed nostrils."

I did not find it funny. "All I can say is you two had better keep your mouths shut about this!" I stuffed the gift back in the bag and hid it under the counter.

If the nose hair trimmer wasn't enough of an insult, later that morning I had a woman who was shopping for a sweater for her husband. When we finally found one that she liked I asked her what size he needed.

"Well, it depends. Sometimes he wears a medium and other times he wears a large."

"Then it sounds like he must be about my size," I said.

"Oh, heaven's no!" She exclaimed. "You're much chubbier than my husband!"

I must have looked pissed by her "chubbier" comment.

"I didn't mean to insult you or anything," she said. "It's not like you are fat. You're just a little porky around the middle."

Actually, she could have stopped with the first insult.

I told her it sounded like he really needed the medium, and I secretly hoped the sweater fit so tightly he couldn't get out of it.

I guess today was kind of a "take aim at Trigsey" day. First, the passive-aggressive anonymous message that my nose hair is offensive and then the blunt in-person "you need to lose some weight" comment. If tomorrow Nettie L'Amour offers me a breath mint, I'm going to quit.

Chapter 21

The Quidnunc

Tuesday, 8-5 Shift

Judge Darnell Beatty's wife Rosemary was in the store this afternoon and as usual she had all kinds of gossip about what was going on at the Sheboygan County Court House.

I could not care less about county politics, but if you really want to know who is porking whom at the courthouse, Rosemary is your go to gal.

While we were shopping, she leaned over and whispered in my ear, "Don't look now, but there is Dorothy Osborn, Judge Wilber Higgenbottom's mistress. She's such a quidnunc!"

That was a word I had never heard before but not wanting to sound like an idiot I smiled and said, "So I've been told."

It seems like you never have a dictionary when you need one. But when I got home tonight, I pulled out my well used Webster's Collegiate and looked up the word.

"Quidnunc: A person who is eager to know the latest gossip; a gossip or busybody."

I had to laugh. The definition could just as well have read, "Rosemary Beatty."

The one thing I will say about that old quidnunc, she never leaves the store without spending at least $500 and when you are working for 1% commission that's another $5.00 bill in my pocket. At least with Rosemary you can be sure she won't be bringing it back.

Chapter 22

Answered Prayers

Tuesday, One Week Later, 7-4 Shift

It was nice to have had a four-day weekend but when I checked on my returns for the days I was off I noticed is that my returns had been 30% higher than days when I am working. Now I know there are times of the year when the return rate is going to be higher, like right after Christmas or Father's Day, but there is something fishy going on.

Every other salesperson's return rate is consistent week after week. Everyone else's except mine, which goes up dramatically every time I take a day off. At the same time Frenchie's return rate is surprisingly always about zero.

I think I am going to call the V. O. Fraud Hotline tomorrow and have them check into it. I just don't trust that woman.

Wednesday, Noon-9 Shift

I had a nice chat with a woman named, Hollyanna at the V. O. Fraud Hotline today who said she would look into my higher than normal returns. She cautioned me that when I'm not there I wouldn't be selling anything to offset the returns I said, "I get that. But even then, I shouldn't consistently have a higher rate of returns on my days I'm off than when I am working."

Today I noticed that Suzanna had a $2,900 return and I don't think she has ever had a $2.900 sale in her life. And of course, it happened on a day when she was off but Frenchie was working. It's just $29 in lost commission dollars that Suzanna will lose, but over time that adds up.

Obviously, something fishy is going on here. It's just not right. *Le poisson pue.*

Friday, 7-4:00 Shift

Kent, Queen, and I got to do a little happy dance this afternoon as everyone in the store watched Frenchie get handcuffed and do the "perp walk" when she was escorted off to jail. Apparently, the Hotline set up a sting and caught her red-handed returning items that she had previously sold on Suzanna's employee number.

For years she has been forcing her co-workers to eat her returns. We're talking thousands of dollars that the little French bitch has been pocketing.

I wish I could have seen the look on Nettie L'Amour's face when she got the news since Frenchie had been Nettie's "Gold Standard" for Customer Service Excellence.

Kent wondered aloud if any of us will ever see any of those fraudulently returned dollars back in our pockets? But, somehow, I doubt it.

All I can say is, "*Au revoir*" to Frenchie. And probably to my commission money too.

One other eventful thing happened today, but I have to explain first that for months now I have been praying every night that something would happen to Debby's charm bracelet. Her constant jingling drives all of us nuts during our shifts. You can be quietly standing there minding your own business and hear Debby jingle jangling like a one-horse open sleigh.

Well today my prayers were answered.

Debby came back from her potty break sobbing uncontrollably. I thought someone had died, but come to find out that when she flushed, her charm bracelet caught on the toilet handle and the bracelet fell off and was sucked down the toilet. Gone forever.

"Oh my God, this is the worst thing that has ever happened to me in my life," she sobbed to us. "I've had that bracelet since I was a little girl. There were over 100 charms on it, from the Wisconsin Dells, the New Ulm Polka Festival, and my honeymoon in Albuquerque."

Newsflash girl – A woman your age should have given up wearing a charm bracelet years ago.

I nodded consolingly.

And who the hell honeymoons in Albuquerque? And besides, you divorced the damn bastard!

By the time she stopped sobbing I was smiling inside. My prayers were answered!

I'm going to just keep on praying. I prayed that we would see the day when Frenchie was no longer here and I prayed that Debby would lose that bracelet. I guess if you just keep at it, sooner or later prayers will be answered.

But who'd a 'thunk' they both would have happened on the same day?

Chapter 23

Stuck in the Ceiling

Saturday, Noon-9 Shift

I got to work a little early so I thought I would relax a little and have a cup of coffee in the lunchroom. The "Sheboygan Press" had a front-page story about how CBRE Commercial Realty had acquired the old Allis-Chalmers factory on Lake Michigan and would be converting it into lofts.

When turning to page six for the conclusion of the story, I saw that most of the page had been unmercifully ripped out of the paper.

I asked my coworkers who were sitting in the lunchroom, "Who the hell ripped something out of today's paper?"

The Bride of Frankenstein looked up from her "National Enquirer" and said, "I'll bet it was Queen from your department. She collects obituaries."

"Obituary collecting? That's a new one," I said. "It seems like you learn something new about co-workers every day."

When I punched in for work and got to the floor, I asked Queen about her "hobby." She told me she's not just interested in just anyone's obituary, she only collects obituaries of "former customers." And apparently, Tootie Friedhof was one of her favorites.

"Oh Mike, you remember Tootie. She was that little old lady with the thick German accent that had a missing tooth and carried that little chihuahua in her purse. I think the dog's name was Cody."

"Now that you mention the dog," I said, "I remember his full name was Cody Pendant. Poor little thing. It had the worst breath."

Queen laughed. "Well, it wasn't as bad as Tootie's gas. OMG that old gal could really let those sauerkraut farts rip."

"That's probably why they called her Tootie," I joked. "And come to think of it, Friedhof is German for cemetery. Sounds like she will be right at home."

It was a fairly quiet for a Saturday but we had a little excitement later in the afternoon when a truck hit a transformer outside the JCPenney store and knocked out the electricity for the entire mall. We had to ask all of our customers to leave because we had no way of ringing up any transactions.

The gates to the mall entrances on all three levels close electronically, but when the power goes off our housekeeping staff had to climb up a ladder and remove a ceiling tile to manually crank the V. O. gates down. Donnetta, the housekeeping supervisor, was so fat that she got wedged into the ceiling tile supports and couldn't get out. We could hear muffled cries of "Help, Help! I'm stuck! Get me out of here."

I'm sure she didn't think it was funny but the rest of the staff sure did! The site of her stubby little legs and big butt hanging from the ceiling was hilarious as we watched by flashlight. Nettie L'Amour was concerned that the entire suspended ceiling might come down from the weight, so she wouldn't allow any of the staff to do anything to help. Poor Donnetta had to just hang there for about a half hour until the Sheboygan Fire Department was able to cut her out with the Jaws of Life.

Wouldn't you know, just as they got her down the power came back on.

Donnetta was so shaken up from the experience that she asked Nettie if she could go home early. I couldn't believe it when that bitch boss said, "Oh honey, you only have about three hours left on your shift and the bathrooms still need to be cleaned."

That woman has no compassion at all. It was just like the time she made Armando, Men's Shoe Assistant Manager, reschedule his wife's C-Section because the couple had the audacity to schedule it for the day we were scheduled to do store inventory!

I wish Nettie would have been stuck up in that ceiling tile instead—and never come down!

Chapter 24

Colonel Clinker

Sunday, 10:45-5 Shift

There are some customers that no one wants. The minute they walk into the department my co-workers and I either immediately have to pee, fake a phone call, or take cover in the backroom.

And the worst customer by far is Colonel Clinker.

You can't miss him because he's the embodiment of the American flag. He's always wearing Red, White, and Blue, along with Stars, Stripes, and Eagles. He's a retired, proud, and very patriotic American veteran who just happens to hate "colored" people, Mexicans, immigrants, Asians, homos, liberals, Muslims, Jews, public school teachers, labor unions, welfare cheats, unwed mothers, Planned Parenthood, tree huggers, Democrats, Communists, Socialists, and the Pope.

Unfortunately, today I got stuck with him. He saw me ringing up a customer and waited until I was done with my transaction. I feigned a smile, and said, "Hello, Colonel Clink. Isn't it a nice day?!"

It should be safe to talk about the weather, right?

"How many times do I have to tell you. It's Clinker! C-L-I-N-K-E-R, Clinker! And what do you mean by nice day? It's windy as hell and it's probably going to rain this afternoon."

That started out well…

"So how can I help you Colonel Clink..," I paused slightly before adding, "er."

He gave me one of his "looks" before he said, "I don't know why your girls down in Alterations can't ever get things right!" He pulled a pair of khakis out of his shopping bag. "These pants are still too long. I think I have been in here at least a half dozen times."

I could see by the alterations slip attached to the pants that he'd actually only been in two times, but decided not to correct his exaggeration. "If you'd like to slip on the pants, I will call Alterations and have someone come out to remeasure them for you."

After about a minute I see our seamstress, Bahija from Kazakhstan, approaching the fitting room. Immediately Col. Clink goes into a conniption fit. "Oh no! Oh no! That woman is not touching me."

I can see that Bahija is understandably shocked by his boorish behavior so I told her that I would get someone else to help the Colonel.

"That woman might be a fancy dresser in HER country, but someone needs to tell her that we don't dress that way in OUR country." He then continued his rant, bellowing, "I've had it with people like her coming over here and taking jobs from hard working Americans. I'm not going to stand here and listen to her Jib Jab butchered English."

He has to know I think he's a freaking asshole, right?

I excused myself and walked with Bahija back to Alterations, apologizing that she had to hear all of his bull$#!+. I explained the situation to Bahija's manager Janita Walker and suggested that under the circumstances she might want to take care of the alteration.

Janita got up from her stool and said, "Listen here, I'm not going to put up with any of his $#!+."

This time instead of staring down at timid Muslim woman in a hijab, the Colonel was looking up at a big boned six-foot two, African American woman with an attitude to match her stature.

"You got a problem?" she barked in her deep smoker's voice.

"Oh no! Nope, nope. No problem here Ma'am!"

"Okay, now that we got that out of the way, stand up straight and get those hands out of your pockets." She gave him a couple of "uh-huhs" as she pinned the pants, then said, "Those will be ready at 6 p.m. in three days."

The Colonel asked if he could have them any sooner.

Janita shot him another look and said, "You want to argue with me? I'm the boss around here when it comes to alterations and when I say three days, I means three days! You got it?"

"Oh no problem…take your time…four, five days, whatever it takes!" He handed her the pants and slithered off without saying another word.

"Guess I showed him who's da boss!"

She sure did! From now on, the minute he comes in the door I'm calling my friend Janita.

Then she added, "Ya know, Mike, sometimes you get some real clunkers."

That's it! Janita has inspired me to give him a new nickname: Colonel Clunker.

Chapter 25

Tight Pants

Monday, 8:00-5 Shift

I don't know why some guys wear their pants so darn tight. Well actually, I do know since I was their age once. But when it comes to being a customer in a store, some guys need to just loosen up.

A few days ago, a guy named Tiger Johnson wanted to buy a pair of Calvin Klein black dress pants for his sister's wedding on Saturday. He tried on several pair and ultimately decided on 32x34, the smaller of the two final options. They certainly emphasized his masculinity but they looked like he could hardly move.

"Are you sure?" I asked. "You know you are going to be sitting down during the wedding, maybe doing some dancing later on. You want to be comfortable."

"Oh no, I like them tight," he assured me. "I like to show off the goods when I'm on the dance floor!"

Well, at least he has the goods to show off.

So today when I got back from lunch, there was Tiger back in the store. I gave him a wave and asked, "Hey Tiger, how was your sister's wedding?"

"Oh, the wedding was great, but you know those pants you sold me? Well, I had a little too much to drink and when I was out on the dance floor, I got a little crazy. I ripped them from the back belt loop all the way to the zipper! Let's just say my family will be talking about it for years."

I laughed and said, "At least you were wearing underwear. I hope they were black."

He blushed and said, "Well Mike, that's the thing…when I was getting dressed, I decided you were right. They were a little too tight, so I went commando."

Oh, my, what an image. All that rubbing against the tight pants must have caused some chafing!

Tiger continued, "So what everyone in the family will remember about Jill's wedding will be Uncle Tiger's lily-white ass making an appearance on the dance floor."

He resisted when I offered to do an exchange. "Thanks for the offer but this was my fault. You warned me. It clearly wasn't Von Oostrom's responsibility. I'm such an idiot."

He's not an idiot. Just a young, foolish guy that probably enjoyed himself a little too much.

I resisted asking him if he got any action that night, but just said goodbye and knew he had learned his lesson.

Later this afternoon I had another young man who was trying on jeans. I still had Tiger's adventures in mind, so I took one look at him and said, "You know buddy those are motel jeans."

"Motel jeans? What do you mean by that?"

He apparently didn't know the joke.

I smiled and said, "No ballroom."

It took a second for my humor to sink in. Finally, he chuckled and said, "That's a good one! I'll have to remember that the next time my dad rags on me for wearing them so tight."

But just like Tiger, he rebuffed my suggestion that there wasn't enough room and said, "Hey, man, I like people to know my religion."

Now I had to think about that for a moment, then took a better look, gave him a thumbs up and said, "Gotcha! You're clearly Jewish and gifted I might add."

Of course, there are plenty of Christians and others that are also circumcised, but it seems like Jewish guys are the only ones who brag about it being based on their religion.

Retail pant fitting isn't rocket science. While the hems can vary a bit, there is stuff you need to cover and stuff others just don't need to see. The crack of the ass is one, and too much bulge is the other. But you'll never convince the young guys. Some of them are real show-offs.

On the other hand, there's Lenny Barnstorm, who has got to be closer to eighty than seventy. I can never convince him to wear age-appropriate jeans.

Skinny jeans on someone that old just doesn't work. When a once firm butt disappears and relocates to the front side and is now hanging over a belt buckle, it's a definite NO!

It's kind of like when an eighty-year old woman wears a tube top. It's something no one wants to see.

You just want to slap 'em and say, "Get a grip buddy. You're too old for that!"

Chapter 26

Hamburgers and Sandwiches

Tuesday – 10-6 Shift

Sometimes I think there should be a four-year class on parenting before people are allowed to have kids. Shortly before lunch I noticed that the shirts near the Brooks Brothers rounder were moving. That's right, they were actually moving around like they were alive. So, I went to investigate.

As I pulled the shirts to the side, I looked on in horror at three little kids, legs crossed, eating McDonald Hamburger Happy Meals on the floor in the center of the rack that held hundreds of dollars of shirts.

I must have blurted out, "For the love of God, who does something like that?" because a woman came up to me saying, "They aren't hurting anything they are just having a picnic!"

Picnic? Surrounded by Brooks Brothers sleeves to wipe their mouths with?

Of course, I couldn't say anything. 'The customer is always right' according to V. O.

But sure as hell, next time someone complains about the ketchup, mustard, or grease stains on a brand new $100 Brooks Brothers shirt I'll just chuckle and say, "Oh it must have been one our little customers having a picnic. Surely you have a Tide stick."

Maybe there was a full moon today but other weird stuff happened in the Brooks Brothers section. Later this afternoon, I saw three college aged boys carrying the life-sized stuffed sheep from the Brooks Brothers display table into a dressing room.

I dashed across the department and could see three sets of feet in the handicapped changing room. Knocking loudly, I said in my best dad voice, "You can't have that sheep in the dressing room!"

One of the boys opened the door a crack. "Sorry, mister, we're just taking pictures," he said. And if I might add, he said it 'sheepishly.'

I grabbed the sheep out of his hand and snapped back, "If you want to take pictures with the sheep you can do it on the sales floor where everyone can see what you are doing."

Apparently, that wasn't the kind of photo the little perverts had in mind. I do have to admit it was kind of funny though—funnier than those little brats eating their picnic in the display.

Wednesday, Noon-9 Shift

As I was about to start my shift, I could not help but notice two very large, masculine women attempting to get on the store's escalator. The larger of the two was so wide it was clear she was not going to fit. Her friend suggested that if she went sideways it might work, but from the look on her face I could tell the escalator was not going to be an option.

I quickly jumped into action. "Come with me ladies I'll take you down the elevator instead."

We headed to the backroom and I opened the door to the freight elevator. Closing its door can be a little frightening but the elevator hummed past second floor and stopped on first.

As the door opened, who do we see but a totally mortified Nettie L'Amour. She looked at me in disgust.

I rushed the women past her as she stomped away; the bigger lady thanked me profusely. As we said our goodbyes the other woman said, "Group hug."

You haven't had a hug until you have been sandwiched between four of the biggest breasts imaginable.

Almost immediately, I heard over the store's public address system, "Will Mike Triggs report to the store manager's office immediately!"

I knew I was in trouble so I took my time and looked at some new Waterford Crystal in the Gift Department.

Soon I was greeted at the top of the escalator by the Groom of the Stool, which is the name Kent and I affectionately call Mr. Krayfisch. In medieval times the Groom of the Stool was a male servant in the household of the king who was responsible for assisting the king in his toileting needs.

As I was ceremoniously escorted into Ms. L'Amour office, the door was slammed as I heard, "Mr. Triggs, what were you thinking taking customers down the freight elevator?"

I shrugged and said, "Did you see the size of those two women? When you add my 168 pounds with the two of them together, we would clearly have exceeded the 900-pound limit in the public elevator."

I could see it was all she could do to keep from laughing but I could tell she so wanted to see another "write up" in my personal file. But this time I escaped with her saying, "Don't let it happen again!"

As I closed her office door behind me, I could hear a burst of unrestrained laughter.

When I returned to my department a lady asked for some help in the underwear department. She wasn't sure if her husband wore the Jockey or Calvin Klein briefs and asked if I remembered what brand he wore.

I had no idea who her husband was or for that matter what brand of tighty whities he wore but suggested the Jockey brand was 20% off this month.

"Oh for Pete's sake, I always like a bargain. I guess I'll take the Jockeys." She squeeled.

She had just gotten out her wallet and was getting ready to pay when a woman behind her said, "I wouldn't buy that brand if I were you."

We both looked a little puzzled by the strangers comment and finally the customer I was helping asked why.

"Well…" she declared, "my neighbor's, brother-in-law's, friend knew someone who bought that brand and they spontaneously combusted on an airplane.

I looked at her in total disbelief and scoffed, "Oh for crying out loud, those underpants are 100% cotton. Why would they possibly go up in flames?"

The crazy woman practically jumped over the counter and screamed, "Are you calling me a liar?"

"Oh no! Not at all. I'm just saying I've never heard of underpants spontaneously combusting"

But before I could say another word in an attempt to calm her down, she screams in an even louder voice. "You might think I'm stupid just because I didn't go to college but I do know what I heard."

I must have rolled my eyes in disbelief because she continued, "Don't you roll your eyes at me you son of a bitch. I learned about spontaneous combustion in a biology class…or maybe it was math!"

With that my customer handed me that package of Jockeys and said, "I think I'm going to pass on the undies. I don't want my husband to blow up on an airplane."

As I watched the two women walk off together, I overheard my customer ask the crazy woman, "Did everyone on the plane die?"

I guess enquiring minds need to know.

Chapter 25

The Holidays

Thanksgiving Eve, After Hours

I have always enjoyed shopping at Von Oostrom during the holidays but never knew what a production it was to transform the store into a Christmas Wonderland.

Unlike most retail stores that put up their Christmas decorations before Halloween, the Von Oostrom family has been committed to keeping holidays separate. The Christmas windows and displays are never seen by customers until store opening on Black Friday.

As an employee, I for one have appreciated the fact that our store is always closed on holidays and we don't open early on Thanksgiving for that early Black Friday tomfoolery.

Obviously, we can't wait until the morning after Thanksgiving to put everything up. Hundreds of hours go into behind the scenes prepping trees, garland, wreaths, and bows for the big day. So, all of them go up the day before Thanksgiving when the store closes at 3:00 in the afternoon.

Once the final customer has left the store every Von Oostrom employee is given their individual assignments and about three hours later the entire store has been decorated. It's an amazing thing to watch it all come together. Of course, they've been doing it for over a hundred years so they've got it down pat.

It may be a little sexist on the company's part, but all the heavy lifting is assigned to the male employees and a couple of really butch lesbians.

My assignment this afternoon was to roll out 47 pre-decorated Christmas trees. It took a while to get the hang of moving them without ornaments falling off and breaking. But by the time I had moved three dozen trees, I was able to move the final 11 without losing a single ornament.

Once the trees were in place, female co-workers would dress them with tree skirts, replace any broken ornaments, plug in the lights and place boxes under the trees that had been identically wrapped in traditional red, green and white Christmas plaid wrapping paper.

I'm looking forward to having Thanksgiving dinner tomorrow with Kent and his parents. I'll have to get up early to make my famous Cinnamon Karo Nut Pie that I'll be bringing for dessert.

Thanksgiving Day

I had such a great time with Kent's family today. His sister, both brothers, their wives and kids were all there his parent's house. Had I tried to do Thanksgiving with my own parents and siblings in Rabbit Gulch. Iowa, I would have spent at least ten hours driving through ice and snow.

I was so stuffed that I hardly can remember what the conversation was about or what we even had. They liked my pie though. There wasn't a piece left.

December 22, 10-7 Shift

I'm not sure where this past month has gone, I had been so good at writing in my journal every night right up to Thanksgiving. But with working holiday shifts, there just weren't enough hours in the day for journaling.

I've been so exhausted, all I have done is sell, sell, sell and box, box, box. I couldn't even wager to guess how many shirts, pajamas, ties, wallets, and Christmas gifts I have sold. But it's a good thing I had all of those sales because every employee in Men's Furnishings had a goal of selling for $3,656 dollars every day during the month of December.

Today during my break to saw Leonard the shoeshine guy. He asked me how I was doing, as usual, and I told him, "Oh, about $457 an hour." All I could do was think about sales goals!

I think I'm going to have an eggnog with a little whiskey in it and go to bed early for a change. I'm so ready for Christmas to be over … but there are still two shopping days left.

And if another pianist plays "Santa Baby" or the "Twelve Days of Christmas" one more time I'm going to kill someone.

Chapter 28

Cha-Ching!

December 23, 8-5, Shift

I have never worked so hard in my life for one customer. Well, actually it was two.

Joan and Robert Benson were the first customers to walk through the doors at 10 a.m. and it was obvious from the start that they had already been drinking.

The first thing I did was to check Joan's floor length red fox fur at the V. O. Concierge Desk. It was the most beautiful fur I had seen since the "shaved beaver" earlier this fall.

I soon learned that Mr. Benson was a Senior Partner at the prestigious Benson, Buxbaum, McCarthy & Yarman Law Firm in Milwaukee. The couple would be spending the Christmas holidays with their family at the swanky Five Star American Club Resort on the shores of Wood Lake in nearby Kohler, WI.

They pulled out a two-page lists of items they needed to buy and asked if it would be possible that I shop with them all over the store. They needed gifts for the entire family and really weren't interested in having to find someone else to assist them.

Cha Ching! That was music to my commission-loving ears.

But little did I know what our shopping spree would entail.

For the next few hours, we shopped throughout the store. First it was for Bob's mother Edith in the Enormé Department. "Edith always thought I married Robert for his money," Joan said.

"Oh honey, you know that's not true," her husband answered.

"It is so! Edith told me herself on our wedding day 37 years ago."

91

We found a really cute salmon aerobics outfit for Joan's sister Judith, who was going through a very difficult divorce.

I really scored in the Infants and Toddlers Department, where we were able to get doubles of everything for their twin granddaughters Annalisa and Marcelene.

While the Bensons were shopping for a Hickey Freeman suit for Robert in Men's Clothing, I called our Tea Room and asked one of the waiters to bring down a Mimosa for Joan along with a Scotch and Soda for Mr. Benson. I probably should have called for Nettie L'Amour's permission, but we had already rang $4,000 in sales, why should I allow her to balk at my requestion.

We picked out a $1500 diamond ankle bracelet for Joan in the Fine Jewelry Department. I watched that slime ball Fine Jewelry Manager Sharonda Fingerphude slip me her employee number on her business card. She whispered in my ear, "Darling, I hope you will ring that bracelet up for me, I'm having a really slow day."

Fat chance that's going to happen. I helped the customer pick it out while you were standing at the cash register giving me the stink eye.

Mr. Benson said, "Michael, I noticed there was a Golf Quest store just outside Von Oostrom. Is there any chance we could leave Von Oostrom to buy a couple of gifts out in the mall?

How can I say no? He is the one with the Black American Express Card that had been burning a hole in his wallet!

At the golf store we bought a putter for their nephew, Tony. Robert said, "The kid thinks he's going to be playing in the PGA someday, but I'd be surprised if that ever happens. Particularly if the PGA does any drug testing."

"Oh Robert, you know he's been through treatment," Joan said, as she wiped a tear from her eye.

"What's it been now, four times?"

"Only three," she responded.

"Whatever."

At the Zondervan Christian Bookstore, the Benson's got into an argument about whether or not they should buy a Bible for Tony's girlfriend, Elaine.

"She's such a Bible thumper. One of those types can never have too many Bibles," Robert said.

While the Bible was being boxed Joan took a look at her shopping list and said, "Well, looking at my list we just need to get something for Barbie and…"

She paused briefly and finally spit out the name, "Dennis!"

"Now who are Barbie and Dennis?" I inquired.

"Barbie's our daughter and Dennis is her husband." Joan almost gagged as she said his name.

Together in unison they said, "We hate him. He's bisexual."

What could I say but, "Oh my!"

Knowing that we would surely find something for the two of them at my store I suggested we head back to Von Oostrom.

Joan was in tears and said, "Maybe we should get her some sexy, bras and panties. Then maybe he'd be more interested in her than in that freaky little boyfriend of his."

We picked out just over $2000 of sexy lingerie, which seemed a little odd for parents to be buying their grown daughter.

If Dennis doesn't get turned on by at least one of those sexy bras, panties or pajamas, he's hopeless. Of course, I haven't met Barbie or his freaky little boyfriend.

Dennis didn't fare as well with the Benson's.

They were inclined to not get him anything but ultimately, they broke down and bought him a $20 nail clipping kit.

All total their gifts came up to $7,520 and that was just in our store. It was my biggest sale ever and it took four hours.

But I wasn't prepared for what I heard next.

Robert said, "Now we're going to need a real tree to be decorated and delivered to the Presidential Suite at the American Club. You'll need to have it set up by tomorrow night at 5:00 when everyone is gathering to exchange gifts."

That was a pretty big request. Then he continued.

"We haven't had lunch yet and all of the gifts need to be wrapped. If you would be so kind to make sure every gift is wrapped and have them delivered to our suite, that way we won't have to be bothered with all that fuss."

Joan added, "You understand we want everything wrapped in its own unique wrapping paper. And please none of it in that cheap Von Oostrom wrap that everybody gets. Nothing but the best is what I always say."

Robert opened his wallet and handed me five new hundred-dollar bills and said, "This should cover it. Keep the change."

My eyes must have popped out of my head. Did I see and hear that right?

I thanked them, wished them a Merry Christmas, and got Mrs. Benson her coat.

The rest of my day was spent finding a 15-foot Frasier Fir, an appropriate tree skirt, lights, and decorations. With the assistance of a couple of The American Club's bellmen and a woman from the front desk staff we got the tree set up, decorated, and each and every gift wrapped and placed under the tree.

We finished just as the Benson's were arriving back at the resort from an afternoon of cocktailing. They were shocked to hear we were finished and said they didn't think we would complete the task until sometime tomorrow.

When it was all done, after expenses I pocketed $187.00 out of the $500, which is going to be my little secret. And that didn't count the commission I would be getting on my next paycheck!

Cha Ching!

Chapter 29

The Long Christmas Eve

Christmas Eve, 8-4 Shift

I knew when I went to work today that I there was no way I could top yesterday's sales. What I wasn't prepared for was all the frantic shoppers trying to get that one last gift before the store closed at 4:00.

It was a madhouse and people were just plain rude. One shopper had the balls to actually say, "Can you box those ties a little faster!"

At one point I ran out of red Christmas shopping bags and had to scrounge around our back room to find some. There wasn't a red bag to be found anywhere, so I brought out a stack of green camouflage bags we had left over from Military Family Appreciation Month.

Of course, Nettie L'Amour saw me give a customer a camouflage bag and totally went ape $#!+ crazy over a freaking shopping bag.

Macy could see that I had reached my boiling point and suggested I go off the floor to cool down. She said that there was a giant plate of Christmas goodies in the lunchroom that Suzanna had brought in to share with our Men's Furnishings staff.

A sugar fix and a giant cup of coffee was exactly what I needed.

I got to the lunchroom just in time to see Sharonda Fingerphude filling a huge Tupperware container with goodies.

"What the hell?" I interrupted her. "Can't you see the sign next to that plate that says 'MEN'S FURNISHING DEPARTMENT ONLY'?"

"Well look who doesn't have the Christmas spirit," she snapped. "If you want to get technical about it, we sell men's stuff in Fine Jewelry too. I'm just taking a few things home for my kids."

"But you're filling a F'ing Tupperware container. And you think I didn't see you stuff those last two pieces of fudge in your mouth when I walked in the door!"

She grinned as I stormed off to get some coffee. But to top it off someone had forgotten to make a new pot when they took the last cup.

The rest of my day was just as bad.

Four o'clock rolled around and security should have been locking the doors. But I found out that someone had called from Fond du Lac and said they had forgotten to pick up the Christmas gifts they left at the store to be wrapped. They asked if we could stay open until they arrived to pick up the packages.

Of course, someone said yes knowing full well that Fond du Lac was 45 miles away. And, of course, every single employee had to stay!

Sweet baby Jesus, an hour later the whole family came rushing in. It was 5:00 on Christmas Eve, when we're all supposed to be home with our loved ones, and these customers decided they needed a few more things. And of course, those "things" needed to be boxed and wrapped as well.

When we finally got them out the door around 5:45, I was looking at a long drive to my parent's place in Rabbit Gulch, Iowa. I had planned on surprising them by showing up unexpectedly for all the Christmas Eve traditions, but now it looked like the surprise was on me.

Now I was going to miss the traditional oyster stew with the family, not see my nieces and nephew open their gifts, and not get to attend Christmas Eve services at the church where I had been baptized. But if I hurried maybe I could get home by 10:00 or 11:00 and catch some of them if they were still awake.

After the day I just experienced, what more could possibly go wrong?

As I headed to my car, Michael Firestone from Men's Suits asked if I could give him a ride to Budget Car Rental at the airport! He said he had been in an accident and wouldn't get his car back from the body shop until the day after Christmas.

I didn't want to do it, but I felt sorry for him. It was Christmas Eve. How could I say no? While anxious to get on the road, I waited at the rental car place to make sure everything went okay with his rental before I headed home to Iowa.

It didn't! The car rental people wouldn't take his personal check. So, Michael came back out to ask if I could put the rental on my credit card and he would pay me back in cash on the 26th.

Reluctantly, I said yes. I had to keep reminding myself it was Christmas Eve.

And wouldn't you know, my long drive home dragged on for an extra two hours because of icy road conditions. I didn't get home until two in the morning.

Mary and Joseph didn't seem to have this much trouble getting to Bethlehem.

Christmas Day, Rabbit Gulch

There is nothing quite like waking up in your old bed to the smell of bacon coming from mom's kitchen.

I quickly threw on some clothes, snuck down the stairs, and surprised my family with a hearty, "MERRY CHRISTMAS!"

My parents were shocked to see me since I had told them I wouldn't be able to make it home for Christmas.

We ended up having a huge breakfast. Eggs, bacon and mom's homemade cinnamon rolls. Christmas was just how it was supposed to be.

The whole family gathered about the dining room table at lunchtime, we opened gifts I had brought with me, and retold stories from past Christmases.

Unfortunately, it all happened too quickly and by three that afternoon I was back in my car headed for Sheboygan since I had to back to work first thing the next next morning.

I can only imagine what a nightmare tomorrow will be when shoppers come through the doors with arm loads of returns. But it couldn't be any worse than what I just went through in order to spend a few great hours with the people who cared about me the most.

Chapter 30

The Busiest Day of the Year

Day after Christmas, 10-7 Shift

I always thought that Black Friday was the busiest shopping day of the year. That was until I worked retail on the day after Christmas!

It's even busier because of the huge number of returns. I've never seen so many unhappy gift receivers in my life. Didn't anybody like the presents they received? Or do they all just want cash (with or without a receipt!)?

My first customer wanted to exchange a pair of Arizona brand boot cut jeans for a smaller size. I told the customer, "These don't look like they came from Von Oostrom."

The customer was indignant, "Yes, they did. They came in a Von Oostrom box."

Trying to be as nice as I could, I said, "If you look around the store you will see that we don't sell Arizona jeans. They are a JCPenney brand."

"My grandma said she bought them in this store," the woman insisted.

"Well listen miss," I said, trying to be gentle with her. "During the Christmas holidays it is easy to forget where everything was purchased."

"Are you calling my Granny a liar? I don't like your attitude. Let me speak to a manager."

I paged a manager to come to my department and cringed when I saw my nemesis, Nettie L'Amour appear.

She immediately threw me under the bus and gave the customer a gift card for $17.24, the price marked on the jeans.

I was even scolded in front of the woman. "Mike should know the rules, no sale is ever final here at Von Oostrom. I'm so sorry he was so ornery. I'll have a little talk with him about our customer service expectations." As she walked away, Nettie gave me one of her classic sneers.

After that disaster I was delighted to see my favorite customers, Colonel Emery Brightman and his wife Kendra waiting at the counter.

"Wasn't she a peach," the Colonel said. "Is she your department manager?"

I rolled my eyes and said with a snort, "Store Manager."

"Well, if that's the case, I wonder why the gal over in Ladies Shoes told me that I couldn't return these shoes because I had them for too long?" Kendra asked.

"I'd be glad to take them back. You heard the lady. No sale is EVER final here!"

In looking at Kendra's receipt after the Brightman's left, I couldn't help but notice that the shoes were eleven years old. But that's the store policy and you have to abide by it. What Ladies Shoes does with an 11-year-old pair of mauve, faux suede shoes with platform heels is not my problem.

I took my lunch today in the mall food court and half way through eating my chicken sandwich I started choking. Try as I might I couldn't dislodge the piece of chicken. I tried to get the couple next to me to do something but the wife kept saying, "Gross! Gross! He needs to go the restroom." The guy on a nearby table just kept doing his crossword puzzle totally oblivious of my gagging and cries for help.

Finally, as I was seeing my life pass before me, a lady rushed up from behind, put her arms around me and gave me five upward thrusts to dislodge the piece of chicken. It flew out of my mouth and landed on the complaining couple's table.

When I turned around to see who had saved my life it was a tiny African-American woman with virtually no teeth. She told me that her name was Wilma and that she works for the mall cleaning tables in the food court.

After thanking her profusely, she told me she had just received training on performing the Heimlich Maneuver and was glad to have the opportunity to do it on a real live person.

"I'm so glad to see it really works," she said.

As I gave her a hug, I decided that I should write a letter to the mall management thanking them for giving their employees the training they might need in emergencies like this.

When I got back to my department after lunch, I saw there was a slip of paper taped to the register stating I needed to cover the Young Men's Department this afternoon. Returns there couldn't be as bad as they were in my department this morning.

Of course, they were worse.

By far the most memorable problem all day was when a young guy handed me a shopping bag with a red hoodie in it. When I took out the receipt, I saw that it wasn't a gift after all. He had purchased it himself on Christmas Eve.

I couldn't help but notice there were big crusty white stains all over the front of the hoodie. I waved my hands and pointed to it, saying, "What happened here?"

Without even flinching, the guy said, "The bitch didn't swallow!"

It took me a few seconds to register what he meant.

Oh my God, the bitch didn't swallow! He must mean...ewwwwww! Who tells a stranger something like that? Do I really need that much information? Shades of Bill Clinton! And couldn't the customer have at least washed the damn thing before returning it?

But rules are rules and "no sale is ever final."

Then I noticed he paid for the hoodie with cash and I didn't have enough money in the drawer to do the return. So I had to call customer service to bring me a cash advance and had to make small talk with him until the money arrived.

What do you say to a young guy that so disrespected women? "Was the blowjob the only gift she gave you for Christmas?"

Once he pocketed his cash, I had to decide what to do with the stained hoodie. Doubting there was a store policy on this kind of disgusting return, I just threw it in the garbage can under the register.

When I telling Macy about the incident later in the day, she said, "Well, I hope you didn't touch it. Everything with body fluids on it needs to go in a HASMAT bag."

Apparently, V. O.'s policy was that anything with human stains, including blood and urine, must be disposed of in a HASMAT bag while wearing rubber gloves. Not only had I touched it, but it was still laying right there in the open trash can for all to see and smell.

But it wasn't like it was radioactive. The stain had been dry for at least a day and as far as I could tell, there wasn't anything life threatening about a stain on a hoody. After all, Monika Lewinsky's famous blue dress may end up in the Smithsonian someday.

My only regret about the incident is that when I handed the young guy his cash I should have said, "Come again soon."

After all, adding a personal touch to customer greetings is part of our V. O. store policies!

Chapter 31

Slow Days with Big Surprises

Monday, 8-5 Shift

When I looked out the window and saw how much snow we receivved last night I just wanted to get back in bed, pull the covers over my head, go back to sleep, and call in later and say I had overslept. But Mr. Perfect Attendance would never do something like that.

Fortunately, the snow plows woke me up early because it took me about forty-five minutes to dig out my driveway.

But then things went from bad to worse.

As I carefully drove the road to work, this bitch was putting on her makeup while driving and came barreling through the intersection and rear ends me.

After giving her a piece of my mind, I knew I had to call the store to tell them I'd been in an accident and would be late arriving to work.

And who answered the phone but Nettie L'Amour?

Did she ask if I was hurt? No! Did she show any empathy or say something like, "I know the roads were bad, take your time coming in?" Of course not. All I heard was, "I'll mark you down as tardy." Then she hung up on me.

I'm standing on the side of I-43 in wingtips, no gloves, with the wind blowing 40 mph, and the bitch says, "I'll mark you down as tardy?"

My blood was boiling even though it was freezing outside. Nettie L'Amour is colder than any Wisconsin winter snow storm!

Once the cops got there and we had filled out the accident report, I decided that if my store manager was marking me down as tardy, I might as well be really tardy. So, I stopped at Perkins for breakfast!

I got to work about two hours late, just in time for the opening announcements at 9:57 a.m. And it was a good thing I showed up, because both Kent and Queen had called in sick.

They didn't really miss anything. It was snowing so hard the store was dead and should have never opened. Of course, the only people out on a day like today were old people with walkers and mothers with newborns. Go figure!

At least I didn't get any returns and tomorrow I start my all-expenses paid one-week vacation skiing in Steamboat, Colorado.

Last fall I seen a Miller Lite ad in Milwaukee's alternative newspaper with a toll-free number you could call for a chance to win the Miller Lite Ski Sweepstakes.

It had been a slow night at work and I thought, what do I have to lose, so I called the number. When I got off the phone I turned to Kent and said, "You're not going to believe this but I just won the Miller Lite Ski Sweepstakes!"

"You're $#!+ting me! You don't even drink beer."

"No, seriously, there was a recording with Bob Uecker, the play-by-play announcer for the Brewers. He said, 'Congratulations - You have just won the Miller Lite Sweepstakes and a ski vacation for two to Steamboat, Colorado.' I had to leave my name and a phone number where I could be reached and he said someone will call back tomorrow."

I learned it was a trip for two that included airfare, lodging at a luxury condo, ski rental and passes, all the Miller Beer you could drink for the week and $1,000 in spending money.

You might know Kent wanted to go with me, but the boss bitch on third floor put the kibosh to that saying there was no way both of us could be gone at the same time.

I hate her so much!

Kent's consolation prize is dropping me off at the airport tomorrow morning and picking me up next week.

Chapter 32

Steamboat Springs

Tuesday night, One Week Later

Wouldn't you know, in my excitement packing for my vacation I forgot to include my journal. It would have been nice to be able to look back on detailed entries from my week in Steamboat Springs.

Kent was there as planned to pick me up today at the Sheboygan International Airport. And he couldn't wait to hear about my vacation. The first thing he said was, "Everyone at work is dying to know who your "plus one" was on the trip?"

Even Rosemary Beatty was asking.

"That old bag?" I said, "I should make up some really juicy story, but with her big mouth that phony story would be broadcast all over town in a flash."

Kent looked like he couldn't wait to hear the details. I tried to keep it simple.

"The truth is when L'Amour wouldn't let you go, I asked a friend from Idaho to meet me there."

"Male or Female?" he asked.

I hesitated, then answered. "It was a guy friend."

"Oooooooooh! I can't wait to hear more," that little gay prick squealed.

"It's not like that all," I assured him. "Parley Pratt is just a friend I used to work with in the state legislature. He moved back to Idaho a couple of years ago to take over his dad's potato farm."

Kent was practically licking his lips wanting to hear something salacious. So, I added, "And he's Mormon."

Kent seemed disappointed. "Mormon? Potato farmer? How fun could that be? I'm guessing you probably left the refrigerator in your condo full of all that Miller Lite. What a waste!"

"Actually, Parley used to work as a ski instructor when he was a student at BYU and he sure taught me a thing or two about maneuvering those black diamond and mogul runs. By the end of the week, he had me skiing like a damn good Midwesterner! Or as Parley would say, 'Gosh darn good Midwesterner.'"

"You're telling me you had to watch your little potty mouth?" Kent laughed.

"We skied every day but Monday and that's because there was a white-out on the mountain. After dinner every night we swam in the condo's pool and rested our tired muscles in the hot tub. It was so freaking cool. They even had an indoor/outdoor heated pool with a tunnel you could swim through connecting the two. There was steam coming off the pool, the mountains in the background, a full moon overhead, and big flakes coming down. It was so much fun. I definitely knew I wasn't in Sheboygan any more. But seriously, I'm glad to be back home."

My rambling seemed to satisfy him. I didn't have to tell him any intimate details.

But just as he was about to drop me off at home I asked, "So did I miss anything at work?"

He laughed, "Queen got a new wig! And she tried her best to get that blond girl at Radio Shack fired. I heard her tell the Radio Shack Manager, 'We don't need people like her skanking up the Mall.'"

"Did it work?"

"Nope, but you know our Queen, she's always got to be stirring something up."

When I opened my front door, I saw there was a large stack of mail inside my mail slot. As I opened my mail, I soon realized almost all of my mail was from my bank.

Ten overdraft charges, each for thirty dollars! I have no idea what that's all about, so I guess I'll have to wait until tomorrow to find out.

Boy a soak in that Steam Boat condo hot tub would sure feel great tonight!

Chapter 33

The Rental Car

Wednesday, 9-6 Shift

When I walked into the store this morning I almost fell over laughing. Queen was wearing a dishwater blond pixie cut wig that looked like a mophead on a black handle.

What the hell was she thinking?

She had come in at 7:00 with Kent, and he had spent that two hours filling her in on my trip details, so I didn't have much left to tell.

Queen did appear to be quite eager to tell me, "I couldn't help but notice there are six or seven phone messages from your bank and four or five from a car rental place. What's that all about?"

So that's what this is about. I gave her a stare, picked up the stack of messages, and took them over to Men's Sportswear department so I could return my calls out of Queen's ear shot. There was no reason that nosy bitch needed to be listening in on my personal calls.

My bank wasn't open yet, so I called Budget Rent-a-Car. I %^<#ing blew a gasket when I found out they wanted to know when I was going to return the car that I had rented on Christmas Eve!

I had to think back to what had happened that night. I had dropped my co-worker, Michael off at the Budget Rent-a-Car place and he was supposed to have returned the car the day after Christmas. But apparently had failed to do so. And since the rental had been on my debit card, I had been charged every day since!

It was now fifteen days later and I was still paying, with overdrafts up the ying-yang.

I immediately called Michael at his home to ream him a new asshole. At first, he was silent. Then he told me something even worse than I had expected.

He had lost the car!

"How do you freaking lose a car!"

The idiot said he had gone home with a girl he had met at a bar on Christmas Eve, spent the night, came out to the car the next morning, and it had a flat tire. He said he tried to go back to her apartment to call AAA, but it was a secure building and he didn't know her name! So, he had no way to contact her. Finally, he took the bus home and now he can't even remember where she lived.

"How the hell does something like that possibly happen?" I screamed.

"Well, you got to realize Mike, I was drunk and horny and the next day I was hungover."

Sweet Baby Jesus tell me this isn't happening!

When I asked if he had any idea where the apartment was located, he said, "Well it might have been near downtown somewhere on Sixth Street or Center Avenue, or it could have been a side street off Riverfront Drive."

"In other words, you have no idea where it is?"

The guy actually laughed and said, "I guess not."

This was no laughing matter. "I don't care what it takes, you're going to find that damn car!"

"You know Mike," he responded, "it really isn't my problem any more. You're the one who rented it. Your name's the one on the bottom line." And he hung up on me.

I tried calling him back numerous times and he didn't answer. It was obvious he was avoiding my calls.

Kent heard me slam the phone and came running saying, "Are you okay, buddy?"

I pushed by him and said, "Call HR and tell them I went home with a migraine headache."

I had to find that car.

I hopped into mine but the heater has been out since I was in that accident ten days ago. I ended up driving around Sheboygan on the coldest day of the year with my windows open to keep them from fogging up.

I started working from the Sheboygan County Court House outward. Hour after hour I must have driven by hundreds of cars.

Finally, after four hours of driving up and down the streets, I found a snow-covered car at 1303 South 11th Street. I got out, scraped off some of the snow, checked the license plate, and it was the rental! Then I checked the door handle and found it had been sitting there unlocked with the keys in the ignition!

I called AAA and had them tow it to Budget Rent-a-Car. Even though I still owed the money to the bank for the overdrafts, I would no longer have to worry about future payments.

Suddenly my headache was magically gone, so I decided to go back to work and finished my shift. I couldn't wait to tell Kent what had happened.

Thursday, Day Off

Boy did I get good news this afternoon.

Kent called me at home and said that Floyd Von Oostrom and his wife Earleen were shopping at our store this morning. He had told them about my fiasco with the car rental. Earleen adores Kent and was absolutely appalled when she heard how I had gotten screwed over by a co-worker in that way. She asked her husband if there wasn't something the company could do to help me out with the situation.

Kent said later in the afternoon Floyd called back and said he had asked Customer Service to pay my expenses out of petty cash and since Michael is showing no remorse or making any attempt to cover the expenses, Von Oostrom will be garnishing his wages to cover the costs for the car rental and my overdraft expenses.

I cried when he told me the news. True friends like Kent are rare and I couldn't help but think how lucky I was to work for Von Oostrom. I guess it pays to have connections in high places.

Chapter 34

The Mad Crapper

Friday, Noon-9 Shift

I wasn't looking forward to going to work this afternoon. It's Friday the 13th, a turbulent storm is whipping up gale-force winds on Lake Michigan, there's a full moon, and we're supposed to have a lunar eclipse later tonight.

And as if that isn't enough, both Mercury and Uranus are retrograde.

As I punched in for my shift at noon, I just knew that one hell of a $#!+ storm was about to happen at work. And it didn't take long to find out I sure called that right.

I was met in my department by one pissed off Kent Patet.

"You owe me big-time! A customer and his niece came in this morning asking for you and I told them you wouldn't be in until noon. They were in kind of a hurry so I offered to help them and it was the biggest mistake of my life!"

"Well, who was it?"

"Oh, some old guy that uses a walker. He had bad toupee and from what I could tell, a pretty advanced case of dementia. He needed a new suit for his ninetieth birthday party. The guy said he used to wear a 54 Long suit, but that clearly wasn't the case anymore."

"Gosh I wonder who that was," I said.

"I can't remember the name; Obviously I musty have written it down on the alterations slip. The guy must have tried on ten suits before we finally found one that fit."

Kent said he escorted the man and his niece back to the fitting room, and the niece told him her uncle would need some assistance as he had braces on his legs that attached to his shoes.

"Once inside the dressing room I had to work around that freaking walker," he continued. "I got down on my knees, disconnected the braces and took off his shoes. All of a sudden, I started to gag from the smell of his feet. As I unhooked his belt and assisted him in removing his trousers, the smell became so intense I realized that it wasn't his feet, but rather he had pooped his pants!"

What?

"I couldn't stop gagging," Kent said. "Then all of a sudden, I felt my stomach rumble and I couldn't hold it in. I puked all over the guy!"

Seriously?

"There was vomit on his shirt, vomit on his pants that were down to his knees, and if that wasn't bad enough there was vomit on his toupee."

I was so shocked I started to laugh

Now that image is funny.

Kent responded saying, "It's not funny Mike. I opened the dressing room door to yell for some assistance but by the time someone could come help, I hurled three more times before I finally made it to the nearby men's room."

I couldn't stop laughing. In fact, I almost threw up myself just listening to Kent's story.

"With the help of housekeeping and his niece we got the old guy and the dressing room cleaned up." he said. "It took a bucket of warm soapy water, a container of baby wipes that a customer had in her diaper bag, and half dozen beach towels that I took of a display table."

My hand was now covering up the smirk on my face.

I was so glad it was Kent and not me that had to deal with it.

Then Kent added, "But the good news is that it was a great sale. I sold him a Hart, Schaffner, Marx suit, a dress shirt, a tie, new boxers, socks, a sweater and a new pair of pants!"

No matter what happens, it's always about the money.

But Kent's story wasn't done. "The guy was a real character. Talk about delusions of grandeur. He actually told me that he used to be the governor and had run for president nine times. As if I was going to believe that."

Governor? Oh, no! I know who that is.

"Well, believe it or not Kent," I said, "the guy was telling the truth. That was former Governor and perennial presidential candidate, Oscar Bjornson."

I had met Governor Bjornson numerous times and knew all about his colorful political history. In 1938, at the age of 31, he became the youngest person ever elected Governor of Wisconsin. He resigned from office in 1942 to become an officer in the U.S. Army. He returned from the war as a highly decorated war hero and was a serious candidate for president in 1948, 1952, and 1964. His name continued to appear on presidential primary ballots six more times, until 1992 when I was working for Papa Bush's re-election.

"As I remember him," I said, "he had been a big, blond, glad-handing Scandinavian who always had an Ole and Lena joke on the tip of his tongue. Obviously, from what you just told me, recent years haven't been so good for the old guy."

Kent didn't know what to say. He was clearly embarrassed that he had thrown up all over one of the most famous men in our state's political history.

"But thanks for stepping in for me this morning," I said. "If there is something good to be said about dementia, tomorrow Governor Bjornson is never going to remember that it ever happened.

"On the other hand, I'm going to remember this story every time the name Oscar Bjornson comes up in a political conversation. I'll be able to say, 'Have I got a story for you!'"

By then, even Kent was able to laugh about it. He still insisted, "You owe me big time!"

To which I responded, "Maybe you owe me for the privilege of being one of the few people to ever see the former governor without his toupee and in his underwear!"

As I was laughing, Kent gagged.

When I took my dinner break, all everyone was talking about in the lunchroom was Kent hurling on a customer. I told them, "I think it has something to do with the full moon and the lunar eclipse."

"You might be right, Mike," Donna Goodhue from Ready to Wear said. "In our department we've got Melinda, the Mad Crapper, who comes out every time there is a full moon."

Once she said the words immediately everyone in the lunchroom seemed to have Mad Crapper stories of their own to share from their own departments.

The little redhead in handbags told how Melinda had lifted her leg and dropped a couple of turdlets in her department next to the Oscar de la Renta case.

My orientation buddy, Tonette, told us how The Mad Crapper had slid across the bench in her dressing room and left skid marks from one side to the other.

"Haven't you heard Customer Service page Housekeeping with 'Code Brown in Intimates?'" she asked. "That's the secret signal for Mad Crapper cleanup."

Imelda Franco, Mr. Krayfisch's assistant, said, "Well, Mike, I heard that a couple of years ago in your department they couldn't figure out where a bad smell was coming from. Finally, after about a week someone found a turd that a customer had left in a Calvin Klein underwear box that had been put back on the rack."

Talk about a $#!+ storm! Who knew this was a retail "thing?"

"I've got a story that will top all of those," bragged Kendra Duvet from the Juniors Department. "Last year, we had someone take ten pink prom dresses into the dressing room and smeared dog poop all over them. She left all ten dresses behind, plus a tooth brush she had used for the dirty deed and a plastic bag of dog poop."

"That's just sick! Why would someone do something like that?" I asked.

"That's easy to figure out," Kendra said. "She had purchased one of those pink dresses and came back to ensure no one else showed up at prom in the same dress. We had to mark $3,000 worth of prom dresses out of stock because of that little bitch."

I bet they had to call in the HAZMAT team to clean up that mess.

What could I say but, "WOW!"

After hearing all the stories, I've decided I'm going to request every full moon off work. It wasn't exactly the dinner table talk I had anticipated when I warmed up my beef tips in brown gravy!

Chapter 35

The Bug Man

Monday, Noon-9 Shift

Over the years I have had people who don't like me for one reason or another. But apparently Bernie Norris really doesn't like me.

Bernie is Sheboygan's Orkin Man. In fact, if I had a problem with termites, roaches, bed bugs, mice or rats the Bug Man would definitely be the first guy I would call.

Since losing 195 pounds, Bernie has become a frequent shopper in the Von Oostrom men's departments. He has shown all my female coworkers pictures of himself in wife beaters, tank tops, and a bright yellow Speedo. When he comes in the store, he likes to lift up his shirt for the girls to show off his abs and often take off his shirt entirely, flexing his muscles and striking a pose in front of the dressing room mirrors.

He was doing his little flexing routine this afternoon when I overheard him complaining to Queen that he had gained 1.8 lbs. since last Saturday.

I couldn't resist inserting myself into their conversation and said, "Oh come on Bernie. One big $#!+ and you'll be back to your girlish figure."

That's all it took. Fire shot out of his eyes as he screamed, "Get out of my face you %^<#ing little faggot."

As I slithered away, I heard him tell Queen, "I'm so sick of that fruitcake prancing around this store like he owns the place. Don't think I haven't seen him and that other faggot that works here peeking around the corners trying to catch a look at my man parts. I know their type. They'd like nothing more than to get in my pants."

Sheeeesh. Who knew The Bug Man was so sensitive. I have to admit he does have a nice body if it wasn't for the face connected to it. His hair always looks like he hasn't washed it in a week. And I don't think there has been a time he's come in when he didn't have a piece of toilet paper stuck to his cheek where he'd nicked himself shaving. And those nicotine-stained teeth, there's only one way to get them clean. Lava soap!

Nope, if I was looking for a hot date, Bernie Norris would be the last person on the planet I'd be searching out.

No sooner than I had escaped the insults of The Bug Man and I get nabbed by Fancy Nancy, the Crazy Cat Woman. There is no getting away from her clutches as she blabs on an on with stories about her cats. Today I got to hear about Tinkles, her Siamese that pees in her toaster oven.

As she takes a picture of Tinkles out of her purse, I said, "Nancy, I really hate cats. When I was three years old, I was bitten 26 times in the arms, legs, back, chest, neck, and cheek by a rabid Siamese cat."

"Oh, but Mike you would love Tinkles. She's such a sweat thing. She can be kinda naughty sometimes, but she's usually a little sweetheart."

I had to get away from her so I faked like I was in pain and said, "Nancy, I'm so sorry I think I'm having a kidney stone attack," and rushed for the men's room.

What kind of nutcase keeps a cat that tinkles in her toaster oven?

Maybe The Bug Man needs to meet Cat Woman Fancy Nancy. Those two crazies would be perfect for each other.

Chapter 36

Rapture

Try as you might, there are some customers that you just can't get away from. Today I had one that I should have tried to escape the minute I laid eyes on her.

She had the crazed look of someone who may have recently escaped from one of the state's mental institutions. And she was carrying a Bible. Not your regular book-shelf sized Bible, but a huge honking Bible that might sit on a church alter. It was gigantic.

The instant I asked if she needed any help, she immediately grabbed me by the shoulder and said, "No you can't young man, but I can feel the Holy Spirit calling me to minister to you today."

She inquired if I was a Christian. I responded in the affirmative in hopes that she might release her iron grip. I am a Christian, after all, though I might attend a much more progressive church than the one she worships in.

She didn't let go and went straight to question number two. "Have you been born again?"

I said, "Well, actually, once was enough for me. It was kind of a traumatic experience. You see I was born breach and the doctors had to use forceps. You can kind of see how my left ear is a bit lower than my right, and the other ear is set a little father back. Do you notice how my sideburns don't quite line up?"

I was kind of excepting a laugh, but instead her face was deadpan. She struck me as one of those people who was born without a sense of humor. Or maybe she had been born with one the first time but got cheated out of a sense of humor the second time around.

As I tried to make a fast escape, the lady grabbed on even tighter. She went into her spiel about the rapture and how I was going to be left behind unless I was born again. She let go of me long enough to open her humongous Bible and turned to the Book of Revelations and started reading me scripture verses. Before I could get away she grabbed onto my shoulder. I didn't see any possible polite way out of her clutches so just listened quietly for a while. When she took a pause to flip to a different section I said, "You know, it was really nice chatting with you, but I need to check in with other customers."

As I tried to move away her, she clutched me even more tightly and she said, "Get down on your knees. I'm going to pray for you."

Is she serious? I only get down on my knees in the dressing room when measuring a hem or an inseam. We're right out in the middle of a major store in a shopping mall, not a church sanctuary, for crying out loud.

She pushed me to my knees, raised the Bible over her head with her left hand, and placed her right hand on my head. Then she prayed out loud. And prayed again. And prayed some more. I just knew everyone in my department was watching me and thinking, "What the hell?"

My knees were getting weak and it seemed like she had been praying for hours. Then all of a sudden, I heard her utter the most glorious word, "Amen." When she lifted her hand from my sweaty head I shouted, "Thank you Jesus!"

Out of the corner of my eye I saw her approach Melvina Skonson who was in a wheelchair. I was half-way expecting to see a miracle but instead she says to Melvina, "Don't you look mean and evil!" and headed toward the cosmetic department.

I rushed over to Melvina, leaned down and said, "I'm so sorry. That was so uncalled for."

She chuckled and said, "No problem honey, I really was trying to smile at her, but as you know I had a stroke recently."

"Oh, Melvina there isn't a sweeter person in the world than you."

My whole body was shaking from the experience and I decided to have a coffee in the espresso bar to settle down. Before heading back to first floor I went to the security office and had them check the cameras to see if she the crazy woman was still on my floor. Thankfully she was gone and it was safe to go back to my department.

Kent was laughing as he saw me return. "If you could have just seen the look on your face! Mike, how in God's name do these things always happen to you?"

Queen also found it rather amusing. "For a minute there I thought I was going to have to whip out my East African voodoo doll and go scare the Bejesus out of her. But I was afraid she might grab me and put me under her spell."

I was just glad it was all over and now I could join in the frivolity. "After all the naughty things I've done lately, I probably needed that prayer." I confessed.

"Yah," Kent said. "When I saw you on your knees, I was thinking you were up to your old naughty tricks."

"You know it's a full moon," Queen said. "All the crazies come out when there's a full moon!"

The woman may not be crazy, and her concern for my soul was well intentioned, but having her gone was a true rapture for me.

Chapter 37

A Gun in the Dressing Room

Thursday, 9-5 Shift

Last week we had a CODE 11–Lost Child. The mother was a mess, the police were called, and every employee was looking in dressing rooms and under fixtures for the little boy.

You never know what could happen in the blink of an eye. Women preaching the rapture aren't the only crazy people out there! Someone could be downright dangerous.

About an hour into the frantic search, I found the little boy in a back-storage room where we keep the 64 fully decorated Christmas trees. The little brat had taken hundreds of glass ornaments off low-hanging branches and was squealing with glee as he threw them on the floor and heard them explode.

You can't blame the kid. He was just two-and-a-half years old. And boys will be boys. But the mom needed to be paying attention and not yapping on her cell phone.

But today we had an incident with a child that really got me riled up.

I was in the dressing room measuring up the father's pants and the mom was on her phone totally oblivious to their four little boys running in and out of dressing rooms, laughing, slamming doors behind them. I was about to say something when their eight-year-old boy tapped me on the shoulder and said, "Hey mister, there's a gun in that room."

"A gun? You mean like a toy gun?"

"It looks real to me mister," he said with confidence.

I got up from my knees to go look and sure enough, there was a real handgun in a leather shoulder holster hanging on a hook in dressing room number 6. I was rattled at first but then knew I had to take control.

All of a sudden, the parents had all four boys corralled and sitting quietly as I removed the gun and carried it to the backroom where I put it in a filing cabinet, locked it and putting the key in my pocket so there was no chance another kid would find it.

I apologized profusely to the parents. But the mother was having none of it.

"What kind of a place is this? One of my boys could have been killed. You know how boys are, they see something that looks like a toy and assume that it is. I can't believe this is really happening."

"Well thankfully your oldest boy realized it wasn't a toy. And hopefully it wasn't loaded," I said.

The dad seemed to be a lot more understanding as he paid for the pants and left the store.

I immediately went to the backroom, unlocked the filing cabinet, and checked to see if the gun was loaded and it was. I had gun safety classes as a kid but I had never held a handgun. Not wanting it to accidentally go off in my hand, I put it back in the holster and took it to customer service where I handed it over to Nancy Sedaka, who was just as mortified as the mother had been.

Four hours later Debby said, "There is a Delmer Bringlestad on the phone and he's wondering if anyone found a gun in our dressing room."

"I'll talk to him," I said.

I tried to compose myself but I was so freaking upset. "Mr. Bringlestad, we have your gun in our Customer Service Department's Lost and Found. And let me just say, you're damn lucky it's in Lost and Found and I didn't call the police to come and pick it up."

He interrupted me and said, "Well, Mr. Smarty Pants, let me tell you I'm a responsible gun owner and a lifetime member of the NRA. That gun was holstered. And I want you to know I have a permit from the State of Wisconsin to carry a concealed weapon."

"Well Mr. Bringlestad, let me tell you something. Anyone who leaves a loaded weapon unattended for four or five hours in a public place is NOT a responsible gun owner in my book. Responsible gun owners don't do something like that! And you should know your gun was found by an eight-year-old. Fortunately, the kid had the good sense to leave it there and tell an adult. But somebody could have been killed and you would be looking forward to prison time for negligent homicide."

I'm not sure if "negligent homicide" is a real thing. But hopefully it scares the $#!+ out of him.

About an hour later I got a call from Nancy Sedaka and she said, "Your 'friend' Mr. Bringlestad was just in to pick up his gun and just so you know I got quite an earful. He said he has never been talked to as rudely as he was today by that, pardon my French, 'little asswipe in Men's Furnishings.' He took his license to carry out of his wallet to show me and said he carries a firearm to protect people like me. "

No surprise there, his type never seems to listen or learn.

"I almost broke out laughing when he said, 'Listen here girlie, I want you to know I'm a good guy with a gun and you'd be mighty glad I'm pack'n heat if some colored person pulled out a gun and started shoot'n up the place."

Of course, in his racist mind the crazed shooter would have to be a "colored person."

"Was he a short little fat guy with a really bushy eyebrows and wearing a camouflage coat?" I asked her.

"That's the guy." Nancy said. "And he was wearing one of those red 'Make America Like it Used to Be' baseball caps."

"Oh, yah, I remember him. Total redneck! When he was here this morning, he picked out a pair of red bikini underpants and asked if he could try them on! To be honest Nancy, I didn't think we had anything big enough to fit his enormous butt. But now I have to wonder why he had to take his shoulder harness off the try on underwear!"

We laughed.

Then she warned me, "Well, just so you know, he has you in his cross hairs. Before he left, he made sure to ask that I report you to store management for your rude unprofessional behavior. He said 'Nobody talks to Delmer Bringlestad like that and gets away with it.' But don't worry about it dear, I got so busy I forgot to mention it to our dear store manager."

"Whew, that's all I need. Another customer complaint. You know I'm skating on thin ice with Nettie."

"That's what I hear," Nancy said. "Our Customer Service girls have got to look out for our little Trigsey."

Chapter 38

Rules for Parents Shopping with Kids

I suppose it's always easy to give advice about how to raise kids when you don't have any of your own. I know I certainly have a list of what parents should NOT do that I would post at the entrance of the store. That is if I was the one that "owned the damn store."

Here are the main ones:

1. Don't bring newborns to the store on the coldest, iciest day of the year.
2. If your kid says, "Mommy, I'm gonna be sick!" don't continue to shop. They're going to be sick.
3. If your kids are sick, stay home.
4. Measles, mumps and chickenpox are all contagious!
5. Pay attention. If your kids are dancing around, crossing their legs tightly, and holding themselves, they have to go to the bathroom. And not later–now!
6. Cash register counters are not baby changing stations.
7. Employees are not a free babysitting service, don't expect us to watch them while you shop.
8. Do not leave dirty diapers in our waste baskets under the counters.
9. We don't do picnics in the store. Take your Kentucky Fried Chicken and McDonalds burgers to a park or the food court. This store is not the place for sticky, greasy fingers.
10. If your toddlers have dry snacks in their stroller, make sure the food is going in their mouths and not leaving a trail for others to step on.
11. Escalators are not amusement park rides for your kids can play on.
12. Don't let your kids run wild. Keep an eye on them at all times.

13. Teenage girls should not dress like hookers.
14. Teenage boys should not be wearing their jeans hanging almost to the knee with their boxer shorts showing.
15. The V. O. piano is a $50,000 finely-tuned instrument. It is not a toy and this is not the place chance for your child to stumble through chopsticks.

I know I'm beginning to sound like a grumpy old man, but jeeeeeez, the things we see.

Von Oostrom's attempt to keep happy customers by allowing kids to do anything they want is actually harming staff members and making other customers unhappy. But of course, we have to just keep our mouths shut and pretend bad things with kids never happened.

Chapter 39

Forget to Take Prozac

Friday, Noon-9 Shift

This afternoon I approached a guy in the underwear section and asked if he needed any assistance. When he didn't respond, I assumed he hadn't heard me so I asked again.

He turned to me and said very indignantly, "If I need your help, I'll ask for it."

"No problem, I'll just let you look! And by the way my name is Mike."

Twenty minutes later he was still putzing around the underwear so I thought I'd try to move the sale along. I slowly sauntered back over to that section, trying to act like I was straitening the racks as I made my approach. Finally, I worked up the courage to say, "Those Calvin Klein's have been a really great seller. They're a cotton/bamboo blend so they'll keep you nice and dry this summer."

I wasn't sure if he was ignoring me or that perhaps he was hard of hearing so I continued, "I might suggest if you do go with the bikini style, you'll probably want to go up a size."

He shot me one of those looks and I knew immediately he was a guy who needed to be left alone.

A few minutes later I noticed that he had two three-packs of Jockey brand in his hand. He walked right by my counter and got in line behind some customers that Queen was helping at her register by the fitting room. Not wanting him to have to wait in line, I said to him, "Sir, if you'd like, I could help you over at this register."

He walked over to my register like he was finally going to allow me to help him. Then I heard him say, "Do you know what your problem is buddy? You're TOO %^<#ING FRIENDLY!"

As he headed back to get in line at Queen's Register, I yelled, "Thanks for the compliment!"

It was one of those days that I was really having a hard time connecting with anyone. The one gentleman who did approach me for assistance asked where we keep our stool softeners.

I couldn't believe my ears. "Stool softeners? This is an upscale department store for crying out loud".

"You don't have to get so huffy! They sell them at Target."

"Well buy them at Target then!" I told him.

Sheeeesh! Stool softeners!

And if all that wasn't enough for one day, the Sheboygan County Tax Assessor, Herb Grussgott comes in just before closing looking for an outfit to wear to Beach Girls.

"Beach Girls. Is that a band?" I asked. "Are they playing at the grandstand at the Sheboygan County Fair?"

Herb burst out laughing and slapped me on the back, "Oh hell no Triggs. It's a titty bar! Are you telling me you've never been there?"

I couldn't even feign interest, but did manage to help him locate a garish Tommy Bahama Hawaiian shirt and some "titty pink" shorts.

Good grief was I ever glad to see my shift end.

I wonder if I forgot to take my Prozac today. Those green and white capsules usually get me through nearly anything, but today something was clearly not working.

Chapter 40

Why I Left Politics

Tuesday, 7-4 Shift

We usually get a huge truck on Tuesdays that we have to unload before the store opens, but for some reason today's truck didn't arrive. Kent and I had shown up for work at 7:00, so we had about three hours to "look busy" before the store opened at 10:00.

Out of the blue Kent said, "I've heard a lot of rumors about why you got fired from Governor Hanson's re-election campaign. Would you be offended if I ask what the real reason was?"

He startled me with his bluntness and I was hesitant to share too much. "Oh, there are some good rumors out there, that's for sure. In fact, some of them are down-right ridiculous."

Kent looked like he was expecting more, so I continued.

"You're probably too young to remember but four years ago Ingmar Hanson's victory was a real fluke. The Republican candidate for governor dropped out of the race ten days before the election in a sex scandal. Since Ing had finished a distant second in the September primary, the Republican Party leadership decided to make him their candidate. Unfortunately, ballots had already been printed so he had to run as a write-in candidate.

"Normally a person would never win in a write-in, but at the last minute the incumbent Democrat had his own juicy scandal and Ing managed to win by 107 votes. It certainly helped having a Norwegian name like Hanson that everyone can spell."

Kent stood waiting to hear more, nodding his head. I wasn't sure how much I should reveal but I figured I could trust him.

"Once Hanson took office many of the conservative activists in the Republican Party didn't like that he supported a woman's right to choose on abortion and that he had recently signed a gay rights bill that made it illegal in Wisconsin to fire someone because of their sexuality.

"Those two things were the kiss of death for many in the far right-wing of the party, so when it was time for the Governor's re-election, many party activists got behind Orville Quisling, a former state legislator from Rhinelander."

"Where did you fit in?" Kent asked.

"I had been kind of a hired gun that the Hanson people bought in to run his re-election campaign. I had a history of being a great political organizer and quickly raised over a million dollars. The campaign committee couldn't have been happier as it appeared everything was going well.

"That was until I started receiving calls from the media saying that Quisling had been shopping around a list he had assembled of 25 gays and lesbians that were supporting Governor Hanson. And guess whose name was at the top of the list?"

"You're kidding me," Kent said. "That's pretty sleazy."

"That's what the press thought. They promised me they weren't going to run with the story. But since my name was number one on the list they wanted a quote from me, just in case some other news outlet ran with the story.

"So, what did you do?"

"Well at that point in my life I had never acted on my sexuality. I had been married to my job putting in 60 to 80 hours a week, never wanting to do anything to cause embarrassment to the elected officials I worked for. I didn't want to go public, so I called Quisling and confronted him."

"Good for you," Kent said.

"Well, it didn't turn out good. I told Quisling, 'You'd better have some pretty good proof to substantiate your claims or you're going to see me in court because I'll be suing you for libel if the story ever ends up in print.'"

"So, did he back off?"

"Hell no! He said his proof was that I wore bow ties and was a 'snappy dresser,' whatever the hell that means! He also said that he happened to know that I did needlepoint!"

"What?"

"Needlepoint for God's sake!

"It was totally true, of course. But how that equates to being gay is beyond me. Come on, NFL great Rosey Greer from the Giants and the Rams even does needlepoint.

"I told Quisling that when I come home at night, I have to do something that totally takes my mind off politics, and needlepointing allowed me to do exactly that. Needlepoint was my guilty pleasure. I'd even won blue ribbons for my work at two State Fairs. But he wasn't going to back down."

Kent just shook his head in disbelief.

"Four other people on my staff were on the list and I knew for a fact that none of them were gay. Prominent businessmen, medical professionals, and other politicians were also on the list. Many were married to women. It should have been obvious to anyone who knew these folks that Quisling's proof was merely speculative.

"Meanwhile, the list kept being passed around political circles. Everywhere I went people were whispering about it. Not knowing when or if the story would ever drop in the press, I started taking over the counter drugs to go to sleep at night, and energy drinks loaded with caffeine to wake up. I stopped eating and within a matter of weeks had lost over 20 pounds."

"Sheesh, that's horrible, Mike."

"I was a wreck," I continued. "Finally, our campaign chairman came to me and said that people close to the Governor had decided that even though the story had managed to stay out of the headlines, it had become a distraction and they thought it was best that I fall on my sword and leave the campaign. And the excuse they would give the media was that I was leaving the campaign due to 'health reasons.'"

"Oh my God Mike, I can't believe that," Kent said sympathetically.

"And it was the 1990s, I was a newly outed gay guy who had all of a sudden lost a ton of weight, and it didn't take much for people to assume the worst."

"Oh, Mike I am so sorry. Of course, the bastards thought you left because you had AIDS."

"And ironically, I was fired by the very guy who just signed the state's Employment Non-Discrimination Act."

"You should have called a press conference and sued," Kent said.

"How was that going to help me? My reputation was already sullied. I'd applied for other jobs in politics to no avail. But because of gossip on Quisling's part, my name was toxic. Realizing I was essentially blackballed, the writing was on the wall, my life in politics was over. So, I packed up my stuff, moved to my parents' cabin on Wood Lake, and took this job until I could figure out what I want to do for the rest of my life."

Big tears were running down both of our cheeks as Kent tried his best to console me.

"So that's my story," I said as we stood alone in the quiet store. "Nothing as salacious as the rumors. No drug bust. No vice squad arrest in a locker room in downtown Milwaukee. No AIDS. I was just guilty of being a snappy dresser and a needlepoint aficionado."

"Unbelievable," Kent lamented.

"You got that right! Unbelievable. But totally true. Sometimes the truth hurts. And the hurt never really goes away."

Chapter 41

Customer Service

Tuesday, Noon-9 Shift

I'm never going to forget Amaryllis Higginbottom, a sweet old lady who shopped with me this evening.

She couldn't possibly have stood five feet tall. As we looked for an umbrella, she told me that she had retired five years ago after working 45 years as the head librarian of the Mead Public Library in downtown Sheboygan.

As librarians go, Amaryllis was right out of central casting. I couldn't help but notice that she suffered from osteoporosis, was all hunched over and walked with a cane. The quirky little spinster wore the cutest hat and white gloves. It's something you don't see all that often anymore.

In fact, she would be the quintessential Miss Marple in an Agatha Christie crime novel.

She told me she was leaving first thing tomorrow morning to visit her cousin in County Cheshire in England.

"Well in that case, I can see why you are definitely going to need an umbrella," I told her. I showed her a beautiful Burberry umbrella that I had in Men's Furnishings.

"Oh, I just love the Burberry," she said. "In fact, I have a Burberry carpetbag that I always travel with."

Carpetbag?! I haven't seen anyone carry a carpetbag since I watched Mary Poppins as a kid.

"You know Mike, my carpetbag is just perfect for my knitting and five or six books. But I was really hoping I could find one of those fold-up umbrellas that I could keep in my bag when it isn't raining."

Not raining in England? Good luck with that!

"Unfortunately, Miss Higginbottom, I don't have any folding umbrellas in my department, but I'm quite sure I've seen them in the Women's Accessories Department." I suggested we go up to third floor and take a look.

Not only did we find folding umbrellas, but we found a folding Burberry umbrella. Knowing she had to exit the store on first floor we returned to my department to ring it up. I wished her bon voyage and said, "Let's hope you won't need your new umbrella." Although the chances were slim to none that would be the case.

Later when I was straightening my department and getting ready for closing, I noticed a Von Oostrom shopping bag sitting unattended on my counter. I sensed immediately that it was Miss Higginbottom's umbrella.

I knew how disappointed she would be when she realized she had left her umbrella at the store. I looked her name up in the phone book and called to offer to drop it off on my way home.

"Oh, Mike you are such a sweetie! That's exactly why I shop at Von Oostrom. You people go out of your way to make your customers happy."

She said she lived at 3210 Maplewood. Since she had already gotten ready for bed, Amaryllis said she would have her porch light on and I should just leave the umbrella inside her screen door.

But it wasn't as easy as I thought. I ended up in the middle of an ice storm and I slid the whole way driving to the northeast side of Sheboygan. When I got to Maplewood Drive, I discovered that 3210 would have to be at least a mile offshore out in Lake Michigan.

I had a Sheboygan street finder guide in my glove box and checked to see if there was another Maplewood in the area. Sure enough, there was a Maplewood Street in Sheboygan Falls. I turned the car around and slid my way ten miles to the village of Sheboygan Falls.

Normally it would have taken about fifteen minutes to make the cross-town trek but with the icy conditions it took me 45 minutes to get to Miss Higginbottom's house, then another 25 to go back to my cabin. I didn't get home until almost 11:00.

Wednesday, 7-4 Shift

Last night when I did my very first Von Oostrom "hand carry" of Miss Higginbottom's umbrella, I came home feeling really good about the experience. But after what happened tonight, I have serious doubts I will ever to offer to do another one.

Late in my shift this afternoon I sold a nice-looking Chicago businessman a $1,000 Hickey Freeman suit. While ringing up the transaction he asked if there was any possibility that I could rush his alterations as he would really like to wear the suit to a business meeting he was attending at the American Club Resort tomorrow.

Since it was just a simple sleeve shortening and pant hem, I said I'd call my Alterations Manager and see if she could accommodate his request.

After hanging up the phone I was happy to tell him, "Our Alterations Manager Janita said we could have it ready for you by seven. I get off at four today and am planning to catch an early movie with a friend after work. I live on Woodlake not far from the American Club, so I'd be delighted to drop your suit off after the movie to save you a trip back to our store."

"Oh my gosh that is so kind of you. If it is no imposition, I'd be glad to make it up to you with a big tip."

I very confidently said, "No, seriously, I do hand carries for customers all the time. It would be my pleasure to help you out."

He didn't need to know that last night was my first hand carry.

After the movie I picked up the customer's suit, checked it out with security, and drove to the American Club. Remembering he said he had a tip for me, I parked the car and called to tell him I was at the front desk.

He said he was in the middle of something and asked if I could bring it up to Room 2411. Once I got to the room, he said he'd really like to try it on to see if everything was okay with the alterations.

Thinking nothing of it, I sat on one of the beds while he took the suit around the corner by the bathroom to try it on.

"So, what movie did you see?" he yelled from other room.

"We saw 'A Fish Called Wanda' with Jamie Lee Curtis."

"You gotta love Jamie Lee," he said loudly. "And talk about an all-star cast! You don't get any funnier than John Cleese and Michael Palin from Monty Python."

Then I heard him pause with a small grunt, and I wondered if the suit was too tight.

Then he yelled, "Oh, and by the way did I mention I have a little tip for you?"

The guy come out from around the corner holding a crisp hundred-dollar bill.

But to my surprise he was not wearing his new Hickey Freeman suit. He was stark naked.

The man had to have sensed that I was visibly upset. As I got up to leave, he grabbed me and shoved me back down on the bed. As I struggled to get up, he said, "I've heard all about you cheap retail whores and the good service you provide. This $100 should pay for everything I need!"

I jolted up and pushed by him. As I left the room I yelled over my shoulder, "You couldn't pay me enough to give that kind of service!"

As I quickly walked down the hall, I wasn't sure what to do. Should I report him to the hotel staff? Should I call the police? But instead of doing either, I drove home. Would anyone have believed me if I did report him? He would have just denied it.

For all my good intentions, I was left feeling used and betrayed. Some salespeople may have found the seduction exciting but the whole experience made me feel dirty.

It's going to be a long time before I'll do another hand carry for Von Oostrom. If ever.

Chapter 42

The Sticker Man

Friday, 1-9 Shift

When it comes to babies, I feel a little like Miss Prissy from "Gone With the Wind" when she said, "I don't know nothin' 'bout birthin' babies." But I do know that when a woman's water breaks it's time for a husband to stop trying on suits and head to the hospital!

That's exactly what happened tonight with one of my regular customers. The wife kept trying to get her husband's attention but he was determined to try on one more suit.

The guy came out of the dressing room and said, "Mike, I like this one." Then turning to his wife said, "Honey, what do you think of it?"

Before she could even mention that the suit was the last thing on her mind, the husband took one look down at the puddle on the floor underneath her and screamed, "Oh my God! Your water just broke!"

I've never seen anyone change his clothes faster.

A day later the proud papa came back to get his measurements on the suit and showed me pictures of their darling baby girl. Somehow, I felt part of their whole birthing process, but sadly they didn't name the girl after me.

There are females named Michael you know!

I may not know much about newborns, but I do know a thing or two about how to handle bratty kids. And my methods virtually always work.

The minute children start to fuss or act up, I say "Hey little cutie" or "Hey little buddy, do you like stickers?" They will undoubtedly stop their tantrums and come running toward me for stickers I've pulled out of the breast pocket of my suit coat.

I usually have princess stickers for girls, sheriff stickers for boys, Disney characters, Scooby Doo, farm animals, dogs, and cats. I've found that kids like choices. And if they are really nice and say thank you, I'll give them more than one.

In fact, on return visits the kids see me and come running saying, "It's the Sticker Man." And I'm proud to be known by that name, it makes me stand out from other salespeople in the store.

This morning before store opening, Nettie L'Amour came on the loud-speaker and said, "I have a KUDO letter from a customer that I would like to read. They she started to read very slowly and loudly so all the staff could hear it clearly.

"'My family and I have been long time Von Oostrom customers and we usually have such pleasant experiences shopping in your store. Recently my children and I were shopping for a birthday gift for my husband in the Men's Department when we were approached by one of your salesmen, who offered a sticker to my four-year-old son, Lincoln.'"

All of a sudden, I realized this Kudo was for me!

Kent frequently gets KUDOs. As does Queen. But today is my big day to come out, take a bow, and collect a $10 reward from the company!

Nettie continued reading slowly and seriously. "'I'm writing this letter to you today because that guy's actions sent our poor little Lincoln into a complete emotional breakdown. It reminded him of his baby brother Jeffrey, who had recently died in a freak sticker accident.'"

What?! This isn't a KUDO, it is a criticism! She's trying to make me look bad!

I immediately broke down in tears, and Kent and Macy came running to console me.

As I tried to pull myself together and could hear Nettie reading something else. But I was so distraught I never heard the tail end of the KUDO letter that explained it all. Nor did I understand why all of my associates were suddenly laughing.

Then I heard Nettie L'Amour end her announcement with, "Thanks to Kent Patet for adding a little levity with this morning's KUDO letter by punking our store's Sticker Man, Mike Triggs. Have a fun April Fool's Day everyone!"

With friends like Kent, who needs enemies like Nettie L'Amour?

Chapter 43

Lies

Tuesday, 8-5 Shift

It is always interesting to hear the intricate lies people tell when they return things that have been previously worn. Dirtied pants they claim fell on the ground when they got out of the car. Stained ties from last night's expensive dinner that they say had been sold to them that way.

Then there was the guy who returned a white dress shirt that he had bought yesterday to attend his grandfather's funeral.

I could clearly see that the shirt had been worn. All of the tags were off, you could see wrinkles on the tails where it had been tucked in, and there were dark sweat stains under the arms.

Instead of just returning it without making a comment, the guy says, "I never, ever, ever, ever wore the shirt!"

He might have had me I might have never given the shirt a second look. But it was the two extra "evers" that left me a little dubious.

I still cheerfully credited his account and said, "Well you know what Mr. Von Oostrom says in our commercials, 'No sale is ever, ever, ever final here, because I'm here, I'm Einar Von Oostrom and I own the damn store."

I hate that commercial. Old Einar has been dead for years and the family has been running the ad since the 1960's.

But customers aren't the only ones that make up elaborate lies, I made sure Debby knew that I had caught her in a real whopper today.

Last week she asked if I would switch shifts with her on Friday. I was originally supposed to open and she was the closer. As you might expect, I always say yes when a coworker asks me to switch shifts.

But then Debby went into this convoluted story about how she was going to visit her sister who was dying of cancer. Because the sister lived on Felch Mountain in Michigan's Upper Peninsula, Debby wanted me to know how she hates driving around the U.P. after dark.

Well today Debby came back to work sporting a beautiful tan and I overhead Wanda from Ready to Wear ask her if she had a good time in Cancun with the new boyfriend over the weekend.

I was guessing the sister with cancer on Felch Mountain was another one of her elaborate lies. So, I confronted her.

She knew she was busted and finally confessed, "Had I told you the truth I'm sure you would have said no because you're so judgmental. And besides my sister IS dying of cancer, so you should be a little more sympathetic. It's so stressful, I needed the beach vacation."

I had to keep from rolling my eyes at her ridiculous excuses.

"Debby, I could care less who you're dating and it's none of my business who you're sleeping with. But let me you this: don't ever ask me to switch shifts with you again. Your sister could be dead and you need time off to attend her funeral and I'll tell you right now the answer is NO!

Maybe I can be a bit judgmental of those that aren't honest. But it's better to tell the truth bluntly than to pretend to be a caring sister and lie about it!

Chapter 44

The Easter Bunny and The Priest

Saturday, Day Off

I looked at the clock. It was 5:48 a.m., and the phone was ringing. Who the hell could be calling at this time of the morning on my day off?

It was Kent. "I hate to be calling this early but I have been up all night vomiting."

"Oh, for crying out loud!" I told him. "You called me at this time in the morning to tell me something like that?"

"You know I normally wouldn't, except that I am supposed to be the bunny at the store's Easter Bunny Breakfast this morning and I was hoping I could get you to fill in for me. Under the circumstances, I'm in no position to do it."

Me having to be the happy Easter Bunny, surrounded by a bunch of bratty kids? It's the one job no one in the store ever wants to do and he thinks I'd be good at tolerating a bunch of brats while stuffed in a hot costume?

Then he moaned and said, "Smelling that food they serve and having to hop around would probably make me puke inside the bunny suit."

My heart went out to him because he sounded terrible, so I reluctantly said I'd do it. "What time and where do I get the costume?"

"Oh, thanks Mike. Everything you need is in our back room at the store. Kelly Wurlitzer from Kids Shoes is in charge of everything and she'll fill you in on all the details when you get there."

The idea of working with kids on my day off didn't get me excited and I let out a sigh.

"You can do this buddy!" He suddenly gave me a pep talk. "I know you can. You just need to be there are 7:30 to get ready to greet the kids when they arrive for breakfast at 8:00."

"Just what I want to do on my day off. You're going to owe me for this one, Kent."

"I know, I know! But I'm guessing you're going to have fun!"

Fun? How could he ever use that word about a grumpy single guy giving up his day off to dress up in a hot costume in a room full of whiny kids? They probably won't even give me breakfast!

I quickly showered and shaved, getting there in plenty of time. When I arrived at the store, I told Kelly I was filling in for Kent.

"I'm so thankful you were willing to pitch in and help," she said. "It's going to be really easy. We are expecting 64 kids, plus parents and grandparents."

That means there might be over one hundred people there for my performance?! One hundred people I have to pretend I'm happy with? What did I get myself into?

Kelly continued. "You meet them at the front door and have your picture taken with each of them individually."

Wow, 64 photos? That's going to take a while. And that bunny suit looks hot.

"Then after breakfast you'll lead the kids in the big Easter Parade about 9:00, and then we'll have an Easter egg hunt on first floor."

Lead an Easter Parade? Egg hunt? This is going to be much more work than I bargained for.

"We do the egg hunt last so the kids aren't all sugared up before break-fast," Kelly added. "Easy peasy! Now get dressed and practice hopping till the kids arrive."

Easy for her to say! Practice hopping? Is she serious?

In the past I had always thought it would be fun to be one of the cos-tumed characters at Disneyland or Disney World. But as I got dressed up, I realized that these outfits are hot, the head is heavy, and it isn't easy to see out the mesh in the rabbit's mouth.

I practiced hopping a little, which was difficult to do with the bulky weight, but soon it was time for my big debut. For the most part the kids were happy to see me and loved getting their pictures taken. But a few of the really young ones were frightened to death and started screaming.

Just as I thought we were finished with the meet and greet portion of the morning I saw a little boy running toward me with hands outstretched. I leaned over thinking he wanted to give me a hug, when all of a sudden, the little bastard high kicked me! Right in the 'tenderest eggs' of my private bunny basket!

I was in so much freaking pain. I wanted to rip off the head off the costume, punch the time clock, and leave. But I knew how disappointed the kids would be if their Easter parade and egg hunt were canceled because the Easter Bunny skipped out while they were eating scrambled eggs and French toast sticks.

Out of the mouth opening I did get to see the little brat's mother grab him by the scruff of his neck and drag him out of the store yelling, "What the hell were you thinking? We're leaving if that's the way you're going to behave."

It sounded like mom was more disappointed to miss the egg hunt than her son.

While the kids were eating breakfast, Bessy from Housekeeping was able to get me an ice pack and a couple of Advil. That helped a little, but I was hopping very gently while leading the parade in order to keep my private eggs from hurting too much. By the time the kids started the hunt this bunny found a place to sit down on his soft, comfy tail.

Thankfully the rest of the breakfast event went off as planned without any more incidents. The customers stuck around afterwards for a bit and by the time they all left I had been in that ridiculous costume for over two hours.

Once I changed and got ready to leave, Kelly unexpectedly handed me a $25 V. O. gift card for helping out. I appreciated the thought, but that worked out to making about minimum wage for a lot of work on my day off. And a V. O. gift card wouldn't help pay for the future doctor's visits I'd have to make for the groin pain!

Monday, 8-5 Shift

Over the next couple of days my attitude changed and I was able to see the humor in the situation. When I finally got to work with Kent this morning I immediately said, "You didn't tell me I needed to wear a jock strap to be the Easter Bunny."

He laughed, "I know, I heard all about it yesterday!"

"Except for that little rat bastard, the kids were really well behaved. And you didn't tell me I'd get a $25 gift card for doing it."

"Oh, you were supposed to give that to me!"

"Yah, right!"

During our break before store opening, I asked Kent, "Did I miss anything yesterday?"

"Miss anything? You sure did! Michael Brownback's big mouth finally got him fired."

"Oh my God, what did he say this time." "A customer came in with six kids, two in a stroller, and the first thing he said was, "Well it looks like you're either Catholic or careless."

We both chuckled, then Kent continued. "Well, the lady didn't think it was at all funny and went up to Nettie L'Amour's office to complain. The next thing we knew Michael was paged to the manager's office and a few minutes later she called me to cover Suits Department, saying Michael wouldn't be coming back."

"We knew it was going to happen sooner or later. The guy was a good salesman but he just couldn't resist the temptation to say whatever was on his mind," I said. "It should probably be a good lesson for both of us."

I kept that in mind this afternoon when Father Tim Schouts from St. Anthony's Catholic parish was in my department. It's rare that I don't see him in all black with a clerical collar. But today he was in workout clothes since he said he was coming from an aerobics class at the YMCA.

"I put on so much weight over the winter I just have to get some of it off," he told me. "I know they say black is supposed to be slimming but it sure isn't working for me."

I suggested that he might want to try wearing Spanx under his clerical clothes.

"That's not like wearing a woman's corset, is it?" he asked.

"Oh heavens no. It's just a man's tee shirt with lots of spandex or Lycra in it. I wear one occasionally when I've missed too many workouts."

Of course, I probably weigh at least 150 pounds less than the good Father.

I showed him where they were and suggested that he was welcome to try one on.

A few minutes later Father Schouts came out of the dressing room and said, "Wow! These things really make a difference. I swear it looks like I have lost at least twenty pounds!"

Even then, he still had more than twenty pounds he needed to lose. But I agreed he looked much better with it on.

"I think I'm going to take one of these," he said as he went back in to change.

A minute later I hear this loud, "Mike, Mike," coming from the dressing room.

I ran back to see how I could help and he shouted, "For the love of God, I can't get this damn thing off!"

It was clearly stuck on him but at least he was laughing about it. His hands were up in the air and the Spanx shirt was totally covering his head. It wasn't going anywhere. The more that the two of us pulled, the more he perspired. It was clear Father Tim was starting to panic.

I called for Kent to come and help, but even with the two extra hands it wasn't coming off.

I kept apologizing and was about to ask Father Tim if he could call on divine help when I suddenly had an idea. I rushed out to our cash wrap desk, grabbed a pair of scissors, and began to very carefully cut him out of his dilemma.

He offered to pay for the ruined Spanx but I told him to forget it. "We'll just mark it out of stock. It's just part of doing business."

After Father Tim got dressed, he said, "Well that idea's obviously not going to work. I'm clearly not going to want to call on Father Duffy or a couple of altar boys to get me out of one of those contraptions."

Not knowing exactly what to say, I responded, "Well, Kent was an altar boy."

The portly Father chuckled and said, "No matter what you hear about us priests, I'm sure Kent never got called into that kind of service!"

Chapter 45

People of the Year

Wednesday, Noon-9 Shift

Standing at the counter, I looked up from what I was doing and Rosemary Beatty, everyone's favorite gossip, was standing in front of me beaming from ear to ear.

"Have you seen the new issue of Wisconsin Law and Politics?" she asked loudly. "You are one of their People of the Year!"

At first, I thought it was another one of Kent's April Fools jokes. But Rosemary opened up the magazine and held the article inches from my face. It was my name and my picture.

As politely as possible, I snatched the magazine out of her hands and started reading.

PEOPLE OF THE YEAR

Our people of the year this year include ousted politicians (Norvid Quisling and Mike Triggs–two names we bet have never before been linked), a quitter (Congressman Tom Pennypacker), con man (Michael DePassquallo), and even a couple of millionaire businessmen (Robert Foster and Knut Knutson). What all of these unlikely linked people share is the actions they took separated them from the crowd– actions that rippled through the Wisconsin zeitgeist last year. These people may not be–indeed, are not, for the most part–powerful in the traditional sense of the word. But their acts have had a power of their own, a power that may influence long after the headline-makers have disappeared from the scene.

There were different stories in the publication, but my eyes were immediately drawn to my story.

MIKE TRIGGS – Knee-capped Quisling – Dismissed from Republican A-List. A New Life for an Old Pol.

It isn't quite Shakespearean, but when you go from the number-one man in the governor's re-election campaign to being a salesperson at the underwear counter at Von Oostrom's, it's quite a fall. But Mike Triggs–who made the trip–wasn't pushed. He says he jumped–and it was a leap for joy, he would tell you.

Until he quit his job last year, Triggs was Governor Ing Hanson's number-one election advisor. Triggs says he has gladly given up 80-hour weeks and a diet of chalky antacids, headache pills, and anti-depressants that couldn't quite do the job. He's gleefully given up high blood pressure and a life of all work and no play. He's also given up a salary of $50,000 a year.

"With 88 cents in my checking account, I'd be lying if I didn't tell you I miss the money," he says, "but life's livable now."

Still, for all the relief he's found, he realizes that everything has its disadvantages. "I've traded the Governor's frantic calls for frantic calls from Visa and Mastercard," he says," but I'm also having a good time."

Triggs is one of the casualties (or, depending on how you look at it, successes) of the split in the today's Republican Party between the old faithful and the religious right. He was hired in 1991 by the old faithful to be the party's executive director, and by all accounts did a smashing job. Then the religious right began taking the party over in caucuses.

Triggs, who clearly identifies himself as a liberal Republican, has hardly been cautious about his opinion of that take-over. He spoke of the "zombie" conservatives he felt were eating the party alive. In a Milwaukee Sentinel op-ed, he wrote, "They were dead in features, totally devoid of a sense of humor, mechanical in action, listlessly voting in a trance-like state for the anti-abortion slate of 'sanitized' candidates." Clearly, he wasn't vying for a position in Norvid Quisling's cabinet.

Before Triggs' political life began to resemble a Grade B horror flick, there was his life in Rabbit Gulch, Iowa, population 1,500. He grew up there in a politically active household and by the third grade was already dabbling at campaign politics, working for his legislator, Frances Hakes, slipping her brochures under windshield wiper blades on Main Street.

He gained experience at many levels in Republican politics in Iowa, North Dakota and Minnesota, even running twice for the Iowa legislature in 1976 and 1984. In 1989 he headed off to Washington to hold political positions in George H. W. Bush's administration before ultimately moving to Wisconsin to assume his fateful positions with the Wisconsin Republican Party and Governor Hanson's campaign.

These days he's not completely out of politics. Instead of designing campaign literature, writing speeches, producing award-winning radio, TV and print ads, he works behind the scenes outfitting the state's best dressed Republicans... and Democrats.

Good times or not, one question still remains. After tasting the political bouillabaisse, can Triggs resist the urge to dive back into the pot? He says he can, but there are many who have their doubts.

Well, I guess I proved them wrong! And kudos to Law and Politics that it didn't feel compelled to mention my sexuality.

"Wow that was quite an article," I told Rosemary. "Thanks for bringing it in for me to see."

"Oh, you keep it," she insisted. "The judge gets a copy at the office and that one came to us at home. I'll bet your mom would probably like to see it."

"I'm sure she would. You know how Moms are."

I showed the article to Kent when he got back from lunch. His reaction upon reading it was, "Nice spin on the story. It's too bad they couldn't have told the truth about how you really got canned."

"Oh well. It's always best to let sleeping dogs lie.

Chapter 46

The Creeper

Friday, 7-4 Shift

The funniest thing happened this morning. A man from China was shopping in the department and in trying to talk with him it became obvious that he was not particularly comfortable with the English language.

After several offers to help, he finally said, "I looky for tongs."

"Oh thongs, we've got those," and I walked him over to the flip-flop section of the Men's Shoe Department.

When I showed him what we had in stock he looked angry and began waving his hands back and forth like a windshield wiper, saying, "No, No, No!" He looked at me and said, "Tongs! Tongs!"

Obviously. I wasn't understanding what he was looking for.

Finally, the disgusted shopper took his finger and ran it up and down the back of his pants and said, "Tong!"

I laughed as I said, "Ah, tongs." I waved my hands back and forth and said, "No, tongs for men."

Over lunch I was retelling the story to others. June La Farge from the Intimate Things and Stuff Department said, "Well we do sell ladies thongs, you could have brought him over to my department."

We all had a good laugh. Maybe he's into that kind of thing. Come to think of it, he was so small that he might have easily fit into a ladies thong!

June then told a great story from one of her first days on the job. A lady came in to Intimate Things with a receipt that she found in her husband's coat pocket. She said, "I see he spent $14.95 in this department on something called Hanky Panky and I wanted to know what it is."

June said she responded with, "Oh, that's the brand name of a company that sells thongs. Maybe he bought it for you for a gift and he just hasn't given it to you yet."

The very indignant woman said, "I don't wear thongs and after 47 years together my husband should know that."

June told us, "I tried to suggest that perhaps it was a just a keying error, but she was hearing none of it."

"Listen here missy," the wife said, "don't think I'm not aware of what's been going on behind my back. I wasn't born yesterday. When I saw Hanky Panky on the receipt I had my suspicion. I just needed to confirm it."

She grabbed the receipt out of June's hand and huffed off.

I was contemplating June's story and all of a sudden blurted out, "You don't suppose that her husband could be a crossdresser and bought them for himself?"

"Could be, but I'm guessing her hubbie might be getting a little action on the side. From the look on that dried up old prune's face, I'm pretty sure it has been years since he gotten any action at home."

After lunch I mentioned to Queen that I'm getting a little nervous about the guy in the trench coat and fedora that has been hanging around our department for the last couple of days.

"He's like something out of a 1940's Raymond Chandler movie the way he lurks around pillars or pops out from behind a pajama fixture," I told her. "He's always there and seems to only be looking at me. It's really creeping me out.

"Maybe he's a private eye or someone from Mall Security" Queen suggested.

"Mall Security guys usually wear those bright yellow polo shirts and I certainly haven't done anything to have a private eye tailing me."

"He's probably just lonely or is one of those customers who can't make up their mind about a purchase. Just ignore him and he'll go away."

"I don't know," I confessed. "He's creeping me out big time."

"Are you sure you've been taking your Prozac lately?" Queen said. "You worry me when you don't take it."

"You are just like my mom. Yes, I took my Prozac! The guy's a creeper...I just know it."

Sunday, Noon-6 Shift

The creeper was back again today. Twice. This is really starting to make me nervous.

He was hanging around the department for about an hour early in the afternoon and I saw him leaning up against the wall outside the store entrance when I left at the end of my shift. Now he probably knows what I drive and might even know where I live.

I talked with the head of our store security team and he said there really isn't anything they can do. Until he makes a threat or does something illegal security can't touch him. He said that a customer just looking at me isn't reason enough for the store to do anything.

Kent, Queen, and several others have all approached the guy asking if he needs help, but his standard line is, "I'm just looking."

It sounds like I just have to put up with his stares.

I've got so many questions. Who is the guy? What does he want? What is he looking for? When will this stop? And why me?

Monday, Day Off

I couldn't sleep at all last night. All I could think about was that guy in the trench coat.

When I was out for a run, I flagged down a Sheboygan police officer and asked what I needed to do to file a police report. He said the same thing as store security, that there is nothing police can do unless a threat is made or some crime is committed.

Sheeeesh, what's it going to take? Are they going to have to find me lying dead on the side of the road before someone will do something?

Tuesday, 10-6 Shift

Taking my afternoon break, I was in the men's restroom and I heard the door creak open. I turned to look, and who saddled up beside me at the urinal but the guy in the trench coat. I was zipped up, washed my hands quickly and got out of there in a flash, and immediately went to talk to someone in Human Resources.

Trying to talk with Krayfisch was no help at all. He kept putting it back on me by suggesting that perhaps I had done something to provoke the unwanted glares.

I was in tears when I left his office and went to the backroom to regain my composure. There I ran into Big Earl from our Shipping Department. Earl is this large, muscular, dumb, former football jock who was the last person in the world you would ever want to see you crying.

But as I shared my fears the guy surprised the $#!+ out of me. Big Earl was better than any therapist I had ever seen. He was so in tune with what was going on and assured me that no one wanted me to get hurt.

After he left the backroom, it took me a while before I could get my tears under control. But once I did, I headed back to the department.

Kent ran up to me and said, "Oh my God Mike you should have been here to see it. Big Earl came out of the backroom and got in your stalker's face screaming, 'Listen here dick head. I don't know who you are or what you're up to but you need to get the hell out of here now or I'm going to beat the $#!+ out of you.' I thought the guy was going to piss himself he was so scared. From the look on his face after Earl was done with him, I'm betting he'll never set foot in this store again."

I sure hope he's right.

I would never have thought that Big Earl would be the guy to put an end to my creeper nightmare but he has definitely become my hero.

Chapter 47

Horses, Vines, and Guns

Saturday, 9:30- 5 Shift

Reginald Schroeder is one of my regulars, he works for the Sheboygan Metropolitan Waste Authority. In other words, he drives a garbage truck. But to see him, you would never know it.

Reggie, as he likes to be called, is quite the natty dresser. In fact, he has an affinity for Robert Graham sports shirts that start at $255 and go all the way up to $450 each. He really loves the gaudier designs.

While they are not exactly something I would ever wear, they are perfect for the best dressed garbage man in Sheboygan. And since I'm working on commission, Reggie would normally be the kind of customer I'd like to have in my Personal Customer Book.

I say "normally," but there is absolutely nothing normal about Reggie. The guy has a wild eye that erratically moves from right to left and sometimes it rolls completely back into his eye socket revealing red spidery veins. All while his other eye is laser focused. The guy never blinks. It's the weirdest thing I have seen in my life.

Once Reggie gloms on, you're stuck listening to him blabber on about everything and nothing for the next forty-five minutes to an hour. Today he mentioned he's is on Match.com and that his Robert Graham shirts give him something to talk about with the ladies.

If true, it confirms a conversation I had with the Robert Graham sales rep a couple of weeks ago when I asked him who the company's target customer was. He replied, "Well, Mike, he's a recently divorced, middle-aged guy who is on the rebound and dating a flight attendant that is younger than his daughter."

Today I wanted to ask about all the women Reggie had been dating, I resisted the temptation and watched the swirling eyeball, while thinking "cha ching, cha ching" as he looked over our latest shipment of Robert Graham's.

It was freaking exhausting, but I hung in there, and finally he plunked down his V. O. credit card for three shirts totaling $835. And I'll really score if he comes back tomorrow for the fourth shirt, he asked me to put on hold.

I had just finished wrapping up Reggie's big sale when a wrinkly, blue-haired prune approached me and said she needed to buy a gift for her 22-year-old great-nephew's graduation.

I suggested, "The Ralph Lauren Polo clothing line is especially popular with young guys. In fact, it's probably our number one choice for men of all ages. I've actually been wearing it since I was in my twenties. It just never goes out of style."

"It's nice, but it's not going to work for Chuckie," she responded. "He was bitten by a pony when he was a little boy and has been traumatized by the sight of horses all his life."

I assured her that there were lots of other options beyond the distinctive Ralph Lauren logo. As we perused the sales floor, I noticed she was eyeing several shirts in one of our other collections.

"These are nice and sporty," she said. "But do boys his age wear plaid?"

"Oh yes, plaids are timeless. The colors you see in the Vineyard Vines collection really pop and they have a cute little whale logo."

"Did you say Vineyard Vines?" she asked. "Oh, I'm afraid that might push him over the top. He's very fragile."

I must have given her a look of total bewilderment. Over the top? Fragile? Afraid of ponies? What kind of freak show is this kid? Did he have an issue with whales too?

She whispered, "He's an alcoholic and spent six weeks in rehab last summer."

"In that case I can see where you wouldn't want to jeopardize his sobriety, but Vineyard Vines really has nothing to do with alcohol. It's just a plaid shirt made in Martha's Vineyard on Cape Cod, Massachusetts."

She made a scrunched-up, disapproving look. Nothing I could say would change her mind and we continued our search for a perfect gift.

After scouring the entire department, she finally picked out a really nice chambray shirt. While wrapping her purchase I casually mentioned that the Rodd and Gunn chambrays launder up so nicely.

"Gun?! Did you say gun?" she asked.

"Not to worry. It's a person's name and is spelled with two n's."

"Oh, I'm very anti-gun! "

Who knew I was going to ignite such a firestorm? For the next ten minutes the old bat went on a rant about school shootings, the NRA, and its support of the Republican Party.

"I know I'm a difficult customer, but you're going to have to find me something else."

Realizing I had run out of options, I asked Macy if she had any suggestions for the young man's graduation and quietly walked away.

A while later I saw Macy boxing up some navy-blue socks and a package of Jockey undershorts. Why didn't I think of that? Underwear was the "perfect" gift for a college graduate from his dear old auntie!

I just hope she doesn't suddenly realize that "socks" and "boxers" might sound a little too violent for her precious Chuckie.

Chapter 48

Swimsuits

Monday, Noon-9 Shift

Kent couldn't wait to tell me the big news. Over the weekend, Debby eloped with Stu the Roto-Rooter man she has been dating. Apparently, she said "I could care less if Stu doesn't have money, his big wiener more than compensates for a big bank account."

Oh my god, our little gold digger has turned over a new leaf. Will wonders never cease?

I had an out-of-town visitor come in today looking for a swimsuit. He was very emphatic when he said, "I don't want the kind with a built-in slingshot."

Now I know what both a swimsuit and a slingshot are, but failed to get the connection.

Finally, it dawned on me what he was talking about. "Oh, you must mean a built-in jock strap."

He chuckled and said, "Ya, that's what I mean. If I can't swim naked, I at least like to have the boys hanging free and natural"

"Well unfortunately, all of our swimsuits have a built-in lining. Of course, you could always cut it out."

He tried on several suits before finally deciding to go with a banana colored, yellow Tommy Bahama swimsuit. In talking, I learned that his family is spending the weekend at the American Club Resort so I suggested that if he wanted to use my scissors, he'd be welcome to do so.

"That's a great idea," he said. "Because I won't have any scissors back at the hotel." He cut the lining out right there in the store.

A couple of hours later the same guy came back in, but this time his face was beet red. Before I could ask how the swimming suit had worked out, he was screaming at the top of his lungs.

"I'm going to sue you and take the Von Oostrom family for everything they're worth!"

He was really pissed. Immediately customers and coworkers were coming from all directions to find out what his outburst was all about.

I said, "Take it easy buddy. Take a deep breath. What's the problem?"

"I went back to the hotel, changed into my swimming suit and met my family at the pool. I jumped in, was swimming around and having fun, but when I got out of the pool I might as well have been wearing Saran Wrap. I could just as well have been swimming naked. Everyone was pointing and laughing. I've never been so humiliated in my life."

It was all I could do to keep from giggling. All I could think of to say was, "I guess there was a reason the suit came with the 'built-in sling shot.' But, unfortunately sir, you were the one who cut the lining out of the suit."

"Ya, but you gave me the suggestion…and they were Von Oostrom's scissors. Someone's going to pay!"

In the end I was able to resolve the situation by returning his money and gave him a black swimsuit for free. It seemed the least I could do to ease his embarrassment of having his family and friends see his "boys."

For the sake of his manhood and reputation, I sure hope the pool was heated!

At least that guy had a sense of modesty. Queen told me that last summer a couple of Dutch guys named Yip and Yanny were not at all concerned about who saw them naked. They stripped right down on the sales floor and tried on swimsuits in front of her and Suzanna.

She laughed and said, "Those were a couple of big Dutch boys."

As I was thinking about the embarrassed guy in the swimsuit and the nude Dutch guys, I saw a good-looking younger man walk in just before closing. He was a cute Delta flight attendant and hung around for a bit before he approached me to say, "You know if you're not doing anything after work, I'm in Room 431 at the Days Inn by the airport."

I thanked him for the offer but told him I already had plans. I gave him one of my cards should he find himself on another layover in Sheboygan.

After he left, I thought, "Damn, maybe he'd be interested in a slightly used, form-fitting Tommy Bahama swimsuit with the lining cut out!"

Chapter 49

The Teen Shoplifter

Thursday, Noon-9 Shift

A very sad thing happened this evening, but hopefully a young man learned something that will change his life forever.

I was working in our Young Men's Department and couldn't help but notice a suspicious-looking teenager. He had been in the store for about forty-five minutes and had turned down my offers of assistance on several occasions.

I've seen enough shoplifting to know there was clearly a struggle going on in this kid's head: *I think I'm going to do it…no, don't you're going to get caught. Oh, go ahead nobody is looking. It will be easy…but you'll be sorry!*

It was a very slow night and he was the only shopper in my area, so I couldn't help but notice that he was carrying three tee shirts on hangers. After his third trip to the dressing room with the same three shirts, I made a call to our store security team and told them I had a suspicious looking kid in Young Men's. The security manager Jim assured me that they had been watching him and that I should just keep an eye on him.

As I hung up the phone, I saw the young man quickly exit the dressing room and return two shirts to the sale rounders before exiting the store. Wanting to give him the benefit of the doubt that he may have left one of the shirts in the fitting room, I went in to check. But all I found was an empty hanger.

I knew what was going to happen next, I've seen it all too many times. As soon as he set foot outside the store our crack security team would make an arrest. They can't arrest him in the store since he can always say he was planning on purchasing it, so we always have to wait until he leaves.

Sure enough, it wasn't more than five minutes before I saw Jim escorting the teen back into the store and heading to the security office.

I got busy with another customer and had forgotten about the whole thing when an hour later a gentleman came up to the counter. He was accompanied by a woman that I assumed was his wife, as well as an older female, a young boy, and a younger girl, all of whom were in tears.

It's not unusual to see little kids cry, but the fact the two women were also in tears seemed highly unusual.

The gentleman quietly asked me where our store security office was located. As I escorted him to the office while the others stayed behind, he told me in slightly broken English that he had received a call saying that his 14-year-old son had been arrested for stealing a shirt. He said he was an immigrant from Mexico and that he had brought his wife, the boy's abuela (which I assumed means grandmother in Spanish), and the sister and brother. He said they all came so that his son could see the shame he had brought on the entire family.

"He has always been such a good boy," the man said. "His brother and sister look up to him. I'm not sure why he did something like this."

"You never know why kids do things," I told him. "Maybe he's gotten in with a wrong crowd. But the good thing is that because he is under age eighteen this arrest won't go on a record and he won't have to go to jail."

"That's what the man told me on the phone."

"So hopefully he will learn his lesson and won't do it again," I said.

I knocked on the security door and told Jim that this was the teenager's father, then returned to the Young Men's Department, where the mother, grandmother, and siblings were waiting, still in tears.

After almost an hour the father returned with the son. Not knowing Spanish, I'm unsure what exactly was said between the family members, but I could clearly understand the shame the young man was feeling and the pain on the faces of his family. That pain is universal and needs no language interpretation.

Before leaving the store, the father thanked me for my assistance and compassion.

Part of me felt badly for them because my call to security was the reason for the boy's arrest. But as I watched them leave, I realized that my call may have changed this young man's life forever in a positive way. And the fact that he has a wise father and loving family to support him means he will have a chance to turn his life around.

When the long work shift had ended, I walked out of the store with Kent. I told him about the shoplifting incident.

"Yah, I saw the whole thing go down earlier tonight. I had a similar thing last Spring."

"What happened?"

"I had twin brothers that stole a couple pair of board shorts for their senior trip to the Dominican Republic. Long story short, as punishment they had to stay home from the trip. Their parents had planned on being chaperones and as part of the punishment the boys had to watch the parents go with his friends on the senior trip without them."

Then Kent added, "You know, I'm a twin so it especially hit home for me. They've got to learn there are consequences for their actions."

"Unfortunately," I said, "Not everyone is as lucky as all three of these boys to have parents who love them enough to steer them back on the right path."

Chapter 50

Shower Buddy

Monday, 8-5 Shift

I couldn't believe my eyes when I saw what Queen was wearing today. She was sporting bright orange thigh-high boots with stiletto heels that were skin tight. They looked like 'pleather' but the only way she could have pulled them on was if they were made from some stretchy material.

Oh, and on the opposite end of her body was a matching neon orange Pippi Longstocking-style wig with braids and over-the-eyebrow bangs.

I wasn't exactly sure what look she was going for. Maybe an African/Swedish school-girl-gone-bad streetwalker?

But any way you looked at it, that getup was not going to pass the Von Oostrom fashion police.

"Those are pretty kinky boots Queen! Did they come from here?" I inquired.

"There is no way our Von Oostrom buyers would have purchased something this cool," she said bluntly. "I got them online at T. B. Dress+."

"I've never heard of it."

"Well, being a man, you wouldn't. They specialize in low-priced, high-end looking women's apparel for full figured women."

A few minutes later Queen got called off the floor by the store's fashion police and was sent home to change into something more "Von Oostrom appropriate."

With Queen gone, I was the only one in the department and we started to get really busy, so I called for some backup.

Wouldn't you know, my two least favorite people in the store showed up to help: Nettie L'Amour and her little weasel sidekick, Homer Krayfisch. What did I do to deserve this?

No sooner had the manager arrived in the department than she said, "Has that person over in loungewear been greeted?"

I gave her an "Are you kidding me?" look. I had three people lined up at the counter. I wouldn't have called if I didn't need help. She then preceded to lecture me on how Von Oostrom rules require every customer to be greeted in 30 seconds and if I can't do the job, "We'll find someone who can."

It was all I could do to not just walk off the floor, but I gave her a smarmy and unctuous, "I'll get right on it."

I apologized to the customers in line at the counter and went off to greet the customer with three seconds to spare. And who was it that I went out of my way for but "Whizzer," a guy from my 98th Street Athletic Club that pisses in the shower.

People at the club have complained about it but his answer is always, "It's just water down the drain."

I suggested that if he needed any help, "Just ask that lady over there," and pointed to Nettie L'Amour.

Of course, he didn't.

When it was time to ring up his sale he came back to my counter.

I rushed through the transaction, hoping he didn't recognize me from the gym. Then out of the blue, he said for half the store to hear, "I know you. You're my shower buddy!"

Ewwwwwww!

He so creeped me out I got goose pimples ringing up his sale and said very quietly, "Oh, yes. I think I remember you."

I quickly put his loungewear in a shopping bag and said, "Thank you for shopping at Von Oostrom."

But it wasn't enough for him to just walk away. He picked up the bag from the counter and said, "See you in the showers!"

I shivered as he sashayed away.

Just then I turned to my left and noticed Krayfisch standing beside me.

"Soooooo, Mr. Triggs, tell me more about your…" adding air quotes, "shower buddy."

I got right in his face, thought twice about how I would repond, and then exploded at him saying, "%^<# YOU!"

Then as I walked away, I announced to the world, "I'm going on my break!"

Chapter 51

Matthew Shephard

Wednesday, 8-5 Shift

I picked up donuts for my Men's Department co-workers, so I got to work about twenty minutes earlier than usual. The last time I brought in Krispy Kremes I got quite a ribbing. I put a note on the box that said, "Please thank the person who brought in the dognuts."

Of course, everyone knew it was me…I'm such a bad speller.

Since I was early, I picked out one of my favorite donuts and began reading the paper in the lunch room. My eyes immediately were drawn to the headline, "Laramie man clings to life - Gay man beaten, burned and left tied to a fence."

In reading the story, a 21-year-old University of Wyoming freshman by the name of Matthew Shephard had been tortured, struck in the head 19 times with a blunt instrument, was tied to a fence, and left to die in the frigid cold. I couldn't help but tear up as I read of the gruesome attack and how he had been found alive by a young man on a bicycle the morning after the brutal beating.

Kent came bouncing into the lunchroom and said, "Hey, I heard there are Krispy Kremes!"

He immediately noticed that I was visibly upset and asked, "What's the matter buddy?"

Seeing the article in front of me he said, "Isn't that horrible. I heard it on NPR on the way in."

He grabbed a donut and I tossed my unfinished one in the wastebasket, then we headed to the floor before we were late for our shift.

When we got to the department there were six big boxes waiting to be unpacked. As Kent sliced them open, he said, "I sure hope the kid lives. On the radio they said he suffered four skull fractures and is in a coma at a Denver hospital. The good thing is the sheriff in Wyoming has arrested a couple of guys who they are pretty sure did the gay bashing."

Good thing. But what possible good could come out of something tragic like this?

I kept thinking about the kid's poor parents watching their only son as he clung to life in that hospital bed.

Kent said, "These gay bashings are happening way too often now."

He went on to tell me about how the boyfriend of a pal of his had been beaten up by six guys outside of a Minneapolis gay bar. They had kicked the guy in the face so many times that his lower jaw had been completely separated from his skull. When the police arrived, his jaw was hanging by a thin piece of skin.

"Did he die?"

"He might as well have. He was in a coma for months then had to learn to walk and talk all over again. While they were able to do reconstructive surgery on his face and jaw, he's never going to be right. The guy is consumed by rage and his anger issues have destroyed a once loving relationship. It was so sad!"

"I know all about that rage he must feel," I said. "I went through something similar years ago."

"What do you mean?" Kent asked.

"You never get over it. I may have told you that in 1984 I was a candidate for the Iowa House of Representatives, but what I'm about to tell you is something I've only shared with a couple of friends and never with any of my family members."

Kent stopped unpacking the box and stared at me.

"I was running for an open seat in the state legislature that had the potential to go either way. There were almost an equal number of Republicans and Democrats in the district. I didn't have as much money as my opponent. But what I lacked in funds I made up for in energy. I started knocking doors with snow on the ground in February and kept knocking every day through the fall.

"By mid-October I had knocked on virtually all of the doors in the district. My strategy was simple: I would knock on their door and when I got home at night would write every voter a follow-up postcard saying I enjoyed meeting them or was sorry they were not home.

"I won my primary by 36 votes and was feeling really good about the fall election. That is, until I knocked on an apartment door on Des Moines' south side."

Kent continued to listen quietly.

"I remember it so clearly; the apartment was across from a laundry room and it was very noisy in the hall, so the man invited me to come inside. Once the door closed, he grabbed me and threw me against the wall and started pounding his fist into my chest, as he kneed me in the groin. Throughout the attack he kept screaming, 'You %^<#ing faggot!'

"It quickly became apparent that he thought I was a different Republican candidate who was openly gay and was running against our longtime incumbent Congressman.

"I tried my best to explain that I wasn't that candidate but he was hearing none of it. I remember he had his hands around my neck and was choking me. I actually saw my life passing before me when all of a sudden, his wife walked in on the attack and said, 'Robert what's going on?' He let loose of me just long enough that I was able to slide out the open door."

"Mike, no. I can't believe it," Kent said. "Did you call the police?"

"No, I didn't, and I didn't go to the emergency room. In my primary there had been a well-organized whisper campaign which was conducted by my primary opponent's campaign manager. The word was spreading that I was gay."

"You've got to remember this was 1984 and while I might have known I was gay in the back of my mind it was the last thing I was going to admit. I had spent decades hiding from the truth."

Kent looked like he wanted to hug me.

"Because of those rumors left over from the primary, I talked over the attack with my campaign manager and we decided to keep it all quiet for fear the story might appear in the newspapers days before the election and it might impact the votes of conservative anti-gay Republicans.

"I'm sure I had broken ribs. I had bruises all over my upper body, particularly my neck where he had me in a choke hold. And the thing I remember most was my scrotum was swollen to the size of a pineapple and the pain it caused me in walking. Instead of seeking any medical help, I took some left-over pain pills I had from having my wisdom teeth out, and wore bulky sweaters and a turtleneck to hide the bruises. If anyone asked why I was limping I said I fell off my bike."

"Jesus, Mike, I can't believe this."

"I know, it's hard to fathom. And to think it was all because of a case of mistaken identity. Needless to say, with three weeks left before the election the last thing I wanted to do was go out door knocking.

"Sensing that the election would be close we did one last big mailing to the Independents in the district. Some over-zealous campaign workers stuffed some left-over literature in some of the envelopes making them too heavy for the first-class postage on the envelope. That meant nearly 5,000 letters arrived at Independent voters' homes the day before the election marked 'Postage Due–11 cents.'"

"Oh, no," Kent responded.

"Oh the phone calls I got from voters who were furious about having to pay that 11 cents. On election night I came up short by a little over 500 votes."

"I bet you were so pissed," Kent said.

"Of course, I was. All that hard work, all those doors knocked, all those postcards and letters mailed, and when it was over, I had nothing to show for it. But sooner or later you get over the loss."

"Mike, I'm so sorry."

"What I never got over was the gay bashing incident. I still remember the apartment number, I still can picture the anger in my attacker's face, and I still can feel how close to death I came. Ultimately, I had to move out of state because every time I drove down Fleur Drive past that apartment building, I would break out into a sweat as I relived the indecent where it happened."

"Ya, it's tough," Kent said. "Instead of Matthew Shephard that could have been you in the news. It's all so senseless."

"Kent, I certainly hope that you can learn from my mistake and be careful out there. I'm more cautious who I place my trust in, I'm constantly aware of my surroundings, and I try to avoid places that could place me in harm's way. The last thing I would ever want is for you to become the next Matthew Shephard."

Matthew Shephard remained in intensive care in the days following the beating and candlelight vigils were held around the world. He was pronounced dead six days after the attack.

Chapter 52

Letters from Trigsey

Thursday, 7-4 Shift

Kent was waiting for me in the parking ramp when I drove in this morning. The minute I got out of my car he said, "Guess what? I'm a grandpa!"

"A grandpa?" I answered. "You're only 24 years old. How is that even possible?"

"Hank's a daddy so I'm a doggie grandpa! When I wasn't looking, he knocked-up our little neighbor doxy and now they have four adorable little dachshund puppies."

As we hurried to punch in, Kent said to me, "I know how much you love Hank, maybe you could take one of the puppies."

I thanked him for thinking of me but said, "This just isn't the right time in my life to have a puppy. But it's funny you mentioned it because I have been thinking of something ever since my flight home from Colorado.

"There were a couple of women across the aisle from me and I happened to overhear one of the women tell the other about a letter writing service she has for kids. The way I understood the concept, she writes letters to kids as if she were a little girl and tells of her various adventures."

Kent said, "Well I can't imagine little boys would enjoy getting a letter from a girl writing about girl stuff."

"That's what I thought! But what about a letter from my dog? Every kid would enjoy a letter from a dog."

"But you don't have a dog!"

"The kids wouldn't have to know I don't have a dog. But if they get a letter signed with a paw print, they are going to believe it's from a real dog. And there is no end to the adventures a dog and his Daddy Mike could have. We could go camping, water skiing, fishing…in fact we could even go skydiving with President Bush and his dog Millie."

Kent thought about it for a minute and said, "You know, Trigsey, you may have really hit on something. And if it works, think of the possibilities. It could lead to a cartoon series, books…you might even get your stories on the radio or TV."

I was happy to hear he sounded excited but I wondered if it could really happen.

"We've got to think up a name," he added. "What are you going to call the dog?"

"I don't know Kent. At this point it's just an idea. I probably won't ever do it."

"You've got to do it, Trigsey. It could be your ticket out of here!"

"Okay. Well, it's going to have to be a wiener dog, so how about calling it 'Letters from Oscar Meyer?'"

Kent gives me an eye roll and said, "Get real. That's a lawsuit waiting to happen."

"'Letters from Kielbasa?'"

"I don't like that either. But what about 'Letters from Trigsey?' I know you told me you hated that nickname as a kid, but Trigsey is a perfect name for a dog. It has a real ring to it!"

"I don't know. I kind of like it. But it's probably a dumb idea and to be honest I don't know where to start in making it work."

"It's NOT a dumb idea and if anyone can make it work, it's you. When you add up everyone you know from your family, people in politics, class-mates, members of your church, breakfast club, customers, and co-workers here at Von Oostrom you probably would have at least 200 subscribers right off the bat. If you charged $25.00 a subscription. That's $5000. You should be able to launch it with that kind of startup.!"

"I don't know, Kent."

"Plus, you will have Hank and me to cheer you on!"

"Well buddy," I responded, "with that kind of encouragement I'm going to have to give that idea some very serious thought."

Little did I know that out of Kent's words of encouragement, Letters from Trigsey would become a real thing. While not a ticket out of retail, for six years there were children in 39 states and 7 foreign countries that received a monthly letter from Trigsey, signed with a rubber stamp of Hank's paw. In addition to the letter, they received special Back to School inserts about Great Dogs in History in September and one in June with Trigsey's Review of Dog Books that children could find at their local library to read over their summer vacation. Years later Trigsey's Letters were expanded into Tales from Trigsey, a weekend Radio show that has been running every weekend since 2016 on Kid's Radio Mania on KDPS-FM in Des Moines. You can stream Kids Radio online at KDPScentral.streamon.fm.

Oh, and I finally had to get a real dog. Of course, I named him Trigsey.

Chapter 53

The Wedding Pig

Tuesday, 7-4 Shift

I heard the funniest story when I had lunch today with Evan and Joanelle Menken. They are both employed at VO: he is the manager of Men's Shoes and she is in charge of the Girl's Department. Up until today there had not been much of an opportunity to get to know either of them.

What a hoot! They talked about their recent wedding at the Port Washington Botanical Gardens.

Since both of them had worked at the store for years I asked if a lot of their Von Oostrom co-workers attended. Evan said since they had recently bought a home together in Sheboygan Falls, they opted to keep the cost down and had a small wedding with a just few family members and friends.

Joanelle added, "The only Von Oostrom employee we invited was Sharonda Fingerphude, who had been a sorority sister of mine. We're really not that close anymore, but I had been one of her bridesmaids 20 years ago, so I kind of felt obligated to at least invite her to our wedding."

I chuckled and said, "As a gay man I know all about the old saying 'Always a bridesmaid, never a bride' and oh yes, I know Sharonda. She's a piece of work."

"You got that right," Evan said. "You're not going to believe what she did at the wedding! Go ahead, Joanelle, you tell him. She's YOUR friend!"

"Not any more…not after the stunt that cheap-assed bitch pulled!"

"Oh my!" my ears perked up. "It wouldn't surprise me after seeing her in our lunchroom. Please tell me more!"

Joanelle responded, "I had better not say anymore since she's an Alpha Xi Delta sister."

Evan jumped in, "Oh, hell, Joanelle, she's no friend of mine, I'll tell."

I couldn't wait to hear about the "stunt!" Evan hesitated, but then opened up.

"Like I said we were trying to keep costs down and when Sharonda sent back her RSVP she had marked on it that her four kids would be coming. We had to let her know that she and her husband were more than welcome, but their children were most definitely not."

We thought she got the message, but at the wedding reception, Sharonda crashed the buffet line ahead of our parents and my grandmother. Then she opened two giant tote bags and whipped out NINE Tupperware containers, yes NINE of them. Then she started filling the Tupperware up with food to take home for her kids!"

"Nine?" I couldn't believe my ears. "Are you telling me she did that before the rest of the wedding guests had gone through the buffet line?"

"Seriously, my mother was right behind her and counted them as Sharonda filled them up! And my mom said they weren't little two-cup containers, these were big honking family style bowls."

"Unfreaking believable!"

"Nothing that woman does surprises me," Joanelle said. "She has been doing $#!+ like this since we were in the sorority house."

"And if that wasn't nervy enough," Evan added, "she had another big container stashed under the table so that once the cake was served, she took home enough cake to feed a small army!"

I had witnessed her lunchroom gluttony when she'd steal from our department Christmas party but this was ridiculous. What a thoughtless pig.

"So, take note Mr. Triggs," Evan said, "should they ever legalize same-sex marriages here in Wisconsin, make sure Sharonda isn't on your wedding invite list."

"Oh, I can assure you she wouldn't be. But the chances of gay marriage ever happening in my lifetime is about as likely as seeing pigs fly."

That isn't to say it wouldn't be nice to find a nice guy and just live in sin until that day comes!

> *Same-sex marriage became legally recognized in the State of Wisconsin on October 6, 2014, upon the resolution of a lawsuit challenging the state's ban on same-sex marriage. A year later, on June 26, 2015 the U. S. Supreme Court held in a 5-4 decision that the Fourteenth Amendment requires all states to grant same-sex-marriages and recognize same-sex marriages in other states.*

Chapter 54

The Personal Ad

Monday, Noon-9 shift

My jaw dropped when I saw the Nordic god Kent was schmoozing in Suits tonight. He was perhaps the most beautiful man I had ever laid eyes on. Tall, blond, chiseled good looks, obviously Scandinavian. He was a total package and then some.

By the time Kent had finished his transaction I was feeling a little moist. "Who in god's name was that Teutonic stud?"

"I saw the way you had your eyes on him!" Kent said. "His name is Torsten Andreassen and he's a neurologist."

Yummy! Educated, successful, rich, and gorgeous!

"I don't think I have ever heard the name Torsten before."

"He said it's the Danish version of Thor, the Norse God of Thunder."

"Well with that blond hair and that magnificent figure I knew he had to be some kind of Scandinavian."

"It's funny that you are so smitten. He kept asking about you during our sale and asked if I would slip you his card."

My jaw dropped. "HE DID NOT! You're making that up!"

"No seriously, he thought you might need some neurological help the way your tongue was wagging."

Grrrr. That Kent! I can never believe a thing he says.

"I should have known you were playing me."

"He did ask if you were single and when I said yes, he wondered if you were dating anyone."

"You know Kent you are one bad liar. And even if I was on the dating circuit, I'm so out of his league. He's a neurologist and I'm a washed-out political whore selling underwear in a department store. I mean come on, what do we have in common?"

"Well did you see those thighs? I'm sure he skis, bikes, and roller blades. All things I know you're into. And you share a common ethnic background. For all I know he might even do needlepoint to wind down after surgery!"

He does look like he's good with his hands!

"No seriously Mike, we need to get you a boyfriend. And every time I throw out a name you have a thousand reasons why they wouldn't be interested. There are tons of guys out there who would be lucky as hell to find someone like you. I'm telling you it's way past time for you to venture out of that deep dark closet and start thinking about you and your future."

I shook my head. Not only did I not like someone trying to fix me up, I like to keep my private life private and away from work.

But Kent kept prodding me. "What about Krayfisch…I hear he might be available."

"Now you're getting silly. Don't you have some work to do?" The kid just wasn't going to give up. "Things are different when you're my age. And besides I'm not really looking."

"Well, you need to be. You need to get out there or else you're going to wake up one day in that twin bed of yours – tired, old and lonely, and you'll have no one to blame but yourself. But it's your choice, go ahead it's your frick'n closet."

As he walked away, he looked over his shoulder and said, "Have you ever thought of running a personal ad in the paper?"

I gave him a "%^<# You" look but deep down I knew he was right. Maybe I'll have to give that hunky neurosurgeon another look. Or at least glance at the personals in the local alternative publication.

Tuesday, Day Off

One of my favorite things to do on my day off is to go downtown to the Paradigm Coffee Shop, sip on an iced double-decaf espresso, and read the "New York Times", "The Milwaukee Sentinel", and "The Instep News", which is Wisconsin's LGBT newspaper.

In reading the Instep's Personal Ads section I got to thinking about what Kent said last night about growing old in my twin bed. While there wasn't a one of the men-for-men ads that piqued my interest, I got to thinking I could write my own. That way I was in control, could do it anonymously so no one had to know it was me.

Chances are I wouldn't get any bites, but you never know there is always that one glimmer of hope that someone is out there just waiting for an old timer like me to come along.

I asked the barista if she had some paper and a pencil, then started drafting my ad. Fortunately that pencil had a new eraser because before I was finished there were lots of edits. But when I was done, I was pleased with my creation.

> "If you like picnics on a whim, have a sense of humor, enjoy a stimulating conversation, the smell of freshly picked lilacs, the sound of snow crunching under your boots, have a library card and use it, can appreciate music that varies from Verde to Rachmaninoff, ABBA to Elton, Bette to Barbara, listen to NPR's 'All Things Considered,' and at this point are perhaps just tiny bit intrigued...
>
> Then it sounds like we may need to meet over a steaming cup of coffee or a glass of Riesling by the fireplace in the American Club Lobby.
>
> I'm an aging preppy, who is as comfortable in my topsiders, chinos, and polo shirt as I am all dressed up and ready for opening night at the Sheboygan Metro Opera. I'm a non-smoking neat freak, who makes time for a weekly massage. I'm a voracious reader, I sing show tunes in the shower, enjoy cross country skiing over the lakes in winter, and biking or rollerblading around them the other three seasons.
>
> I'm 5'9", 165 lbs., approaching 40, still have a full head of hair and all my teeth.
>
> Curious about the knucklehead who wrote this? Take a chance. Write back.
>
> What do you have to lose? Hey, it's the cost of a postage stamp!"

I counted the words in the ad and saw that there were 210. At ten cents a word, it was going to cost me $21.00. There's a good chance no one will reply but who knows, "Instep" is distributed statewide and with a little bit of luck there might be some dork that lives within a couple hours of Sheboygan that might be a good match or become a good friend.

Before losing my courage, I headed for the post office, bought a pre-stamped envelope, wrote out a check, and dropped my ad in the mail.

Then I felt sick to my stomach. What had I just done? I took some antac-ids when I got home and started crossing my fingers that I just didn't make the biggest mistake of my life.

Saturday, 9:45-6 Shift

When I got to work this morning, Kent was waiting for me in the parking garage with the biggest grin on his face.

"Hey, remember when I suggested that you should check out the personal ads?" He handed me the latest issue of "The Instep" and pointed to an ad he had highlighted in yellow.

I took a quick glance and saw that the one he had highlighted was mine. I smiled and said, "I don't know…he sounds kind of dorky to me."

"It's the perfect guy for you! Why are you so damn picky? You've got the same interests, you're the same age, and for Pete's sake he lives right here in Sheboygan!"

I wasn't about to show my cards or admit that I had placed the ad so I shot him my most disgusted look and tossed the newspaper back to him, saying, "I appreciate your new found interest in my personal life, but leave my dating life alone!"

As we punched in, I could tell Kent was really pissed. But believe it or not, he took my advice and the subject of the ad never came up the rest of the day. He did, however, make a point of telling me that Dr. Torsten Andreassen had come in to pick up his alterations.

I'm going to have to start calling that little $#!+ Yenta since he wants to be a matchmaker so badly! But with any luck I'll be making myself a match soon.

Chapter 55

The Personal Ad's Responses

Saturday, 9:45-6 Shift

I was so glad to get out of the store today, it was just one cluster %^<# after another.

Right off the bat this morning, someone called in sick in the Infants and Toddlers Department and I got a called to cover until their evening shift employee came in at noon. Two hours of screaming kids is about all I can handle.

Then I got to my department just in time to hear a "Code Brown in Men's Furnishings" announcement over the PA system.

The Mad Crapper had struck again!

She'd left a turd trail from the belt racks to the Men's Fragrance Department counter.

I can't understand why they don't just ban her from the store. She has to be on security cameras. But of course, I don't make the rules!

Then just as I'm ringing up a big $1,200 sale, the customer asks to open a Von Oostrom Account. After ten minutes of trying to open a new account, the customer found out he had only been approved for a $300 credit limit. The guy was so pissed he told me I could shove the sale up my ass.

There has to be a full moon out tonight.

Fortunately, I did have one customer who really made me laugh. The sweetest old lady said that her husband has poor circulation in his legs and was looking for some socks that might not have any elastic in them.

I told her she had come to the right place. "We've got a sock by Gold Toe that is just what you're looking for."

She took a look at the sock and said, "These are black. My husband needs navy."

"Well unfortunately, they only come in one color. But you know, lots of us men have a hard time telling the difference between black and navy. I'm guessing if you put them in your husband's sock drawer, he'd never know the difference."

"You know, you're probably right. But I'm going to only buy one pair in case he throws a fit."

When she wrote out the check, I noticed the names in the left-hand corner were Dr. Rosco Fingerman and Myrtle Fingerman. Out of curiosity I asked, "What kind of doctor is your husband, Mrs. Fingerman?"

She gave me the biggest smile and then cackled, "He's a proctologist."

I had to stifle a giggle.

But she continued. "Ever since he's been in practice the Fingerman name has been the 'butt' of a lot of jokes!"

We had a good laugh together and I said, "Did you ever think of keeping your maiden name?"

"Oh, heavens no honey. I was a Mucklemeyer and Myrtle Mucklemeyer wasn't that much better."

I thanked her for adding a little levity to my otherwise horrible day.

When I got home from work, I checked my mailbox and there was a bulky manila envelope with a return address that said "Instep Magazine." I sat down at my dining room table and opened it.

I couldn't believe it! There were 47 envelopes with postmarks from Green Bay, Racine, Baraboo, Madison, Milwaukee, Fond du Lac, Sturgeon Bay, Manitowoc, and a surprising number from Sheboygan and neighboring cities.

I ripped open the first one and the words on the page were so foul I couldn't help but think, "Oh my, someone has quite the potty mouth. He probably grunts like a caveman too."

I set it in a "not interested" pile.

As I started to go through other letters, I was disappointed that many weren't much better. I wondered why some of the guys had even taken the time to write. It was obvious we had absolutely nothing in common. Many didn't even seem to read my entire ad.

But there were some worth seriously considering. One was from a former Barnum and Bailey circus clown that works at the Circus World Museum in Baraboo. He sounds kind of interesting and my dad was a Shrine Clown, so at least we'd have a clown connection. Unfortunately, Baraboo is half way across the state and over two hours away.

Then I opened three envelopes in a row from teachers in Milwaukee. All of them sounded nice. Maybe I could take a quick hour's drive down there and audition all three in one trip with breakfast, lunch, and dinner dates.

There was another guy who said he's a member of the Wisconsin Nude Dudes. I wonder if he knew my former coworker Byron, who was in that club. And the guy sent a picture. Oooooh baby, I spent a long time looking at that nice full-body tan!

I enjoyed the envelopes that included photos, but I noticed that quite a few of those I ended up putting in the reject pile had sent nude pictures. And all of the photos were taken from the shoulders down. Am I a prude or am I just more attracted to faces? Maybe I could write back, "Nice belly button. But sorry, I'm really into outies."

One came from a funeral director in Fond du Lac who said he enjoys giving massages and has his own table. He definitely sounds interesting. He got bonus points for reading biographies. His picture was of him lying on a towel on a nude beach with palm trees in the background, maybe in Florida. He's a real Hottie McBody!

As I stared at the naked body parts I couldn't help but wonder where they get their film developed. Aren't these photos illegal?

There was a letter from a guy in Madison who said he's an organist at an Episcopal Church. I recall during the governor's campaign I went to an organ concert. I can't remember if it was an Episcopal or Lutheran church. I do remember, however, that the organist was really cute and did some really fancy footwork. Looked like he knew how to use his fingers as well! He might be worth checking out.

Maybe it's a coincidence, but many of the letters that ended up in the "interested" pile mentioned that they are spiritual. I like a spiritual connection but I sure hope it doesn't mean they are into that New Age metaphysics, crystal healing, or mystic stuff. My customer Wanda Winkleman is really into that $#!+. She is always telling me that I have an aura about me. It really creeps me out.

Then there was a letter from a Jeffrey at the Columbia Correctional Institution in Portage who said he's interested in serial killers and loves to eat meat.

That's got to be someone's idea of a bad joke. I do like a guy with a sense of humor and was tempted to put in the "maybe" pile. But now that I think about it from Kent! He's such a prankster.

After almost two hours of fun reading my mail, I noticed there was one letter left to read and I couldn't help but notice it had a Sheboygan postmark. As I sliced the envelope open, something fell out on the floor. When I picked it up, I couldn't believe my eyes.

It was a picture of Mr. Krayfisch! Only instead of his usual V. O. attire, he was wearing a black jock strap with his arms and legs were tied to the four corners of a bed!

The only one in the whole bunch that sent a face picture, and I know him! He wrote that he is into S&M and likes being dominated. Well, the guy works for that evil bitch of a store manager, so I am not surprised!

My first reaction was, "Kent has got to see this." But then I wondered how to show him without him knowing about my personal ad. I've got to think about how much I want to share with Kent.

When I was done reading all the letters, I counted up my piles. There were 27 "not interested" that went into the trash. Well, actually 26. I decided to keep Krayfisch's bondage letter, it's way too good to toss and maybe I could use it for blackmail the next time he writes me up for some trumped up infraction.

I was surprised when I counted 20 letters that were definitely worth giving another look. While none of them were 100% my type, the chances of ever finding a perfect match would be damn near impossible.

While none of them may end up being the love connection Kent was thinking I needed, I might just end up with some really good friends out of it.

And if I'm ever desperate enough, I can just take a pair of handcuffs and a whip up to Krayfisch's office! Or maybe I'll just give him a nice hard slap on the ass the next time I see him walking the floor at the store.

Chapter 56

Three Dates in Milwaukee

Saturday, Day off

I really did not know what to expect when I got in the car and made the hour drive south to Milwaukee for my three dates. All I knew for sure was that I was meeting guys named Tony, Calvin, and Jahn. They happened to all be Milwaukee teachers.

My first date at a place called the Honeypie Café in the Bay View neighborhood south of downtown. Driving down Kinnickinnic Avenue, I could see it wasn't exactly the best part of the city and got to thinking maybe this wasn't a good idea after all. But Tony had told me that it was his favorite place for breakfast and it did have a whimsical curbside appeal.

When we arranged our date, Tony said he would be wearing a red Bucky Badger hoodie, which made him easy to spot when I walked into the restaurant. While he wasn't exactly the George Clooney I had envisioned, he was a nice-looking guy in his mid-thirties.

It was obvious we were both new to this and weren't quite sure where to start, so I took the plunge and said, "Tell me Tony, do you bring all your honeypies here?"

We both laughed and that was just the icebreaker we needed.

"Well actually, you're my first if you can believe that," he said. "I'm kind of new to this whole dating thing. I guess you could say I've always been married to my job and haven't given much thought to finding someone to share my life with until recently."

I assured him that I was in the same boat. "Well, I guess if finding a honeypie is what's on both our minds this looks like we've come to the right spot. I saw the pies in the counter when I walked in and they look amazing."

On our waiter's recommendation I ordered the Ham and Cheese Hand Pie, which he described as their version of a Cornish pasty filled with ham and cheesy hash browns.

While waiting for our food, Tony told me he teaches high school mathematics and coaches the men's soccer team. Hoping I wasn't being too forward, I patted him on the thigh and said, "Well, I was pretty sure with those thighs you were an athlete of some sort."

He recoiled a bit, and I could sense that I had crossed the line in touching him.

Tony went on to tell me that he sings tenor with One Voice, which is Milwaukee's chorus for gay men and their allies.

"Oh, that sounds fun. I used to sing. Maybe I could drive down and catch your next concert."

He kind of hesitated. "Well, that's not…going to be possible…you see I don't perform with them; I just rehearse with them. I really don't want anyone at work to be know that I'm gay."

I reassured him that I had been there, done that for most of my life but I was at a point where I needed to be a little more honest and open about who I was. Everyone's on a slightly different path.

You could see the disappointment in his face when I said that, but as we continued our breakfast it became more and more obvious to both of us that being on two different sides of the closet door probably wasn't going to allow either of us to meet in the middle for any type of meaningful relationship.

I left Tony knowing I'd never see him again, and headed downtown for my second date of the day. It was at the elite Milwaukee Athletic Club or The MAC as the good old boys like to refer to it.

During my political career I had been to The MAC many times, schmoozing the party's major donors, so I kind of knew my way around the place.

I got there a little early and told the gentleman at the front desk that I was meeting Calvin Wentworth for lunch. He invited me to have a chair in the wood-paneled lounge and said that he would inform Mr. Wentworth that I was waiting when he arrived.

All of the memories of political high rolling in private clubs, the leather wingback chairs, the white-haired old men smoking cigars and sipping brandy, were coming back to me. As I looked around the club it surprised me, but I no longer missed it.

I was beginning to think I had been stood up when an adorable white-haired young guy in a bow tie arrived and said, "You must be Mike, Mr. Humphries told me you were waiting."

He apologized for running late but said that he had been in a counseling session that had run over the scheduled time.

I had to wonder what school teacher has a counseling session on a weekend?

In a somewhat condescending way, he said, "Working in retail I thought you might enjoy having lunch at The MAC."

I threw the attitude right back at him and said, "Oh, I've had lunch here many times."

He apologized for the way that came out. "Growing up a Wentworth in Milwaukee, it's just the only place my family ever thinks of going. I guess you could say I'm in a rut."

"Not a problem," I responded. "The food here has always been delicious. I have to admit when I saw the name Wentworth on your letter, I couldn't help but wonder if you were one of 'the' Wentworth's. But had come to the conclusion that since you were a teacher you probably weren't."

He laughed. "I guess you could say I was always the black sheep in the family. I was the only one of the four Wentworth boys who did not go back into the family business. Actually, I think my Grandpa Cal always respected me for being my own man and going down another path. He just always wanted me to know that the family perks that my brothers have are also available to me. So, today's lunch is on Grandpa's tab. Heck, he's just going to write it off as a business expense, so we might as well enjoy the meal."

My first impression of Calvin was much different than the man I got to know over lunch. He was smart, articulate, well read, and, like me, had a real passion for history. I could see why his students would like him.

The more we talked the more I saw things we had in common. We both share a special affection for bow ties, cross-country skiing, and historical fiction. The similarities were so spooky that at one point I said, "You don't do needlepoint, do you?"

He gave me a "What the hell?" look, so I took that as a no.

But the thing that impressed me most about Calvin was he seemed to be genuinely interested in me, which is something you rarely see with guys you meet in the gay community. Usually, their universe centers around them and them alone.

The waiter was clearing the table and Calvin said, "Since I'm downtown, I thought I might work out here at the club. You'd be more than welcome to join me if you'd like."

I knew I had a couple hours to kill so I said, "That sounds like fun, I've got my gym bag out in the car." He walked out to the parking ramp with me and when I opened my trunk he said, "I can't believe it you drive the same Honda Civic that I do."

"Civic? I expected took you for a BMW kind of guy."

"Ha, you sure pegged me wrong. You must have me confused with my dad and oldest brother."

Together we spent the afternoon in a cardio class, lifting weights, and working out on the stationary bikes. We were about to head for the shower when he said, "What do you say we swim a few laps to cool down?"

"Oh gosh it sounds fun, but I don't have a swimsuit in my gym bag."

He laughed and said, "This is The MAC, it's a Men's Club and virtually no one wears a swim suit!"

So, we went swimming…nude!

Calvin was a much better swimmer than I am. But the nice thing about swimming laps it really doesn't matter how fast you go; you just have to stay in your own lane.

After we showered and dressed, Calvin said as we walked to the cars, "You know Mike, this has really been a fun afternoon! I sure hope I get a chance to see you again soon!"

"Sounds like a plan! Maybe, next time I can show you my 98th Street Athletic Club in Sheboygan!"

As he unlocked his matching Honda, he flipped me a thumbs up and said, "It's a date."

My speed dating was going much better than I had ever expected and I was tempted to just call it a day and skip teacher #3. But since I was already in town, I figured I might as well see what Jahn was like.

When I talked on the phone with Jahn I asked about his slight accent and unusual name. After I learned he moved here from Germany I suggested that maybe we could go out for some "real" German food and agreed to meet at Mader's.

Neither of us had any idea what the other looked like, so it had the potential for disaster. I looked for someone who was as befuddled looking as I'm sure I was.

If I was casting a Friar Tuck for a Robin Hood remake, Jahn would have been the perfect pick. He was short, stocky, and had just a little hair around the back and edges. Where Calvin could have walked off the pages of GQ magazine, Jahn was the epitome of frumpiness.

But what he lacked in sartorial elegance, he more than made up for it in personality. The guy should be doing stand-up comedy. I don't think I have ever laughed so hard in my life.

At one point he was telling a story about one of his students and I spit-sprayed Riesling all over him. I was so embarrassed and offered to pay for his dry cleaning, but he said, "Everything I own is wash and wear and it's white wine, it's going to dry and no one will ever know."

We were enjoying some of Mader's famous strudel when I noticed two Catholic priests in their black suits with white clerical collars waiting for the maître d' to seat them. Jahn noticed the two and then waved, shouting, "Tony, Calvin, come over and meet my friend Mike Triggs from Sheboygan."

Did he say Tony? Calvin? That was quite a coincidence to have the two priests be the same names as my first two dates.

Then I saw their faces approaching. They WERE Tony and Calvin!

I'm not sure who was more red-faced, date #1, date #2, or me!

Priest #1 Tony jumped in and said, "I know Mike, we had breakfast at Honeypie this morning."

"Isn't that interesting," said Priest #2 Calvin, "I also know Mike. He was swimming nude in the lane next to me at The MAC this afternoon."

Jahn looked at me. "Well, what a coincidence that you would meet all three of us on the same day." Even though we were in the middle of dessert, Jahn insisted that they join us.

What an awkward situation. But to add some levity I said, "So Jahn, something tells me you might also have a clerical collar at home in your closet."

I guess that was one little detail that all three seemed to have forgotten to mention in their letters, on the phone, or during our dates!

I learned all three are Jesuit priests that live in the same Jesuit residence. They all teach at St. Ignatius Boys Catholic Prep School.

It was all coming together now. Tony's earlier comment that he was "married to the job" made perfect sense. When Calvin said he was doing some counseling, he must have been in the confessional. They were dressed in their clerical collars tonight because they were coming from Saturday night mass. And the reason I associated Jahn's look to Friar Tuck was that he was actually a man of the cloth, albeit a little more disheveled.

While awkward at the time, I was glad that Jahn had asked the other two to join us. And before the night was over Tony actually lightened up a bit. I noticed at one point his hand was resting on my knee under the table.

We spent close to four hours together before ultimately saying our good-byes. Who would have thought that this Protestant, gay guy could have so much fun carousing with three gay Catholic priests?

While ultimately, I think the vows each of them took when they entered the priesthood will win out, I am quite sure that I'm going to be friends with all three for years to come.

Chapter 57

Elizabeth Taylor

Friday, 7-4 Shift

One thing you can always be sure of is that Von Oostrom will have a huge truck with new merchandise every Friday morning.

Today was the exception. And it made for a very boring three hours until the store opened.

When Queen, Kent, and I arrived for our 7 a.m. shift, we found a note on the loading dock saying that today's truck had been canceled.

"Darn, if I they would have told us that last night, I would have brought in a dozen donuts," Kent said.

Trying to be the responsible one I said, "Well we could always dust."

That prompted a loud chorus of, "No!"

"Or one of us could vacuum. I don't remember the last time anyone vacuumed."

Neither of them was taking me up on my suggestion.

Queen piped up with her idea. "Or even better, I move we just 'act busy' until store opening."

Kent quickly said, "I'll second Queen's motion."

I was the new kid on the block, but for some reason they were looking for my approval. Finally, I acquiesced. "Alright I'll make it unanimous."

So, we headed for the back room and for the next three hours we acted busy, got caught up on store gossip, Kent talked about plans for his weekend in Chicago, and Queen filled us in on her noisy neighbor.

After clearing all those subjects from the table, Kent looked and me and said, "So Trigsey, the other day I heard you used to be Elizabeth Taylor's chauffeur."

"Now Kent, where would you have heard something like that?"

"That's what the new girl in Activewear was telling me. She said you mentioned it in your orientation class but you didn't give them any specifics."

Before I could respond, Queen asked, "Who's Elizabeth Taylor?"

Kent shot me one of those "Oh my gawd" looks that only a gay man can give. "You don't know who Elizabeth Taylor is?" he said. "Where've you been girl friend? She's just one of the biggest movie stars of all time!"

Queen appeared confused so he filled her in. "Purple eyes, she was married to Richard Burton twice, "Cat on a Hot Tin Roof", "Who's Afraid of Virginia Woolf", "Cleopatra". Come on girl, you're supposed to be an African Queen. You've never seen Cleopatra?"

It was obvious from the stunned look on her face, our African Queen didn't have a clue that a very white British woman played one of Queen's possible ancestors.

"So, tell us about your chauffeur gig. I'm just dying to know more."

"Actually, it was years ago when she was married to her sixth husband, Senator John Warner from Virginia. I was this hot shot young Republican and just happened to be at the right place at the right time. Senator Warner was scheduled to be the keynote speaker at the Republican Party's annual Lincoln Day Dinner and fortunately for me, the person who had been scheduled to drive the senator and Ms. Taylor had a family emergency. So 'voila' I just happened to be available when my state party chairman, Steve Roberts called."

Kent couldn't control his excitement, "So did you get to drive a limousine? Was she nice? Did you get her autograph?"

I answered his questions with a "No, no, and no!" I could see the disappointment on his face.

"Actually, I drove a new Cadillac Fleetwood that I picked up at Betts Cadillac on the way to the airport. When the Warners arrived, I couldn't help but notice that everything she was wearing was way too tight. It looked like the once beautiful diva would have been right at home holding a corn dog at the Iowa State Fair. She had a scarf pulled up over her hair, partially masking her face, and wore giant sunglasses.

"We could have probably walked through the airport concourse unnoticed had it not been for the fact that her high heels were monogrammed ET and reporters were there snapping pictures as they were met by Iowa's Republican Senator Roger Jepsen, who rode with us to their hotel."

"So, tell me, what did you talk about?" Kent asked.

"Well, I might as well have been invisible, but the senators engaged in a political discussion, which I could tell through my rear-view mirror was of no interest to ET. In fact, the only words out of her mouth were, 'What a retched downtown' as we approached the hotel."

"MEEEEOOOOOOOW!" Kent said cattily. "She sounds like a bitch!"

"I remembered Senator Warner saying she was suffering from one of her migraines," I added, "so I wrote off her bad behavior to not feeling well.

"Senator Jepsen's wife was there to greet them at the Hotel Fort Des Moines. As they exited the Caddie, Senator Jepsen introduced the Warners to his wife, Dee. ET looked at her with a sneer and said, 'We've met at a Senate Wives Club Luncheon,' and gave her the obligatory kisses on the cheek.

"As they were entering the hotel, she turned to me and said, 'I'll be waiting for my bags, I hope they arrive soon.'

"We had been told ahead of time that Ms. Taylor doesn't travel lightly and that we should arrange for a truck to transport her luggage. About twenty minutes later two Louis Vuitton suitcases, a trunk, and a wig case were delivered to her room.

"The fundraising event that night was quite a success. In fact, it was sold out as Iowa Republicans from across the state flocked to meet the famed Elizabeth Taylor. Unfortunately, she arrived in the ballroom just as dinner was about to be served and managed to exit the speaker's dais via the curtains and escaped through a backroom.

"She did look ravishing. Her hair and makeup were exquisite. Although, her lime green chiffon floor length gown looked a bit out of place in a room full of Red, White and Blue attired Iowa Republican women.

"I do remember her looking a bit bored during the speeches. But ravishing, throughout the event.

"The next day, I arrived at the hotel at 6:45 to drive the Warners to the airport. Roger and Dee Jepsen were waiting under the hotel's Porta Cochere to see them off."

"So, what was she wearing when she left?" Kent squealed.

"I knew you were going to ask. She had a red blazer, black Capri pants, and one of those puffy blouses…you know the kind from the Seinfeld episode."

"Ewwwww!" Kent responded.

"Obviously not interested in the senators' small talk, ET headed toward the car. Mrs. Jepsen followed her, but to her disappointment ET had snapped the door car shut before she could say goodbye. Mrs. Jepsen attempted to get Mrs. Warner to roll down the window but rather than being a gracious guest she fumbled through her handbag, took out her compact, and checked her makeup. She did manage to touch her lips and smear the window in a feeble attempt at 'see you later.' I felt sorry for Mrs. Jepsen, you could see the disappointment on face.

"Once the senators shook hands and said their final goodbyes, we were off to the airport.

"I hadn't been driving for more than ten seconds and I hear her say 'Music please' from the back seat. It startled me. Should I sing the Iowa Fight Song or a chorus from the Pirates of Penzance? But opted to turn on the radio. And what do we hear but a commercial saying, 'Do your hogs have bloody scours?'

"Oh my god, I think they were talking about pig diarrhea! Of course, the radio had been set to WHO radio's farm show. I quickly changed channels until I found Iowa Public Radio's classical station. It must have pleased her, because I heard 'Oh heavenly' from the backseat.

"As I turned the corner onto Fleur Drive, I said, 'If you look out the windows on your right you can see Terrace Hill, our Governor's Mansion.'

"She snarled, 'Oh yes, Governor Bob Ray…and his lovely wife, BILLIE!' She spit out her name with such disgust I thought I caught some of that spit on the back of my neck.

"The next thing I heard was, 'Johhhhhhhn, I sure do love my new red blazer. How did you ever know my size?'

"'Oh, I knew,' he lovingly replied.

"'Well, it's a little tight through the boobs,' she told him.

"I adjusted my rear-view mirror and had to agree. Everything I had seen her wear was too tight.

"Pretty soon I heard…'Johhhhhhhn, what are we having for dinner?'

"It was 7:00 in the morning and she was already wondering what was for dinner!"

Kent and Queen laughed but seem enthralled.

"Senator Warner responded, 'You can have anything you want dear!'

She asked for fried chicken, and the Senator told her he would call from the airport to make sure they had it!

"Then she purred, 'I sure hope Miss Pam doesn't make it. Her chicken is so greasy!' to which he said, 'Oh, sweetheart I will make sure Sue Ellen fries up the chicken for you.'

"Then Liz said in a cutesy voice, 'Oh GOODIE! Her chicken is so crispy!'"

Kent was really enjoying the story and laughing loudly. He said, "I can't believe that two of the richest people in America were actually having a conversation about fried chicken at seven in the morning!"

I agreed, adding, "They could have just picked up a bucket of KFC's extra crispy on the way home like the rest of us!"

As we laughed, Queen wanted to know if anything else happened and I had to tell them about the airport.

I pulled up in front of United Airlines, got out of the car, opened the trunk and handed the senator his overnight bag. Everything of hers had been sent ahead. As I closed the trunk of the car, he grabbed my right hand and started pumping it. It was extremely awkward as the keys were between the palm of our hands. Trying to be sincere, he said, "Now what was your name?"

"I told him my name and he quickly replied, "Michael how can we ever thank you for taking time out of your busy schedule to shuttle us to and from the airport?"

I responded that the pleasure was all mine. And really it was a pleasure to see how common famous people can be. Then he released his grip, and as I turned to get back in the driver's seat he said, "Oh Michael, there is one more bag you forgot."

I gave him a startled look and thought, 'One more bag?' I knew he brought only one. I was sure the trunk was empty.

"Then he pointed to the back seat and winked at me.

"There she sat. His other bag.

"He and I shared a brief chuckle. As I opened the back door and she rolled out I said, 'Enjoy your chicken dinner!'

"She barely even acknowledged me. As she walked away, I noticed that she had left a People magazine in the back seat. And on the cover was a headline

'Washington's Favorite Hostess' with a picture of Elizabeth Taylor holding a platter of fried chicken. I smiled and thought that fried chicken story will stick in my mind for the rest of my life."

Kent and Queen applauded when I finished.

"Mike, you have led an amazing life. You need to publish that story to reveal the truth behind the famous Elizabeth Taylor," he said.

He was right. I probably should put all my experiences down on paper. But would anyone believe them?

Chapter 58

The Over/Under Event

Saturday, 7:45 - 4:00 Shift

When I looked at my schedule for this morning, I thought there was a typo. Our Saturday shifts always start fifteen minutes before store opening at ten, but today I was scheduled to be there at 7:45.

I knew there had to be some special event. I just didn't know how "special" that event would actually turn out to be.

I saw Sharonda Fingerphude at the time clock and asked why we were scheduled so early.

"Oh honey, today is Von Oostrom's Semi-Annual Over/Under Event and we open two hours early for it. Twice a year we bring in sizes that we normally wouldn't carry for the hard-to-fit ladies. We'll have gals driving in from Milwaukee, Racine, Green Bay, and the Fox Cities. I always volunteer to work the food station where we'll have coffee, mimosas, mini muffins, and bagel bites."

Now that didn't surprise me. I could see that Sharonda had brought along a couple of tote bags with empty Tupperware containers to take home any leftovers.

On third floor they had set up tables with piles and piles of big girl bras, bustiers, butt-huggers, camisoles, panties, negligees, and all kinds of unmentionables. There was even a table with king-sized panty hose. Who knew? Apparently, according to Sharonda, V. O. normally only stocks up to queen size?

It's too bad I didn't know about this event a couple of days ago. I could have invited my hard-to-fit customer with the ginormous breasts.

Usually, I ride the escalator straight down to first floor, but today I was curious to know what was happening in the second-floor departments for the special event.

Our Enorme Department is the place we send our full-figured Von Oostrom clientele. I guess I had always assumed we carry sizes as big as they come. But surprise, surprise…I saw four rolling racks of coats and dresses that could have more appropriately been sold at Sheboygan Tent and Awning.

Not wanting to be outdone, the Fine Jewelry Department had jumbo-sized toe rings and bracelets that would fit the wrists or ankles of a stylish sumo wrestler.

Just as I was removing my shoe and stocking to try on a mannish toe ring, Nettie L'Amour grabbed me by the neck and snarled, "What the hell are you doing in this department? I have you scheduled to work in the Women's Shoe Department this morning. Get down there now!"

I quickly tied my shoe and headed to first floor. Along the way I spotted shoeshine guy Leonard Jackson, who had come in early for the event as well.

"Looks like your shoes need a shine, Mike."

"Not now, Leonard," I said as I rushed past. "Maybe later. I've got to get into Women's Shoes.""

He let out a laugh, and I did too once I figured out how funny that must have sounded.

As I descended the escalator, I could see that the main event was by far special sized shoes for women. There were tables and racks of them on every aisle throughout the first floor.

Flora Bunda, the Women's Shoe Manager, met me as I got off the escalator and told me I'd be in the high-end party section that was located in Men's Sportswear. But she informed me I needed to line up with all the other V. O. employees inside the first-floor entrance for "the clap."

The clap sounded like a venereal disease, but as the store's entrance was unlocked, I found myself applauding and cheering wildly as a herd of big-boned women came storming through the doors. Some were actually pulling wagons to cart off their finds. Fortunately, to keep from getting crushed the really little shoppers were the last to arrive at the big Over/Under event.

I swear every drag queen in the state of Wisconsin was shopping for high heeled pumps and stilettos. It was a like a scene right out of Cinderella where the ugly stepsisters were attempting to force their bovine hooves into a size 14 glittery pump. But once on, those queens sure knew how to work the crowd as they sashayed through the aisles like models on a runway.

I had a delightful drag queen named Cornita Cobb from Oconomowoc who loaded her wagon with eleven pair of shoes. She wasn't the prettiest queen in the store, in fact she had a hint of mustache and a 4-inch wild hair on her chin that was oh so annoying. It was all I could do to reach over the counter and pluck it. But I knew she was giving me my biggest sale of the day and I was just going to have to resist the temptation. Oddly, she reminded me of my dear Aunt Mavis back in Rabbit Gulch.

When Cornita handed me her check for $847.23, I couldn't help but notice the name printed on the check was Melvin "Butch" Bedvetter.

As I put the check in my cash register, I had visions of how I was going to spend my $8.47 commission check from that big sale!

I've never worked so hard in my life. This two-hour event was bigger than Christmas, Father's Day, and prom season all rolled into one. My cash register never stopped humming.

By 9:30 everything in my section was gone. Well, I should say almost everything. There was that one pair of size 19 avocado green, faux-suede, platform clompers that looked like they had been around since the disco era. Seriously, that pair of shoes was so butt ugly, not a single shopper gave them a second look.

It only took me five minutes to take down the empty tables in my section and cart them to the loading dock. I was hoping I might be able to snarf down a couple mini-muffins before store opening but between those big-boned vultures and Sharonda there wasn't a crumb to be found.

When I surveyed the Von Oostrom staff that were working the Over/Under sale I was certainly one of the smallest in the store. So, I guess you could say I represented the "Under Shoppers," but Sharonda was definitely the biggest "Over." She could stand to take home a few less filled Tupperware containers!

Chapter 59

Kids Shoes

Tuesday, Noon-9 Shift

Oh, my gawd. I was stuck in Kids Shoes for four hours this afternoon. There isn't a department in the store I would rather not get assigned to cover.

As soon as I arrived on the floor a mother was waiting at the counter with six shoes in her hand and asked if I had them in her daughter's size.

"Well, what size is she?" I inquired.

"I don't know anymore. My little sweetheart Juanita used to be a size 4 but lately she's been growing like a weed."

Chubby little Juanita was anything but a sweetheart. In fact, she was more like a noxious weed. I tried my best to get her to stand still as I measured her foot in the metal foot measuring thingy, but the little brat kept hopping around.

I told the mom, "I don't normally work in this department and to be honest I don't have a clue what I'm doing, but it looks like she's going to be a size 5."

Of course, the mom insisted I bring both a size 5 and 6 for the little brat to try on.

The shoes are all arranged in the stockroom in alphabetical order by vendor on three different levels. Twenty minutes later, I carried out six loose shoes and twelve boxes, trying my best not to fall down the steps. But I came out on the floor to find no mom, no kid--just a big wet spot on the chair that little Juanita had been sitting.

I was so freaking disgusted. I knew I needed to page housekeeping, but couldn't remember the color code for that type of accident so I called customer service. Silly me. As soon as I hung up the phone I heard, "Housekeeping–Code Yellow in Kid's Shoes."

The mother and Juanita never did come back, which meant I had to schlep the shoes back to their proper place on the shelves.

Other than children that haven't taken their Ritalin, kids are usually pretty cute when they come to V. O. to shop. And they do say some of the funniest things.

One little girl looked at me and said, "Hey Mister, I like your bow." I appreciated the compliment and said, "Thank you honey. Aren't you just the cutest little thing!"

Obviously, she had been told that many times because she responded, "I know!"

Two little boys also noticed my bow tie. One asked, "Are you a clown?" And the other one said, "Are you the mayor?"

They are cute when they are little. But unfortunately, they grow up, and their attitude's grow with them. Especially the girls.

I had a mother who suggested a particular shoe, only to be totally rebuffed by her teenage daughter who said, "Oh mom I would be so embarrassed to wear THAT! No one at my school wears THAT BRAND anymore!"

A little later I overheard that same sassy girl talking on the phone to a friend. She said, "I totally get it. Adults have friends too. Like our neighbor Tom who comes over and drinks beer with my dad in our garage."

Not sure what that conversation was about. But yes, we do have friends too. I totally get it! And when I see children who behave as badly as that teenager, I'm thankful I don't have any kids of my own.

Chapter 60

Suzanna's Polish Adventure

Wednesday, 8-5 Shift

It is such a joy to work with Suzanna. Today was her first day back after a medical leave of absence.

For years Suzanna and her husband Tadeusz had dreamed of going back to Poland where they had immigrated in 1968. However, being in the restaurant business in America, their return to the homeland never became a reality. But once Tadeusz sold the business last February, they finally decided to go back to Krakow for two months.

Sadly, on their second day back in Poland, Suzanna fell down the steps of the Basilica and broke both legs, fractured her hip and she had a ruptured spleen. If that wasn't bad enough, in all the commotion of the accident and being transported to the hospital she lost the upper plate of her dentures and her hearing aids.

So obviously it didn't turn out to be the dream vacation she had planned. She spent about six weeks in a Krakow hospital and went through months and months of physical therapy once she got back to Sheboygan.

Quite frankly, after all she went through, I never expected her to come back to work. But she's a scrappy little thing and we're glad to have her back. And like Suzanna always says, "Whatcha to do?!"

When I was working with my first customers this morning, Suzanna interrupted us and said, "Excuse me, but do you happen to be Dr. Steven Gannon?"

He replied, "I am."

She immediately lit into him and said, "Well, I've got a bone to pick with you."

The doctor looked so surprised.

"You gave my husband Tadeusz a prescription for Viagra and I don't have time for his four-hour erections. I'm 78 years old and just recovered from two broken legs, a fractured hip and a ruptured spleen."

It was apparent the doctor didn't know what to say, but finally uttered, "We probably need to get you both to come in to talk about this and perhaps I can get him on a lower dose."

"Lower dose?!" She shrieked.

It was obvious that wasn't going to be an option as far as Suzanna was concerned.

"He's 84 years old! Those blue pills you prescribed have him hopped up like an 18-year-old boy in a whore house! At his age I'm concerned he's going to have another heart attack. And besides that, I lost interest in stuff like that years ago."

Oh my, the old girl did make a good point about a heart attack.

Conveniently, the doctor's pager went off and he was able to quickly apologize by saying he'd be back to finish shopping another day.

Hopefully he'll call ahead to make sure Suzanna isn't working.

Chapter 61

Goodwill Celebrities

Wednesday, 12-9 Shift

Probably the number one reason I never watch our local Sheboygan TV station is I can't stand it's sports guy, Holden McWiener. He tries so hard to be funny and relevant, but he's really nothing more than an overweight pompous ass with bad makeup and too much hair spray.

Today I had the pleasure of helping not only KSHB's sports boob, but also his wife, Gayle, a former Iowa State Fair Pork Princess.

Gayle thinks of herself as equally important as Holden because she was once on "The Price is Right." I'd encountered Gayle previously when she was buying a couple of ties and she had inquired if Von Oostrom gives "celebrity discounts."

First off, a second-string weekend sports guy is not a "celebrity," nor is a woman who lost the showcase round on a TV game show. And second, what store in the middle of Wisconsin would actually give "celebrity discounts" anyway?

I tried my best to avoid the obnoxious couple as they shopped today, but apparently, I wasn't the only one who had that thought. I could see that all of my co-workers were making a quick escape to the stockroom once our local "celebrities" appeared.

In my smarmiest voice I said, "Well look who's here. It's Sheboygan's favorite TV personality. What can I help Mr. and Mrs. McWiener's with today?"

You could see on Holden's puffy face that he soaked up my phony compliment like a sponge.

"You probably have heard that I'm emceeing this year's Fibromyalgia Ball and since it's a Caribbean theme I'm looking for a Cuban shirt to wear."

"Actually, Holden, I hadn't heard. Since I've been working this retail gig, I'm kind of out of the Sheboygan high society loop," I said with a hint of sarcasm that went over his head. "But what an honor for you. From what I've heard the Fibromyalgia Ball is the place to be seen, if you're into that sort of thing."

He again beamed, thinking I was putting him on a pedestal.

"Let's take a look and see what I have for Guayabera's." I'd never had a Spanish class in my life but for some odd reason the name for those Cuban-style shirts popped into the back corner of my brain.

I took the McWiener's over to our Men's Sportswear Tropical Apparel section and took a quick glance at what we had in stock. "I'm so sorry Holden, it looks like you're out of luck today. No Guayabera shirts, but I do have some really nice Tommy Bahama shirts. You know the Bahamas are just a couple islands away from Cuba."

I could see the disappointment on Gayle's face. She said, "Everyone will be wearing Tommy Bahama. I really want Holden to be wearing something authentic and not some tropical knockoff made in China."

I forced a smile as she continued her pouty rant. I haven't liked that whiny little bitch since she overbid on a ten-day trip to India, telling Bob Barker that she "wanted to help deliver necessities like makeup and hair spray to the poor foreign woman around the world."

Just when I thought she was done, she added, "What's wrong with this place? I can't believe you don't have any Cuban shirts! When we were in Miami, we saw Cuban shirts in every department store. Macy's had them, so did Neiman Marcus and Nordstrom."

Holden tried his best to calm her down saying, "Now, honey, this is Sheboygan after all. It's not like we have a lot of Cubans here."

"I can't wait for you to be out of this God forsaken Sheboygan media market. If you're looking for anything but Bratwurst or cheese curds, you're never going to find it here."

I decided to respond with as much sarcasm as I could muster. "You know Holden, my management wouldn't want me to tell you this, but the other day I was in Goodwill and I saw the most beautiful hand embroidered Cuban shirt. I'm sure it was your size. If you hurry right over there you could probably snatch it off the rack for five dollars."

His eyes glistened while she rolled hers.

"Now I have to be honest, there was a stain on it. But if you take it to Imogene's Dry Cleaners, she can get stains out of anything!"

Gayle made a disgusted "tsk" sound but her husband is such a cheap ass, the thought of a $5.00 shirt was music to his ears and they were off to chase a bargain.

Wouldn't you know the minute they left the store my co-workers miraculously reappeared.

It wasn"t the only time I recommended Goodwill to a local celebrity today. Sheboygan County Supervisor, Tad Godbersen and his wife Toni were in with their teen brat Chaz, a freshman at the University of Wisconsin in Madison.

Apparently, Chaz had put all of his clothes in his dorm's laundry room washing machine and had forgotten all about them. Three days later he came back and everything was gone so he needed to replace his entire wardrobe. Maybe he was practicing to be a future wasteful politician like his father.

At one point while shopping with them I overheard Toni say, "Oh look Chaz these polo shirts are on sale, three for a hundred dollars."

The spoiled little brat said, "Oh mom, you know I don't wear sale clothes!"

I turned to his dad and said, "You know Tad, if my kid talked to his mother like that I'd be saying, 'After a careless stunt like you pulled, we're heading to Goodwill and you'll be wearing someone else's used clothes for the rest of your freshman year.'"

Did the spineless bastard take my advice? Hell no. He caved in and let his entitled little brat spend $2,200 for a completely new, full-priced wardrobe. Absolutely nothing they purchased was on sale.

As I finish writing in my journal I decided after a day like today I'm going to treat myself to a big bowl of Ben and Jerry's Chunky Monkey before heading to bed. It's as close as I'll ever get to splurging like a celebrity.

Chapter 62

A Day That Will Live in History

Saturday, 9:30 – 5 Shift

I always dread coming to work on Saturdays because we are required to attend Nettie L'Amour's 9:45 pep talks before the store opens at ten. I think that Nettie was one of those girls who always dreamed of being a cheerleader but never got picked for the squad so Saturday is her chance to lead the masses in one of her little cheers.

Frankly I could care less whether first, second or third floor can scream "Von Oostrom rocks" the loudest.

Today's big announcement was that Clovis Footdragger, of Fort Wayne, Indiana would be coming through our front door in fifteen minutes.

Nettie could hardly contain her glee as told us that in a few minutes Miss Footdragger will be fulfilling her 11-year dream of shopping in all 37 Von Oostrom stores and she had saved our Sheboygan store for her final destination.

Whoop-D-F'ing-Do!

Nettie told us how proud she was that we would be part of "a day that will live in history." I'm not sure how many history books keep track of stores that people shop in, but I shouldn't complain since this was one of our manager's rare positive moments.

One of the girls in the Cosmetics Department had made up a giant sign with today's date and check marks beside each of the 36 previous stores our shopper had visited. All she had to do was to make her final check on the giant poster and Miss Footdragger's quest to visit every Von Oostrom store would be complete.

The Channel 17 news team and a Sheboygan Press reporter and photographer were there to cover the historic event. Of course, all employees had to line up at the front entrance as Nettie led us in a couple practice rounds of clapping and cheering loudly in preparation for the big arrival.

At ten seconds to 10:00 we did a countdown for the unlocking of the door.

"Ten, Nine, Eight..."

This is the kind of thing I hate.

"Seven, Six, Five, Four..."

I don't care who in the world walks through our door!

"Three, Two, One!"

Can't we please just get this done?

Everyone started to scream wildly. Balloons dropped from third floor, the doors to the store flew open and...no Clovis Footdragger.

To everyone's surprise the only person waiting at the door was longtime customer Rosemary Beatty, who seem bewildered by the cheering, applause and balloons.

All the store employees waited at the door for about ten minutes but no special shopper from Indiana appeared. Apparently, after all the hoopla, she was a no show.

At lunch I heard the shocking news.

Miss Footdragger had died the previous day and thus would be unable to drag her foot through the final door on her quest to make history.

Apparently. her family had failed to notify us of her untimely demise.

Never-the-less, every employee was able to enjoy the cake with the big "37 Stores" on it. Sharonda Fingerphude had of course volunteered to cut the fairly small pieces so that she would be able to stuff the leftovers in the Tupperware containers she just happened to bring to work that day.

If there was any other silver lining to that dark cloud, Nettie L'Amour announced that she was going home early with a throbbing migraine headache. Unfortunately, before leaving the store, she stopped by our department to ask me if I could represent the store at this evening's The Best of Sheboygan Awards Banquet. She said that Von Oostrom had been nominated in six different categories and she thought I was the perfect individual to stand in for her.

The bitch has never said anything nice to me in the past, which left me highly suspicious of her motives, but for whatever reason I agreed to represent the store at the event.

She thanked me profusely and gave me an unwelcome hug. This truly was a day that would live in history. Then as she released her embrace she said, "Now be sure to wear your tuxedo, it's a formal event."

When I arrived at the event, much to my surprise I was the only one wearing a tuxedo. In fact, I was the only one in a jacket or tie. Everyone was wearing casual attire. I knew I should have never trusted that woman.

For some reason I thought at a swanky event like this we would be dining or prime rib or fillet mignon. But oh no, tonight's entrée was a classic Wisconsin Fish Fry, and for the next two hours we kept hearing Tina Turner belting out "Simply the best, better than all the rest" as each award was announced.

Who really gives a $#!+ who has the best hamburger, cheese curds, protein drink or is Sheboygan's best dog groomer?

When it came time for the Apparel Awards, I thought I better sit up and look interested. In fact, I have a new appreciation for the Academy Award nominees that are forced to smile and applaud nicely while watching someone else take home the award. After meeting Oscar-winner Liz Taylor I now know how important faking a smile can be for us "celebrities."

Eight times I had to watch that phony Marlys Fudgeball, the CEO of our rival H.C. Prange Company, accept awards for Best Department Store, Best Women's Shoe Department, Best Men's Department, and on and on and on.

I thought the event was finally over and I could go home to get into some cozy clothes when the emcee said, "We have one final award to present, the coveted Best Mall Restroom. "

Oh, Lord, what lame store would want to win such a ridiculous prize?

I almost got up to leave as I heard the emcee say, "And this year's coveted award goes to…. " He slit open the envelope, they once again DJ started up the "Simply the best" track, and I hear him yell, "the restroom at Von Oostrom!"

The applause was nothing short of awesome. You'd think it was like we had just won the Nobel Peace Prize.

Then the emcee continued, "Accepting the award for Von Oostrom's Store Manager Nettie L'Amour is Mike Triggs from the store's Men's Department. And I must say, he is looking mighty dapper tonight in his penguin costume."

All of a sudden, I found myself on stage, accepting the award for the Best F'ing Mall Restroom. And I was expected to say something!

For the first time in my life, I was speechless, there were simply no words. Finally, I composed myself enough to say, "Well ladies and gentlemen, if you have to tinkle or take a load, you now know the place that has Simply the Best potties in town."

It got a good laugh, but it was humiliating standing in a tuxedo in front of Sheboygan's movers and shakers, clutching a plastic frame from the dollar store and a certificate for the best john in town. It certainly was a day that will live on in my personal history.

Now I know why Nettie L'Amour sent me in her place. She thinks my work belongs in our award-winning toilet.

Chapter 63

Blowing It

Tuesday, 8-4 Shift

When I got to work this morning, I heard an announcement over the store public address system that the Men's Sportswear department needed additional help with their stock. I had wanted to get to know their new manager, Mervin Purvis so I answered the call.

It was a good thing I did because they received 43 huge boxes of winter coats, sweaters and corduroys. That's probably four times what they normally have to unpack.

Mervin is what you would call odd. He's 6'7" tall, built like a pencil, and he struck me as being more suited for a career as a funeral director than retail.

Maybe he was just nervous, but I swear he responded to everything I said with either "yep" or "yepper." Is that even a word?

I also couldn't help but notice that he had so much goo on his hair that a fly had gotten stuck. Seriously.

For almost two hours I kept wondering if I should I tell him there was a fly in his hair goo or just hope the poor creature would find a way to escape the sticky mess. I opted to ignore it.

But the thing I couldn't ignore was his putrid body odor and bad breath. It was worse than cabbage farts.

All of a sudden, I noticed the fly had given up trying to get loose and apparently died of the stench. May he rest in peace.

I offered Mervin one of my Listerine Breath strips, which he accepted without thought, but my kind gesture appeared to have absolutely no effect on his severe halitosis.

At 10 a.m. the store opened and I was finally able to escape to my own department. But even there it was apparent the stench had wafted onto what I was wearing and I sure as hell didn't want anyone to think it was me. I sprayed myself from head to toe with the Hugo Boss cologne tester that was on my counter.

Wouldn't you know, from behind me I heard Nettie L'Amour snap, "Those testers are for customers. If you want to wear cologne you should use your 20% employee discount and buy your own!"

As she walked away, I was careful to utter the word "BITCH" under my breath.

My first customer of the day was a beautiful woman in a low cut, sexy red dress with high heels. When she passed me she smiled and said, "Don't you smell delicious. I wish all the men I work around smelled like you."

I thanked her for the compliment, picked up the tester and said, "It's the new Hugo Boss scent."

I know we are advised to not make comments about how customers are dressed, but I complimented her on how nice she looked and how fond I had always been of women in high heels. You could see she hadn't taken it the wrong way. Or maybe she picked up on the fact that I was gay.

"I have to tell you a story about 5-inch spike heels," I said. "My grand-mother, bless her heart, went to the Mayo Clinic for a checkup when she was 99 and her doctor told her that at her age, she shouldn't be wearing high heels. Having none of it she said, 'I don't feel dressed up unless I'm in heels. In fact, I even wear high-heeled snow boots.'

"And let me tell you, after wearing heels all those years she didn't have a single varicose vein. In fact, her legs were so beautiful she looked like a dancer. I would have put her gams up against Eleanor Powell, Ginger Rogers, Leslie Caron or Tina Turner."

My customer smiled and said, "Funny you should mention it, I'm also a dancer."

"I knew it!" I said, "With those long beautiful legs, you could be high kicking with the New York City Rockettes."

When the lady paid for the shirt that she was buying, she used 97 crinkled one-dollar bills. The more she counted out the bills, the stronger the stench. They almost had bar smell to them?

That's when I surmised, she must be a different type of dancer than I was thinking, but I didn't ask any more questions. I simply admired her legs as she confidently left the store.

When my shift was over, I walked out to the parking ramp and noticed Mervin. He seemed to be waiting for me, thanking me profusely for helping him get out the winter apparel.

"No problem, I was glad to help out," I said. "We're a team here at Von Oostrom and that's what team members do."

"In that case," he said, "I was wondering if I could ask a favor."

I remembered the last time I offered to do a co-worker a favor by renting a car, so I was a little reluctant to do another one. But of course, nice guy Mike acquiesced and said, "Sure, anything for a co-worker."

"Remember that Listerine breath strip you gave me this morning?" he asked.

"Yah, what about it? Do you need another one?" I offered.

"Oh no. It's just that I have a breathalyzer on the steering wheel of my car and the strip might have had a trace of alcohol in it. I'm afraid it might be detected."

I just stood there looking at him. Now I knew why he smelled so bad.

Is he asking me to blow into it for him so it won't detect that he has been drinking? You've got to be freaking kidding me!

He looked at me with a pitiful face and said, "I'd really hate to lose my work permit license. I need my car to get back and forth to work. Oh, come on Mike, we're a team and your team member needs your help."

I guess he got me with the "team" thing. So, I reluctantly got behind the wheel of his car. "Okay, what do I do?"

Mervin stood by me with the door wide open, reaching in to show me where to blow. I tipped my head down and put my mouth on the breathalyzer as he was leaning on me.

But after puffing some air I immediately felt sick. I yelled as I got out and pushed him away, "That is the most disgusting thing I have ever tasted! Don't you ever ask me to put my mouth on it again!"

Just then I heard giggling from behind the car. I turned and saw Krayfisch was walking past, grinning from ear to ear! He had heard everything.

"So, you had your mouth on it, did you Mike?" he asked. "Couldn't you wait and just take Mervin home?"

"It's not what you think!" I said, turning red. "Let me explain what happened."

The douchebag gave me one of his smarmy little looks and said, "Oh honey, I wasn't born yesterday! I've heard of parking garage blow jobs before, but Mike, you seem like an expert. I just thought you were classier than that."

He got in his car, gave me a prissy little wave, and drove off.

I was shocked that he thought I'd stoop to something so low in public. And Mervin just stood there clueless about what had just happened.

With the foul taste of the breathalyzer still in my mouth, I reached into my pocket for a breath strip. Wouldn't you know the one time I really needed it I had given out my last strip.

I had never been so anxious to get home and brush my teeth. I won't be blowing anything for a long time.

Chapter 64

Cup Size

Wednesday, 8-5 Shift

We got slammed with new stock again today. It was a miracle that we were able to get it all out on the floor before the store opened. In fact, I was still opening the register and counting the coins when my first customer walked up to the counter.

She was an extremely mammorous, I mean glamorous, full-figured African American woman. I've never seen so much cleavage in my entire life. My eyeballs must have been popping out of my eye sockets when she asked, "What's the largest cup-size you sell here at Von Oostrom?"

"Cup size?" I queried. My mind wasn't registering what she meant since she was in the Men's Department. "I'm sorry but we don't sell athletic supporters here," I said as I stared at the enormous breasts that were hanging over the counter.

She looked at me like I was the stupidest person in the world and said, "BRASSIERES! I'm talking about brassieres!"

"Oh, you mean cup sizes for you!" I blushed. "Let me call our Intimate Things and Stuff Department to find out."

Without trying to gawk, I picked up the phone and called June LaFarge. "Hey June, it's Mike. Mike Triggs from Men's Furnishings. Hey, what's your largest cup size?"

She shrieked, "You perve!" And hung up on me.

I dialed again and in my sweetest voice I said, "June, it's Mike again. We must have gotten cut off."

"Is this some kind of sick joke?" she said loudly.

"No June, I really need to know what's the largest cup size we carry. I have a customer in the Men's Department who wants to know."

I heard her let out a disgusted sigh. "Calm down," I said, "it's a woman asking."

I got a response, thanked her for her help, and hung up. Then I smiled at the customer and said, "I think she thought it was a crank call."

"So, did she tell you their biggest size?"

"She did. I'm not sure what she meant, but we have sizes up to 44-Triple D."

"Oh Lordy, that's not gonna be near big enough," the woman said.

Seeing her disappointment, I said, "Ma'am, I am so sorry I couldn't help you today, perhaps you can try JCPenney or Target."

"Oh honey, don't call me Ma'am. My name is Jai. Jai Norma Stitz."

"So nice to meet you, Jai." I smiled as we shook hands.

As Jai walked away, I noticed Kent had saddled up beside me and was smiling from ear to ear.

"What are you smiling about?" I asked.

With a cherubic look he said, "Oh, I'm just thinking about a scripture verse I learned as a boy from the old King James Bible."

"A Bible verse?" I scoffed. "What Bible verse did she make you think of?!"

"It was in the 23rd Psalm. Her cup runneth over!"

Leave it to Kent to make the Bible sound naughty.

Chapter 65

Grandmas

Wednesday, 8-5 Shift

If it's Wednesday, you know for sure that the first customers to walk through the doors will be the Kraft sisters and their 97-year-old Nana.

It doesn't matter if it is a sweltering 97 degrees out or thirty degrees below zero, Nana will be wearing her knee-length wool coat with a muskrat fur collar. Apparently, the Kraft family matriarch thinks Von Oostrom's is always freezing.

I'm really not sure why the girls even bother bringing Nana along because the instant they arrive they plop her down in a wingback chair by the fireplace in our department, where she sits patiently for the next couple of hours while her granddaughters shop in other departments.

Technically, the fireplace is supposed to be turned off from April 1st through September 30th, but Nettie L'Amour says the twins spend so much money at V. O. that if the old lady wants it toasty then someone in our department needs to start her a fire. And since I had once been an Eagle Scout, that fire-starting responsibility usually falls on me.

Actually, it's a gas fireplace so it just amounts to flipping a switch to turn on the gas. But Nana doesn't have to know that.

While the Kraft girls are twins you would never know it to see them. Velveeta always looks like she walked off a Paris, Milan, or New York fashion runway. You just know Vel's makeup will always be flawless, her hair elaborately coiffed, her French manicure exquisite, and she'll make a beeline to the Shoes, Glorious Shoes department where the salespeople will fight over who gets to help Velveeta today.

I hear she has a serious "shoe fetish" but since we're not supposed to gossip about customers, I'll just leave it at that.

On the other hand, her sister Valvoline (who I call Val) couldn't be more different than her twin. While Vel has to be wearing the newest Stuart Weitzman Tanzanite Heels, Val is totally comfortable looking a little dumpy in an ankle-length poly/cotton Peasant Skirt and her twenty-year-old Birkenstocks. It also doesn't seem to bother her if her waist-length hair is straight and greasy or if she has a little dirt under her fingernails. That's just the way she is.

Neither sister currently has a man in her life, so they never actually shop in my department. But I do enjoy chatting with them each week when they meet to pick up Nana in Men's Furnishings.

Today Velveeta walked up just as Valvoline was telling me about the perfect gift she had purchased for Nana's birthday. Of course, Nana wasn't sitting far away but she would have a hard time hearing a fire alarm go off.

"So, what did you buy for Nana?" Vel asked.

"I bought her a masturbator."

Vel gasped, obviously horrified. Quite frankly I was taken aback as well.

"No, no, no…I mean, it's a vibrator not a masturbator," Val said sheepishly.

"A vibrator for crying out loud! Val, she's going to turn 98 years old!"

"NO! I don't mean a vibrator! It's a foot massager thing," Val said. "It's like a pillow with little slits you can put your toes into while it massages your feet."

"Oh, I know what you mean," I said. "It's called Tingle Toes. I saw them advertised the other night on TV. I might have to think about getting one for my Grandma Vivian."

Before they left, I had to tell the twins about my grandma's annual physical at the Mayo Clinic. "Grandma Viv is the same age as your Nana and her doctor said it was time for her to give up her five-inch spike high heels. Heck she even had snow boots with high heels!"

"Did she do what the doctor said and give them up?" Val asked.

"Of course, she didn't! She says she doesn't feel dressed up without her pumps. She'll be wearing high heels until the day she dies and probably has it in her will that she has to be buried with them on her feet!"

My grandma story is always good for a laugh. Leonard the shoeshine guy always asks me to tell it when he's having a slow day.

But Nana looked over at us chuckling and I hoped she didn't think we were making light of an old lady dying.

Vel said, "Your grandma sounds like someone I'd like. I sure hope I'm still in heels when I'm her age."

She then looked down at her sister's feet and said, "Of course when Valvoline is 98, she'll probably be wearing that same pair of Birkenstocks!"

Chapter 66

Small and Short

Thursday, Noon-9 Shift

One night a couple weeks ago I was standing at Cash Wrap #39 and happened to look out into the mall. I noticed a couple of shady-looking characters enter Tinias Small and Short Superior Menswear.

To be honest, I see suspicious people at the mall all the time, but there was something really unusual about those two, especially when the manager of the store locked the door from the inside and escorted them to the backroom.

I probably would never have thought twice about it had it not happened again and again on a number of different nights over the past few weeks. It seemed like it always happened about 8:15 pm. Like clockwork they would enter the store, the door was locked, they would go in the back room and a few minutes later they would exit the backroom, the door would be unlocked, and the two shady characters would leave the store.

It really wasn't any of my business but I got to thinking that if it were my name on the door, I'd want to know what was going on behind locked doors during mall hours.

On my way back from coffee one day, I walked into the Tinias store and chatted with the manager. I casually asked how many Small & Short stores are in their chain.

"Oh, we've got seven now. In addition to this store in Sheboygan they're across the Midwest in Freemont, Winona, Fairmont, Brookings, Waterloo, and our headquarters in a small town in northwest Iowa called Primghar. I think that adds up to seven."

"Yep, that sounds like seven to me. You've certainly carved out a market for Small and Short menswear," I said with a smile.

That's why we call it Tinyass Menswear behind their backs!

When I got back from my break, I called directory assistance and got the number for the Tinias store in Primghar, Iowa and spoke with Norbert Tinias, the company's CEO.

I told him I felt a little awkward calling him with what could be nothing serious, but explained what I had been observing.

At first, he seemed skeptical. "Ronnie has always seemed like such a good young man I have a hard time imagining he would ever do anything like you are describing. But thank you for calling and for watching out for my store's best interest."

After talking to Mr. Tinias, I never really gave it another thought until early this afternoon, when a well-dressed diminutive older gentleman came into the store asking for me.

When I said, "I'm Mike Triggs," he responded, "Oh Mike I am so glad to meet you. I'm Norbert Tinias and I wanted to stop in to personally thank you for your call a few weeks ago."

"I'm sorry, when I called, I felt a little like Gladys Kravitz, the nosy neighbor from the old TV sitcom Bewitched."

"No, No! You have nothing to be sorry about. I was a little dubious when you called because the impression the manager had given me was that he was a 'good Christian man.' But I decided to have surveillance cameras secretly installed in the back room. Working with Mall Security and the Sheboygan Police Department, we were able to put the kibosh to the drug deals he was running out of our store."

"Drug deals?" I was a bit surprised but happy that my nosiness paid off. In appreciation, the owner gave me a $200 Tinias gift card.

While it was a very nice gesture, having been in his store I knew they don't have a single thing that would fit a "normal" size guy like me.

After he left and I headed to lunch, I was surprised when I talked with Jim Patrick from the Men's Sportswear Department. He was much shorter and I immediately said, "Jim, have I got a surprise for you."

While we sat together and I gave him the gift card and he started telling stories. I had worked with him almost a year now and thought I knew almost everything about him, but today discovered Jim was one of the original members of the Doo-Wop group, The Monotones!

In 1958, he, his brother Charles, and four other guys from a Newark, New Jersey formed The Monotones. They saw their single, "The Book of Love," peak at number five on the Billboard Top 100 chart.

I'd always "wondered, wondered who, who-oo-ooh, who…who wrote the Book of Love?" Now I know! And I was so happy to be able to share the gift card with him. He said he used to be much taller, closer to my height, but had shrunk as he aged.

Later that evening before closing I had a teenage boy who was shopping for some Under Armour gym shorts with his mother, grandmother and two sisters. I couldn't determine if he was a small or a medium so sent him back to the fitting room to try them on. I told the kid's mom there were a couple of chairs in the fitting room area if she and the grandma would like to have a seat.

But before they could sit down the boy's two sisters plopped down in the chairs and began fiddling with their cellphones.

The mom said to the boy, "Now you come out and model those shorts for us girls."

Ten minutes later the mother said, "For cripes sake Gordy how long does it take to try on two pair of shorts? Your old Granny has to pee! What's taking you so long?"

She got up, threw open the fitting room door and said, "Get out here NOW!"

The poor kid was obviously embarrassed because it looked like he had a tent pole trying to poke through the gym shorts. Instead of respecting her son's privacy, mama said, "Look girls, Gordy's got a stiffy!"

All four of them were pointing and laughing as the mom struggled with the teen to keep him from closing the door.

The kid was wiping tears from his eyes when he later came out of the dressing room. He put the gym shorts on my counter but his mom looked at the size of the shorts and said, "Oh honey, from the looks of that boner you're going to need a much bigger size."

All four of the family members appeared to enjoy another good laugh at his expense. But he was horrified.

It was all I could do to keep from smacking the mother. At his age those things just happen and the last thing a boy needs is to have his own mother humiliating him.

As he turned to walk away, I noticed his tears and whispered in his ear, "I'm sorry! No one deserves to be treated like that."

Chapter 67

Purses

I knew the minute I walked in the department this morning that Queen was in a pissy mood because every time she wears her black wig with the white stripe down the back, I know her inner skunk is going to show its dark side.

And I was right. Apparently, she is feuding again with her neighbor in the apartment below her. According to Queen, the guy is a bartender who gets home about two in the morning and plays loud country music until five o'clock when he finally decides to go to sleep. And she can feel that loud bass beat vibrating her floor.

"I usually let him sleep for a couple hours before I retaliate."

"Retaliate…what do you mean?"

Queen let out one of her maniacal laughs and said, "Well, this morning I took one of my old honk'n purses from the 70s, filled it with kitchen utensils, and then slammed it the floor. But that didn't do anything. It just ripped my purse. Then I gave him the bowling ball treatment."

"Bowling ball? I didn't know you bowled."

"I don't. I bought it at a garage sale for a dollar. I thought it would make a good torture devise. Just when I hear him start to snore, I start dropping the bowling ball. I think this morning I dropped it about ten to fifteen times. I just do it enough to give him a really bad ass headache."

> *Note to self: Don't ever piss this woman off and never, ever move anywhere remotely close to her. Queen is definitely someone I wouldn't want as a neighbor.*

"Sometimes when I get to work, I'll dial my own number and just let the phone ring until the store opens at ten. And one of my other favorite ways to drive him nuts is to play mariachi music real loud."

She then did one of her crazy laughs.

I slowly backed away, wondering if she knew how insane she sounded. I was going to ask if she ever thought of just knocking on his door to asking him to turn the down the music, but figured it was better to not make her upset!

Then as soon as the store opened at ten, I got a call from Judy in Human Resources saying she needed me to cover the Women's Accessories Department until noon. I thought it was an odd request because Von Oostrom has a policy that forbids men from working in women's departments, but Judy said the store was really short of staff this morning and it would just be for a couple of hours.

How difficult could it possibly be selling ladies purses, neck scarfs, or sunglasses? I can do this!

As I got on the escalator and headed to second floor, there was a customer who was waiting and I made my first mistake. I said, "It looks like you are looking for a purse."

A customer immediately set me straight when she said, "Oh honey, purses are so yesterday. Purses were something your mother carried. Today we call them 'handbags.'"

Well, now I know.

So, I guess if I carried a "man purse" it would be called a "manbag?"

I actually went into sticker shock when I saw the prices on some of the women's handbags and accessories. I had no idea women paid those kinds of prices just to spruce up an outfit.

The Handbag Department is right next to Ladies Swimwear and at one point I got a call from Swimwear Manager Joni asking if I would be willing to come to her department for a moment. She said one of her customers was wanting a man's opinion.

I'm a man who definitely has opinions, but I probably shouldn't have remarked that I'd never seen a bikini bottom with "fur" trim on it.

Only apparently the trim wasn't part of the swimsuit. Oops.

Not only did that honest mistake cause me to get slapped, but I received a call to report to Nettie L'Amour's office, where I was written up for "borderline sexual harassment of a customer."

Jeeez Louise, how the heck was I to know that it wasn't fur? It's not like I spend a lot of time looking at women in their bikini bottoms!

And what's this "borderline harassment" crap? Either it is or it isn't.

I guess I'm just lucky I got away with a warning to engage my brain before opening my mouth and wasn't fired.

I'm going to assume I won't be sent to second floor for to cover any women's departments anytime in the future. Although I wouldn't mind collecting the commission on some of those high-end PURSES! Ha!

After lunch I came back to my more familiar surroundings in the men's area where I met Dr. Harris Newgaard, a professor from the University of Wisconsin in Madison. He was shopping for a vest with pockets.

While trying on various vests I casually asked what he teaches at UW and he said he was the Chairman of the East African Studies Department.

"East African Studies, well I need to introduce you to one of my co-workers who is from Zambonika."

"Zambonika?" He looked puzzled. "Now that's a new one even for me. But you know how these African counties are they are always changing their names."

"Oh, you'll enjoy meeting her. She's actually that country's Queen in exile since her parents were killed in a bloody coup."

You could tell from the look on the professor's face that he was definitely intrigued.

We finished our sale and I walked him over the back counter. "Queen, I'd like to introduce you to Professor Harris Newgaard. He's the head of the East African Studies Department at the UW Madison."

They shook hands, but I could tell Queen was nonplussed because she said, "It's nice meeting you, but I need to be going to lunch."

After she quickly departed, I said, "I'm so sorry that was really rude. I would have thought you two would have enjoyed chatting."

The professor laughed. "I hate to break this to you Mike, but there isn't a country in Africa called Zambonika and I'm afraid your coworker is a fraud."

That was no surprise to me, but what he said next, was.

"The reason she made the quick exit was that she and I have known each other for years. We graduated together at Milwaukee West High School in 1982. Her real name is Precious Littlebaby."

"Precious Littlebaby! Shut the front door!"

"I know," he said, "Who the hell names their kid Precious? Especially if your last name is Littlebaby. Oh, she was teased unmercifully about her name, so I can see how she might want to reinvent herself. But a queen she is not!"

I thanked Dr. Newgaard again for his sale and for shedding light on the secret.

When Queen came back from lunch, I must have still been laughing about what I had discovered because she said, "What are you smiling about?"

"Oh, that skunky wig of yours always brings a smile to my face."

She gave me a glare and said, "You better watch out buddy, I could get you written up for borderline sexual harassment. I might need to get my purse and whack you over the head with it."

Obviously, someone had loose lips in the lunchroom. News travels fast at V. O.

It's too bad Kent's on vacation in Europe. I can't wait to tell him about our little Precious Littlebaby.

Chapter 68

Goodbye Kent

Thursday, Noon-9:00 Shift

Today started out like every other. I was excited that Kent was returning from vacation today and rushing to beat the time clock, when suddenly I dropped my lunch bag just inside the employee entrance and got chicken noodle soup all over my shoes, socks, and the carpet!

Wouldn't you know, Nettie L'Amour was standing just inside the door and said, "Triggs, you had better make damn sure you clean that up so other employees aren't tracking it all over the store!"

I shot her a look and snapped, "Can I punch in first? You wouldn't want me to be freaking tardy!"

Without even giving her a chance to respond, I headed to the time clock. I thought I was being discreet when I under my breath I whispered, "Bitch!" But obviously not discreet enough, as the bitch snapped back, "I HEARD THAT!"

After cleaning up my mess I went to put my stuff in my locker when I noticed that Kent's locker door was wide open and was completely empty. That was very odd, given the fact that he usually has so much junk in it that he can hardly get it to close.

When I finally made it down to first floor, I found Queen and Suzanna in tears. They were so upset that my first instinct was to give them a hug but knew I would get hauled before the V. O. sexual harassment court if I did.

"It's Kent," Queen sobbed. "Nettie just had him escorted out of the store by security."

"Kent? Oh, no! What did he do?"

"We don't know," said Suzanna. "All Mr. Krayfisch told us is that if someone calls for Kent, we are supposed to tell them he doesn't work here anymore."

I just knew it couldn't be for theft or anything nefarious like that. He must have gotten a really bad customer complaint. "Has anyone called him to actually find out what happened?"

"We wanted to," Queen started, but she was sobbing with such intensity that she had to stop and blow her nose before she could say more. She finally blurted out, "Krayfisch said we are forbidden to talk to Kent, that it was a 'corporate' decision that is way above our pay grade."

"Well, that little weasel can take his little pay grade chart and shove it sideways up his keister," I responded. "Krayfisch never told me I couldn't talk to Kent, so if I want to call a friend of mine no one is going to stop me!"

I picked up the phone and called Kent's cell number. It immediately went to voice mail and a recording came on saying that his mailbox was full.

I tried all afternoon and evening to reach him but kept getting the full mailbox message. Of course, everybody in the store was calling our department wanting to know what happened but all we could tell them was what we knew, which was nothing.

I finally reached Kent about 10:30 tonight and he sounded surprisingly happy when he picked up. Like maybe too happy—had he been drinking?

He assured me that there was nothing to be worried about, that leaving was his decision. He had accepted a great job offer to go to work for Nordstrom in Chicago as one of their men's sportswear buyers.

"As a courtesy I gave Human Resources my two-week notice," he said, "but when Nettie L'Amour got word she went bat $#!+ ballistic and had me terminated on the spot."

I really had him laughing when I told him the girls in the department had gone through a couple of boxes of Kleenex soaking up tears. "Little buddy, I have to tell you, while I'm sad for our team, I'm happy that you are finally getting your chance to make it in the big city and Nordstrom is such a well thought of company."

Then I told him that late this afternoon L'Amour had already named his replacement and Kent acted kind of shocked.

"Replacement?! You know I can't be replaced in the Men's Department!"

Of course, he was right. Kent Patet was one employee that was absolutely irreplaceable.

"I know that Kent and everyone in the store knows that, but starting at 8 a.m. tomorrow you are being replaced by none other than June La Farge."

I heard a thud. He had fallen off the chair laughing.

"Triggs, you have got to be $#!+ting me! You mean to tell me I'm they're replacing me with that ass-kisser from our Intimate Things and Stuff department?"

"You heard me right pal. You've been replaced by a woman with more hair on her upper lip than you will ever have."

"I know for years you have dreamed of getting this buyer's job, but you're going to miss all the fun stuff that happens on the floor. You can't tell me you won't miss us."

He was still laughing, so I continued.

"Like today, this gentleman came up to the counter complaining about a pubic hair that he had spotted in a hanging Calvin Klein boxer brief. I checked it out and sure enough, stuck in the fly was a short and curly hair."

"Gross!" Kent said. "You know, Triggs, you really need to stop trying on the merchandise and leaving evidence behind after you're done adjusting you hairy junk!"

"You know I'd never do that!" I scoffed.

Kent laughed loudly at my continuing to take him so seriously.

"Anyway, I told him, 'Well sir, you're absolutely right, there is a hair, but I don't have the forensic background to determine if it is in fact a public hair. For all I know it could be a hair from someone's underarm or maybe it fell off someone's beard. As a matter of fact, that's a pretty bushy beard you're sporting, mister. Are sure you didn't give them a big sniff before bringing them over to show me?'

"You could see that the guy was mortified by the thought and left without saying a word."

"Now that you're almost gone, I have to let you in on a secret. A couple of months ago, on your suggestion, I ran a personal ad. You'll never guess who responded to my ad and sent a very risque picture with their response!"

"Nettie L'Amour? NUDE?"

"God no! But almost as good. It was Homer Krayfisch and he was just about as buck naked as you can get. He was wearing a leather jockstrap. And get this, he was handcuffed to his bedposts!"

On hearing that Kent couldn't control his laughter. "Oh my god, oh my god, oh my god! Promise me you will email me that picture…then again it might scar me for life. No, go ahead and send it."

We both had a good laugh before Kent said, "You know Trigsey, you're right. I am going to miss that place. And I'm really doing to miss you."

"I'm going to miss you too, buddy. I didn't even get a chance to say goodbye, Kent."

"Well pal, I'll be back to visit! It's crazy all the stuff that happens on the floor of Von Oostrom's."

Then he added, "One of us should have been writing this stuff down. It would make a heck of a story. But then again, nobody would ever believe it."

Chapter 69

Position Wanted

Saturday, Day Off

After three days I already miss Kent. Life at Von Oostrom just isn't the same without him around.

And with him gone I've come to realize how sick I am of working this retail gig. I keep wondering what else I could be doing with my skills, other than politics or retail. It has given me a reason to think outside the box and start to pursue other options.

I actually had started glancing at the job openings online weeks ago after being so mistreated by my store manager. I had thought I had found a job where I was a perfect match, only to receive an email yesterday saying:

> *After a review of your qualifications and those of the other candidates, we have decided to hire someone whose background and experience more closely match our needs. We appreciate your interest in this position and wish you every success in your job search.*

After receiving that "easy letdown" I was wondering what kind of job would call for a silver-haired, aging preppy who has a sense of style and elegance, a passion for serving guests, works well under pressure, and who looks good in suit or a tuxedo?

I wrestled with the idea all night and was catching up on "The Nanny" before coming up with the solution: I could become a butler!

I think in most cases today they title this job a "personal assistant." But I'm so ready for a change, I'd gladly answer to whatever.

I've always been drawn to butlers. "Batman" (Alfred Pennyworth) or "Richie Rich" (Cadbury) were comic books I read as a child. I enjoy reading murder mysteries where the butler plays a prominent role.

On television I was attracted to shows that had a butler in the family's employ, like "The Addams Family" (Lurch), "Mr. Belvedere," and "Benson." And as I matured, I found my sophisticated tastes were drawn to the butler on "Upstairs Downstairs" (Angus Hudson).

Phileas Fogg had his Passepartout, Daddy Warbucks had Drake, Inspector Jacques Clouseau had his Cato, and "The Birdcage" guys had the FABULOUS Agador Spartacus. Even Jeeves has his own search engine for Pete's sake!

Being a butler would fit me perfectly!

I could be extremely loyal, make travel plans, drive Miss Daisy (I have a clean driving record), do airport runs, walk the dog, and fix meals. Did I mention that I can roll a mean Swedish meatball and bake a mouthwatering apple pie?

I could pick up the laundry at the dry cleaners and make sure the car was always washed. Keep the wine cellar stocked and be trusted not to take a sip. Serve appetizers with panache on very little notice. Even pack luggage and make sure it gets where it needs to go, as my close personal friend Elizabeth Taylor can confirm!

I'm very good with names, am an amazing storyteller, know how to keep a secret, and could accompany the Mrs. or Grandma to the Sheboygan Metro Opera or lunch at the Von Oostrom Tea Room.

And did I mention I have great fashion sense with great industry contacts that could keep my man's closet full of the latest fashions?

In mysteries they say "the butler did it." Well maybe I should do it too. What the hell, I have the day off today. I'll spend my day writing a "Position Wanted" ad that could run in the "Sheboygan Press" and post it on some of the internet job search sites as well.

What have I got to lose? It's a cold, windy, rainy day. I might as well be doing something productive instead of moaning about Kent flying off to his new high-profile gig.

And like they say here in Wisconsin, "The fish aren't going to bite unless they see bait on the hook."

Chapter 70

The Secret

Monday, 8-5 Shift

Could that freaking truck we unloaded this morning have been any bigger? Queen and I had four full carts and two rolling racks of merchandise to get out on the floor. In fact, it took the two of us until 3:00 to finish with all of the stock work.

When we were done my suit looked like a mess, all dusty and smelly. And my shoes were all scuffed up. So, before I headed home, I decided to check in with my friend Leonard, the Von Oostrom shoeshine guy that always has a smile on his face. He still had another hour before he packed up.

"Your shoes sure look beat up," he said immediately. "I don't think I've ever seen them so dirty."

"Well pal, we've never had a load like we had to put out today. It took us over six hours, and we had to help customers while doing it!"

Leonard asked me what I was up to lately and I told him about Kent leaving and how it made me want to find a new job as well.

"Can you keep a secret?" I asked him.

"You know me, Mike. I don't know nothin' about nothin'."

I shared with him my desire to become a butler or personal assistant for someone rich or powerful. And that I had just posted a Position Wanted ad online.

"Mike, you may not believe this, but I have a secret too. I don't tell many people this, but right after high school I was a butler for a rich Atlanta family."

I had no idea! Leonard went on to tell me his father and grandfather had served the family since just after the Civil War on what used to be a plantation.

"Dad always said they treated him more like an employee, not servants or anything. He said they were like family to us, so it was natural that when I graduated from high school my father wanted to train me in his work to take over for him some day."

I love American history and found his story fascinating.

"I just wasn't cut out for it," Leonard said. "When I got my first job I wasn't as lucky as my daddy had been. I didn't really like being bossed around by uppity white folks. I wanted to be my own boss. I left their household and started shining shoes in downtown Atlanta. That led me to eventually work at the first mall department store there, and the rest is history! "

I prodded him to tell me more about his family story of working on a former plantation in the South. He talked about the tough times during his boyhood, the KKK burning a cross at his home, and being trained as a butler in the 1960s, when he was still just treated like one of "the help."

As much as I wanted to hear all the fascinating details, my eyes started to close after the exhausting day of cleaning up the boxes. He brushed my shoes, kept talking, and soon I was dozing off, my mind thinking about the more he talked the more I wanted to make this career changed and become a butler.

Chapter 71

The Personal Assistant

Monday Evening

I heard my telephone ringing when I approached my home and rushed to get the door unlocked to answer it.

"Hello, this is Mike Triggs."

There was a long pause and then I heard, "Mike Triggs? Really? It's, um, Kramer Rockwell."

It had been years since I had seen or talked to Kramer. Early in my political career as a young "hired gun" I had managed Kramer's campaign for the State Senate in Green Bay back in 1988.

For the next twenty minutes we reminisced about how we almost knocked off old Larry McAlpine. We laughed about how I had slept on an army cot in the basement of the campaign headquarters and showered next door at the YMCA. All to keep costs down for the campaign,

Finally, Kramer said, "So Mike, you're probably wondering why I was calling."

"Well," I laughed, "I'm pretty sure you aren't calling for tickets to tour the White House since you've already called in that favor."

"Actually, it's about the classified ad you ran. When I called, I didn't actually expect you to be on the other end of the line until I heard your voice on the phone. While I should have retired a couple years ago, I'm still in the head-hunting business and am representing a high-profile client who is looking to replace a personal assistant who has been with him for the past ten years."

I have to admit that I was as surprised as he was.

"However," he continued, "now that I know that it was you who placed the ad, I am not at all surprised that both my client and I were absolutely blown away with what you wrote. In fact, it's just freaking weird that nearly everything you wrote in your ad was spelled out in my client's job description."

I was not only interested, but now getting excited by what I was hearing.

He continued. "Well, buddy, here's the deal: my client's current personal assistant has worked for him for ten years and will be leaving the first of the month so he's hoping to act quickly to get someone hired and trained before the other guy's last day."

The first of the month? Did he just say he wants to get someone trained in the next couple weeks? Talk about last minute!

"Wait, wait just a minute," I stopped him. "You are kind of catching me off guard. I just walked in the door and haven't even taken off my coat."

He laughed, sounding like it had caught him off guard as well that someone he knew had placed the ad.

"In fact, I have to tell you Kramer, I ran the ad on a lark. I have to know, who's your 'high profile' client? Obviously, he's not from Sheboygan, so where does he live? And what specifically is he looking for? I'm not even sure if I'm qualified for the job!"

"Just listen up," Kramer interrupted. "You're going to want the job. Ironically my client is Ragnar Thoresen, a former college roommate of mine. Of course, you have heard of him because he's a big political donor."

"Heard of him, of course I have. He was one of George H. W. Bush's major donors and was appointed ambassador to one of the Scandinavian countries."

"It was Norway actually," Kramer reminded me. "Marilyn and I had a chance to stay with him and his late wife, Elsa, at the ambassador's residence in Oslo. The guy has made a ton of money in the aeronautics and off-shore oil industries. Let's just say the has more money than he'll ever be able to spend.

"He has homes in Scottsdale, San Diego, a condo in Park City, a penthouse apartment in New York, and spends the summers at his home on Grindstone Lake here in Northern Wisconsin."

My mind was swirling trying to picture what I just heard and I couldn't even respond.

"So, here's the deal," he continued. "If you are interested, he'd like to meet with you on Wednesday."

"Wednesday? The day after tomorrow?"

"Well actually, he's looking at both Wednesday and Thursday. In talking with him, it sounds like this might be more of an audition than a traditional job interview. You don't have to drive clear across the state, he is offering to send his private plane to pick you up in Sheboygan and will be flying you to Hayward. You will be spending the night as his guest at Valhalla on Grindstone Lake."

"Valhalla? Is that a resort?"

"No, it's the name of his home. You will want to Google it. From what I hear this isn't your typical Wisconsin fishing cottage."

I was dumbfounded by this sudden offer. "Oh my God Kramer, of course I'm interested but this is a lot to contemplate. Can I sleep on it?"

"Of course! I'll let the ambassador know that we spoke and that we'll talk again tomorrow to hopefully finalize plans for your trip to Valhalla."

I thanked him for his call and as I hung up the phone all I could think was "Oh My God." In fact, I pinched myself. Was this really happening? Sure enough, the caller ID said "Kramer Rockwell."

I quickly ordered a pizza and spent the next couple of hours learning much as I could about Ragnar Thoresen, Valhalla, Intrepid Aeronautics Industries, and Odin Offshore, Inc.

Tuesday Morning

I had just stepped out of the shower and was toweling off when my phone rang. It was Kramer calling back.

"Hey buddy, Kramer here. I hope I didn't get you up."

"No, not at all. In fact, after sleeping on it I'm really intrigued with the possibility."

"That's terrific! You will need to be at Burrows Aviation at the Sheboygan County Memorial Airport at eight o'clock tomorrow morning where you will be met by his pilot, Skyler. I have to tell you, I know Rags, I mean the ambassador, will be very impressed once he meets you."

Then there was a pause until Kramer's voice changed a bit. "Oh, Mike, there's just one more thing. His three grandkids are staying with him for a couple days and he asked if you might pick up some pajamas for them. His oldest Thor is seven, the middle child Loki is five, and his granddaughter Elsa

232

is almost four. Apparently, he has a Von Oostrom account, so just charge the pajamas to it."

When I got to work, I immediately went to the Children's Department and picked out some super hero jammers for Thor, dinosaur PJs for Loki, and Disney princess pajamas for Elsa. Knowing how I enjoyed unwrapping gifts when I was a kid, I had their gifts wrapped. If it's one thing that Von Oostrom does well, it's their over-the-top gift wrapping.

Needless to say, I had a hard time staying focusing on my job all day with the potential for something really exciting ahead.

Wednesday

When I went to bed last night, I thought that I would probably have trouble sleeping. But the truth is I slept like a baby. Had it not been for the garbage truck outside this morning I would have probably overslept. Thankfully I had packed my bag the night before.

I drove to Burrow Aviation, parked my car, and was met by Ambassador Thoreson's current personal assistant Bryce Underhill, who looked very young for his years of experience and was very attractive. He took me to the jet where I met pilot Skyler Lincoln, a thin African-American who had a relaxed smile on his face that reminded me of Leonard the shoeshine guy.

We climbed the steps and entered the jet. Skyler explained that we would be flying on a Learjet 60SE, which was a seven-passenger plane that oozed luxury. I looked around the cabin and noticed that the jet had fawn-colored leather seats and the cabin was decorated in high gloss Teak wood trim. Very Scandinavian.

I couldn't hold back saying, "Just curious, if I were going to buy one of these, what are they going for?"

Skyler laughed. "I'd have to check with corporate to see if it's for sale. But just guessing, you could probably buy this one used for about $2.25 million. Should I tell my boss I have a buyer that is interested?"

I almost fell over. "Ohhhhh, probably not on my current salary."

As Bryce and I buckled in to get ready for take-off, he explained that our flight to Hayward would be approximately an hour and ten minutes, which was far shorter than the five and a half hours it would have taken me to drive the 346 miles.

Once the wheels were up and we had reached our cruising altitude I heard Skyler announce that we were free to remove our seat belts and move about the cabin.

Before I knew it, Bryce was up and serving me coffee with a cherry Danish from the galley at the front of the cabin.

Once Bryce returned to his seat he said, "So I'm guessing you have lots of questions for me before we arrive at Valhalla."

"I sure do. From what Kramer told me about the job it sure sounds intriguing but I have to ask why you are leaving?"

"Well, I have worked for Ambassador Thoreson ever since his wife Elsa died of pancreatic cancer. Elsa had always kept his life organized and on track. For a couple of months after she was gone, he struggled with trying to keep his home and affairs in order."

I empathized, knowing a number of widowers who had trouble living without their late spouses.

Bryce continued. "At the time I was actually his massage therapist and during the many hours he spent on my table we had developed an amazing rapport. One day when he was bemoaning how his life was spinning out of control he asked if I might be interested in coming to work for him. When he asked if I would become his personal assistant, I had no idea what the job entailed and I don't think he did either. Let's just say it just kind of evolved."

I nodded, feeling that I was unclear as well.

"Looking back," Bryce added, "it was by far the best ten years of my life. But I'm 42 years old and I just think it's probably time to move on. I've taken a job as Head Concierge at the Phoenician Resort in Scottsdale and plan to get back to doing some massage on the side.

"This really is an amazing gig. Should you get the job, I think you'll find the ambassador expects a lot from his staff. But he is a very generous man and understands that if he wants to keep good people, he needs to pay them well and reward them with the time off they need to rebound."

"What are we talking about in terms of hours?" I asked. "And Kramer never actually mentioned a salary."

"Well, I actually live at his estate in a casita on the back of his property in Scottsdale and have a room above the boathouse at Valhalla, which is part of my compensation package. Consequently, I haven't had to buy groceries or pay rent for the past ten years. That perk has allowed me to squirrel away a substantial portion of what I have earned."

That certainly intrigued me. But then he added, "The downside to living on site means you are at his beck and call at all times of the day and night. It's not everyone that can provide that kind of service."

"Oh, listen," I responded, "I've worked for politicians. I remember the governor calling at one in the morning, saying he wants something on his desk at 5:30 a.m., and he didn't care if I had to work all night to make sure it was there."

"Well, if that's the case it sounds like politicians and business execs are cut from the same cloth," Bryce quipped. "The nice thing about the job is that no day will ever be the same. You could be fixing appetizers to serve lakeside on the cook's day off or be responsible for taking his schnauzers, Tristan and Isolde on walks. So, I sure hope you like cooking and dogs!"

I nodded and before I could respond that I'm a real dog lover, he had gone on to say I would need to make sure the cars were always washed and that the boats or other watercraft were gassed and ready to go.

"When his grandkids are visiting, I find my inner Mary Poppins comes out reading books, playing games, and watching movies. Ambassador Thoreson loves his grandkids and showers them with lots of attention and gifts."

"Yes," I said, "he asked me to bring some gifts for the kids."

"I know. The interesting thing is that the gifts are never from him. He wants the kids to think that the gifts are from the housekeeper, gardener, cook, or me. I haven't quite figured out why he does it, unless he wants the children to love and respect the staff as much as he does. So, when the pajamas you brought are presented, I'm quite confident that he will say they are from you."

I made notes while Bryce was talking, which he picked up on. "I see you are taking notes. The ambassador doesn't like to say things twice. Note taking and follow-through is a good thing."

"What does he like to do for fun?" I asked.

"He's a voracious reader, he bikes, likes to go hiking, fishing, he's a pinball fanatic, and loves downhill and cross-country skiing.

I saw the opportunity and jumped in saying, "Wow, those are all things I enjoy! In fact, a couple of years ago I skied the Birkebeiner Ski Race in Hayward."

"The only time the ambassador returns to Valhalla during the winter months is during Birkebeiner week. All of the guestrooms are filled with skiing friends from all the world. I think I mentioned he loves to entertain."

"It's good to hear you enjoy those activities because you'll get many opportunities to ski, bike, hike, and fish with him, since he never likes doing anything alone."

I smiled picturing myself next to the Ambassador on the slopes.

"He also loves talking about politics. I can't tell you the number of times we have stayed up into all hours of the night talking about campaigns, elections, and public policy.

"Of course," Bryce continued, "you know he has always been known as a big-time Republican, but I will let you in on a little secret: in recent years he has felt his party has moved so far to the right that he has found himself donating more and more to candidates of the other party. And frankly, I wouldn't be surprised if one of these days he ends up switching his registration and becomes either an Independent or Democrat."

"I feel kind of the same way about the party," I added. "As a moderate, pro-choice, gay man, it has become harder and harder to call myself a Republican. I sure hope being gay won't be an issue."

"Oh, heaven's no. His son Erik is gay. Erik and his partner Richard are the parents of the grandchildren you will soon meet.

"I'm also gay and I sing with the Phoenix Gay Men's Chorus. He always makes sure I have every Monday night off for practice and each year he has allowed me to host an annual pool party for the chorus at the end of our concert season."

I smiled.

"Oh, and one other thing," Bryce said. "I sure hope you enjoy opera. His wife had been a past President of the Phoenix Opera Guild and opera was a passion they shared. I think you will find that when he is home opera can be heard throughout the house."

That didn't surprise me. "I gathered that anyone who would name his dogs Tristan and Isolde who have to be an opera fan. I saw my first opera when I was a student in Vienna in 1975 and immediately became an opera aficionado."

That hour-long flight went by very quickly and before we knew it, we were on the ground, taking the short 15-minute drive to Valhalla.

I almost wish we had been in the car longer because I had arrived at peak season for fall colors. Several times I asked if we could pull over so I could take some pictures, but Bryce assured me that the colors would only get better as we got closer to Grindstone Lake.

Everywhere I looked could have been a postcard. The oaks and maples were ablaze with the most radiant shades of red and orange. The ash, basswood, and birch were a deep rich gold and yellow hues. When paired with the spruce and white pine's lush forest greens it was a simply breathtaking drive. It was like a dream.

Only God could have created something this beautiful!

As we made our final turn off of County Highway K, I couldn't help but notice a rough-hewn sign that said, "Velkommen til Valhalla." And there before me the sat largest log home I had ever set eyes upon. "Oh my God," I exclaimed, "this is the most beautiful log home I have ever seen!"

Bryce laughed and said, "This is the back side of the house, wait until you see it from the lake."

We entered through the back door and were immediately greeted by Ambassador Thorsen and his two schnauzers, Tristan and Isolde, who seemed very excited to meet me.

While I had seen pictures of him when doing my research, it was now obvious they were taken fifteen to twenty years ago when he was ambassador. But like a fine wine, his good looks certainly improved with age. In fact, it was uncanny how much he resembled Peter Graves from the old Mission Impossible TV series.

After he welcomed me and our introductions were out of the way, he asked if I would care for something to drink. "I have ice tea, a glass of wine, and I'm certain there is a fresh pot of coffee. I also have some delightful Wisconsin pale ales or a Leinenkugel Oktoberfest."

"I think I'll have a Leinie!"

Bryce left with the schnauzers and then immediately returned alone with bottles of the Oktoberfest brew and a couple of frosty beer glasses. Tristan got a little excited and hopped in front of Bryce, causing him to stumble a bit and slosh the brew.

"You dogs! Go lay down and leave us alone! Capisce?"

I thanked him for the otherwise perfect head on the beer he just poured and said, "Bryce, even with the dogs running around, you balanced all that like a Hofbräuhaus beer maid."

"You should see me balancing eight steins while wearing a dirndl!" We all had a good laugh, which broke up the tension that I always feel when walking into a job interview.

Ambassador Thorsen motioned for me to sit in one of the wingback chairs by the massive granite fireplace at the end of the great room. I couldn't help but notice that American and Norwegian flags were centered to the right and left of the fireplace, with a giant moose head mounted in the middle.

As I sipped my beer I said, "It looks like you must be a hunter."

"Oh heaven's no. I don't even own a gun. Sadly, about six years ago that beauty got caught in a steel trap in the woods and had to be put down by my property caretakers. I was so saddened to see that majestic animal tragically taken by one of those damn traps that I asked one our local taxidermists to preserve the head so he might live on forever here at Valhalla."

After finishing our beers, the ambassador showed me around his 4,600 square foot summer home. It was fascinating to hear that the house was constructed from timber logged in British Columbia and transported by train to Thunder Bay, where it was loaded onto a Lake Superior freighter and the logs were ultimately transported to this location by truck from Duluth.

The dining room had a fireplace of its own and a massive iron chandelier that was constructed to look like it was made of deer antlers. It was all finely crafted metal by a female artist in Sedona, Arizona. She had also crafted the iron work on the back door, the property's fencing, and the beautiful iron gates we had driven through.

The ambassador said that the dining room table was made of white pine, hand crafted and imported from Norway. "While it usually seats ten, I have additional leaves for the table and chairs to accommodate a party of twenty-four."

Twenty-four?! That must be quite a dinner party.

"We only do that during Birkebeiner week in February when all eight guest bedrooms and the bunkhouse in the basement are occupied. And we always do that dinner smorgasbord style, which is easier to serve."

Then we walked in the kitchen and I immediately noticed it was massive. In fact, the kitchen was bigger than most starter homes. It was there, in the kitchen that I got to meet housekeeper Bridgett and Millie the cook, who told me the French La Cornue eight-burner range had been inspired by the late Julia Child.

That kitchen would be every foodie's dream come true. It had everything you would ever need. And what a shame it's only used about five and a half months of the year.

The master suite was on the opposite end of the great room. It had a masculine look and feel. The bedroom was decorated in the same rich red, orange, yellow, and green colors we had seen earlier on our drive. There was an exquisite rustic wood king size four-poster bed with two identical miniature beds for Tristan and Isolde near the fireplace hearth.

As hard as it was to believe, his en suite bathroom was bigger than the bedroom and walk-in closet combined. It was huge.

The ambassador said the Kohler Company, located just outside of Sheboygan, had actually designed his bathroom and spa. The bathroom was on one end and the spa on the other. How many people have a bathroom equipped with a massage table, a steam shower, a soaking tub, free weights, a treadmill and other exercise equipment?

Ambassador Thorsen said, "This is where Bryce works his massage magic. I don't suppose you do massage, do you?"

"I'm not professionally trained. But I've spent lots of time on massage tables over the years and I know what I like and what feels good. I've been told I give a pretty good back rub and foot massage."

He smiled and said, "Maybe I could sign you up for some classes."

We walked outside and the dogs followed us. I could see what Bryce was talking about. The view of the house was nothing short of amazing. "I can see why you called it Valhalla."

The ambassador said there was 1400 feet of shoreline on the property with a beautiful sand beach. I could see three docks, a skiing boat, a fishing boat, a pontoon, and several small water craft.

I pointed and said, "Is that what I think it is?"

He smiled as said, "It sure is! It's a Finnish sauna that I brought over and had reassembled at lakeside. You can't see it from this angle but it has its own dock that you can run out and dive into the lake after your sauna. We've even cut a hole in the ice for dips in the lake after taking a sauna during Birke week."

I shook my head and said, "I don't know about that."

He smiled. "Maybe after dinner I'll have Bryce fire it up and we can all take a sauna. It's always a nice way to wind down after a long day."

I smiled.

"Oh, by the way," he added. "Bryce's apartment is located above the boathouse. It's only about 900 square feet but during the summer he doesn't spend much time inside his apartment."

The ambassador turned and led us back to the house. "We need to go inside and meet the grandkids. Since it's a little nippy out today I'm guessing they are on third floor in the game room. They love it up there. We've got pinball machines, a little two-lane bowling alley, and toys galore. Let's go meet them."

He pulled out a whistle out of his breast pocket, put it to his lips 'weet-whoohweetweetwoohwoohwooh." It was almost like the scene where Captain von Trapp blew the whistle in "The Sound of Music," but instead of the children suddenly appearing, Tristan and Isolde came running from the shoreline where they had been watching some ducks.

When they lined up at his feet, he reached in his pant pocket and rewarded them with a treat. "Those little German dogs never learned the word 'come' but they know when they hear the whistle there is a treat waiting for them."

I chuckled and said, "I'll try to remember that."

We went back in the house and climbed the ten-foot-wide staircase that split in the middle with steps continuing up to the right and left. Come to think of it, it also reminded me of "The Sound of Music" where the von Trapp children ascended singing "So Long, Farewell."

While climbing we took the stairs to the left and at the top of the stairs the ambassador said, "there are four guest rooms on each side. They are all named after forest animals. You will be sleeping in my favorite the Wolf Room, which is the first room on the right."

As we entered, I could see my overnight bag and the grandchildren's gifts were sitting on a bench at the foot of the bed. "I hope you don't wake up tonight and get scared by that ferocious looking timber wolf in the picture. Why don't you grab the gifts, since you know which is which I'll let you give them to the kids."

We climbed the stairs to the third floor. Before opening the door, he said, "I've had the room sound proofed so guests aren't disturbed by the pinball machines or children screeching."

Upon entering the room, the children came running screaming, "Farfar, Farfar." He turned to me and said, "It's Norwegian for grandfather."

"Oh, it's the same in Swedish."

"Children this is my friend Mike. He will be staying with us this evening. Mike, this is my oldest grandson, Thor."

He extended his hand and said, "Pleased to meet you Mr. Mike."

"And this is my little Loki, he can be a little mischievous at times."

The middle boy also shook my hand and said, "Hello there Mr. Mike. I like your bow tie."

"And this is my little Princess Elsa."

As I bent down to meet her, she gave me a hug.

The ambassador added, "That was my wife's name so I was so pleased when my son and his partner chose that for her name."

"Well kids, guess what! Mr. Mike has brought some presents for you."

I gave them each their gifts and after thanking me, we watched them frantically rip open the wrapping paper. Who knew kids could get that excited about pajamas? In fact, before I knew it little Elsa was changing into hers.

Tristen and Isolde looked rather disappointed that they didn't get any gifts. But they did have fun playing in the wrapping paper.

Loki said, "Farfar, can you and Mr. Mike stay and play pinball with us?"

"Not right now Loki, but maybe later."

Before leaving their play room the children gave me a group hug and again thanked me for their PJs.

As he closed the door the ambassador said, "I hate to tell you this Mike, but I have a meeting that has come up with the DNR this afternoon. It shouldn't take more than a couple of hours. However, I thought maybe while I am gone you might be able to make one of those famous apple pies you wrote about. I'm sure Millie has plenty of apples and a Pillsbury Pie Crust in the refrigerator."

"I'd be glad to make a pie," I said. "But I have to tell you, I make my own crusts."

"Wow! Millie doesn't even do that. I'm sure you'll have fun in the kitchen. I'll see you in a couple hours."

I went to my room to change into something more comfortable before heading downstairs to do some baking.

As I walked into the kitchen, Millie said, "I hear you are you going to be baking an apple pie for tonight's dinner."

"Gee, word must get around quickly in these parts of Wisconsin. I just found out myself a few minutes ago."

She laughed, "Actually the ambassador told me yesterday that he was going to ask you to do that so I picked up some apples at our local orchard. I bought some Courtlands, Honeycrisps, and Granny Smiths. I hope one of those kinds will be okay for you."

"Why don't I use a couple of each. I always use six apples in my pies."

She said, "The pantry is on your left, spices are in the top cabinet to the right of the oven, and the refrigerator is on your right. You should find everything you need but if you don't, just ask."

"I just hope I don't get in your way," I said.

"Oh, heaven's no! During Birke week I bring in about a half dozen ladies to help out. There's so much room in here we never bump elbows."

In the pantry I found a big mixing bowl, measuring cups, a pie dish, flour, and sugar. I was about to start measuring some flour when Millie said, "Oh honey, I forgot to tell you I picked up a Pillsbury Pie Crust at the market. It's in the refrigerator on the second shelf."

"Oh, that was nice of you Millie, but I always make my own crust."

She gave me a sneer that reminded me of Nettie L'Amour and sarcastically quipped, "Well aren't you just the professional little baker man. The next thing I know I'll be replaced too!"

"Come on, Millie," I scoffed. "From what I've heard you are an amazing cook and definitely irreplaceable. I wouldn't worry about your job if I were you. Pies are just my thing."

When I was getting butter for the crusts, I decided to add an extra stick of butter and some more flour so I would have enough dough for an extra crust for some appetizers.

As I was mixing up my dough, Millie remarked, "That looks like you're using way too much butter."

I laughed and said, "I'm kind of like Paula Dean, you can never use too much butter."

I could tell she didn't like having someone else in her kitchen and snapped, "Well, I always use Crisco when I'm baking."

I ignored her comment and went about forming the dough into three equal sized balls, rolled them in wax paper, and placed them in the refrigerator to chill for an hour.

As I started to peal the apples I said, "Millie these apples look amazing."

Either she didn't hear me or was ignoring me, pissed that I wasn't using Crisco. I cut up the apples, added the white and brown sugar, cinnamon, nutmeg, a dash of salt, a couple of tablespoons of flour, some corn starch, a couple of extra tablespoons of butter, and some lemon juice to keep the apples from turning brown. All the while, I could tell I had two eyes watching every move I made.

When I finished my pie filling, I got out a block of Gruyere cheese and started to grate it.

Millie said, "I've never heard of putting cheese in apple pie."

"Oh, you haven't? My mom always says 'Apple pie without the cheese, is like a kiss without the squeeze.'"

She chuckled and said, "Well, let me tell you, it's been a long time since this old girl has had a kiss or a squeeze."

I smiled, hoping that wasn't an invitation but just meant that she was relaxing with me a bit more.

"I saw a mini muffin pan in the pantry and thought I'd make some tiny quiches for appetizers. Say, what kind of smoked fish is that in the refrigerator?"

She made a face and said, "It's smoked walleye. Don't tell me you're thinking of putting it in the pie!"

"No, actually I was going to put it in the quiche," I told her. "Can't say I have ever used smoked walleye before, but I've used smoked salmon so it's worth a try."

She rolled her eyes.

After mixing all my eggs, cheese, mayonnaise, milk, and flour, I added some chopped green onions and the smoked walleye, then put it in the refrigerator to chill.

I rolled out my first crust, put it in the pie pan, poured in my apple mixture, rolled another crust and placed it on top, fluted the crust, sprinkled it with sugar, set my timer, and put my pie in the oven.

Then I rolled out my third crust and used a water glass to cut out little circles for my individual mini quiches. After finishing, I put the muffin tin in the refrigerator to chill. I'd wait until just before dinner to pop them in the oven to bake.

The buzzer went off just as I finished cleaning up my mess. I took the pie out of the oven and I couldn't have been happier with the way it looked.

"Well sir, I have to tell you I am very impressed," Millie said. "And to think you did that without ever looking at a recipe."

Just then the ambassador walked into the kitchen and said, "I could smell that pie the minute I walked in the house. Do I get to have a piece now or do I have to wait until dessert?"

Millie said, "You better wait. Pies are always better if you let them cool down for a couple of hours."

He looked disappointed but said, "Mike we have lots more to talk about regarding the job. Can I get you another Leinenkugel?"

We headed into the other room and while he was stoking the fire the dogs jumped up in my lap. I asked, "Is it okay if the dogs are on the furniture?"

"Oh, heavens yes. They can be anywhere they want except my bed. That's where I draw the line."

The more he told me about the job, the more interested I became and the more apparent it became that Tristan and Isolde had a new friend.

After a couple of hours of chatting, we finished up and he said, "Well dinner is at six, so you'll have some time now to relax a few minutes before we eat."

"How about I take these two for a walk?" I volunteered.

"Oh, I'm sure they will enjoy that!"

The dogs loved the exercise and at 5:30 I came down to put my mini quiches in the oven. Once they were done everything was ready.

When dinner was served it took some convincing to get the kids to try the quiche, but it was even better tasting than I had hoped. And I really hit a home run with my apple pie. Little Elsa said this is the best pie she had ever eaten.

After dinner the kids got in their new pajamas and I read them what seemed like ten stories before it was their bedtime. But before sending them up that grand staircase, I sang them a couple of verses of "So Long, Farewell."

"Well, Mr. Triggs, let me tell you--between the quiche, the pie, your stories, and that song, you have made quite an impression on not only me, but the grandkids and the dogs as well. What do you say we head out to the sauna for a good sweat? I told Bryce that we would meet him out there as soon as the kids were in bed. It should be nice and toasty in there by now."

There's nothing like sitting naked with your potential employer during a job interview! But what a delightful evening it was in that ten-by-ten-foot Finnish sauna, talking about state and national politics. About three or four times we got so hot we had to jump in the lake before returning for more political talk.

Finally, the ambassador said, "I don't know about you, but I've had enough. Let's toss some lake water on those ashes and call it a night."

What a day and night it had been. I knew I was going to sleep well tonight.

Thursday Morning

I was sleeping like a baby until I was awakened by a "woof." It wasn't the howl of a timber wolf but I thought maybe I was dreaming.

Then I heard it again, this time it seemed like it was coming from the hallway outside my door. I got out of bed to open the door and there sat Tristen and Isolde. They must have thought I was inviting them to join me because they rushed in and jumped up on the bed, which I knew was against house rules.

We cuddled for a while and they both got petted. But try as I might, I couldn't get Isolde to stop woofing. Finally, I decided she must need to go for a walk. So, I got dressed, went downstairs where their leashes were hanging by the door, and took them out.

We walked and walked and walked. Of course, Tristen lifted her leg on the first bush but do you think little bitch would pee? She would get into position and then she would be distracted by a bird. The next time she squatted she saw a squirrel she wanted to chase. We must have been out for forty-five minutes before she finally decided to do her duty.

When we finally got back to the house, I could smell coffee and hear people talking. I followed the dogs to the kitchen where we were met by Ambassador Thoreson and Millie.

"I see the dogs must have gotten you up," he said. "When I hit the snooze alarm, they must have decided they could get their new friend to take them out."

"Oh, they did, but I'm actually an early riser and it was a beautiful morning for a walk on the path through the woods. We even saw a herd of deer and the dogs chased a raccoon up a tree."

"Well pour yourself a cup of coffee Mike," he said. "We have some things we need to chat about before you head back to Sheboygan."

I got my coffee and he led me back into the great room where we took a seat by the fireplace.

"Mike, I want you to know what a pleasure it has been to meet and spend some time with you."

"Oh, it's been my pleasure."

"This has been a real challenge to find someone to fill Bryce's position. After being with me for the past ten years I've come to the conclusion that I will never be able to truly replace him, but nevertheless I need someone in his place quickly.

"I've interviewed five individuals, of which you are one. It was obvious from the start that the two women I interviewed were more interested in eventually becoming my wife than the personal assistant that I need, so I have ruled them out of consideration."

That made sense to me and I smiled as he continued.

"The other two men bring a great deal of experience to the table. One of them has worked for a professional colleague of mine for 19 years and the other has been Senator Wilfred Easton's butler at his home in Savannah, Georgia."

My smile went away, knowing now what the competition was.

Is this when he tells me that I was one of many qualified candidates but that he was going in another direction?

"And then there was you," he said. "You have an amazing background in politics and customer service, with a warm and engaging personality. But as you might expect, when comparing the experiences that the other two gentlemen have as a personal assistant and a butler, you are clearly are not what I was looking for when I began this job search."

Oh, no.

My eyes started to tear a bit and my lip was quivering as I readied myself for the big letdown.

He continued, "This was a tough decision, Mike."

I knew it was because I couldn't help but notice tears were starting to form in his eyes as well.

"Michael, I had to make a decision quickly, and..." He took a handkerchief out of his pocket and dabbed his tears. "Ultimately, I watched the way you engaged my staff, charmed my grandkids with your stories and song, and how my dear pets took to you. Ultimately, those were the things that made me decide you are the most important one to me and I'd like to offer you the job. I hope you will say yes!"

I wasn't sure I had actually heard what I just heard; I was so ready for a letdown. My mouth was open but nothing came out.

Yippee! My dreams have come true!

The ambassador continued. "Oh, and let me tell you. That pie of yours really sealed the deal. Millie and I had the last two pieces this morning while you were walking the dogs, and even she was blown away with your culinary talents. Elsa was right. That was the best Apple pie any of us has ever eaten!"

Thank you Paula Dean! An extra stick of butter never hurts!

"So do you accept the position?" he asked.

My tears were now running down my face at a rapid clip. I reached across, shook his hand, and said, "Yes! Of course! I'd be delighted to come to work for you!"

He stood and gave me a hug. "Welcome! Now let's get you some breakfast and back to Sheboygan. You've got some packing to do because I'd like you to start a week from Monday."

Oh my gosh! I've got to turn in my notice and pack up my place and say goodbye to everyone at work!

During breakfast the ambassador said, "You know, we never talked about salary or benefits. You might want to reconsider when you hear what I was thinking."

"Well, go ahead lay all your cards out on the table."

"I'm not sure what you are making now…"

I interrupted, "Oh I'm sure whatever you are offering is more than I'm making now."

He laughed and said, "You haven't heard what I was thinking."

"Trust me, I'm currently making $9.50 an hour and 1% commission, it has to be better than that!"

He acted surprised and said, "Wow! I had no idea your commission rate was so low. But yes, I was prepared to beat that. I was thinking of starting you at an annual salary of $85,000. Of course, that would also include the Casita in Arizona and the boathouse apartment here at the lake. Bryce will also be relinquishing the Honda Fit he drives on his last day. It's a couple years old but once the lease runs out, we could make a change if you'd like to drive something different. After you have worked for six-months, we can renegotiate your salary."

My jaw dropped and I kind of stammered as I said, "Yes, I think that will work for me."

"If it's alright with you, I'll have my attorney draw up a contract. I'll have her email that and the other insurance and 401k information in a couple days."

"Since Bryce has already moved into his new condo in Phoenix, we'll have all of your personal possessions moved to Arizona. My secretary Emily will work with you and the movers.

"But for now, I'll have Bryce quickly show you around the boathouse apartment where you will be living next summer. Then once you are packed, I'll meet you back in the great room and you can say goodbye to Bridgett, Millie and the grandkids.

I was a little disappointed when I saw that the boathouse apartment was a typical Wisconsin cabin. It was actually kind of shabby. I guess Bryce was one of those gay guys who didn't get the "decorating gene." Of course, after being a guest at Valhalla, any other place on the lake is going to look a little shabby.

It didn't take me long to pack my overnight bag and say my goodbyes to Millie and Bridgett. The kids, on the other hand were not as easy.

Thor said, "I hear you're going to be the new Bryce."

I laughed, "Well I'm going to try. But those are some mighty big shoes to fill."

It was nice knowing that the two little ones didn't want me to leave. I gave them all a hug and the schnauzers got one last petting.

Finally, I said goodbye to the ambassador, and thanked him for the opportunity he was giving me to come to work for him.

"Oh, it was my pleasure. I just know this is going to work out well for all of us. With that, I'll see you a week from Monday in Arizona."

We shook hands, then Bryce and I got in the car and headed to the airport.

While driving, Bryce told me how happy he was that I had made the final cut.

"I was sure he was going to hire that senator's butler. I wish you could have seen what an ass kisser the guy was during his interview. He certainly had done his research and knew every button of the ambassador's to push. And he knew just the right words to say in that syrupy sweet Southern accent. But I didn't trust him."

I laughed and said, "Oh Bryce. tell me what you really think about the guy!"

"Seriously Mike. Everything about him screamed smarmy. He was just a big fat smarm ball. Then you came along and the whole equation changed."

"Well, I must admit it appears I've got one hell of an adventure ahead of me."

"You'll do just fine and if you ever have any questions, you've got my number."

Once we arrived at the airport, we were met by Skyler's big smile. "It looks like a beautiful day for a flight to Sheboygan. I see you are going to be my only passenger this flight."

I turned to Bryce and said, "What? You're not going?"

He winked and said, "Actually there is no place I rather fly to than Sheboygan. But we are in the process of closing down Valhalla for the winter and there is a lot of work to do in the next couple of days. Just enjoy the flight. It isn't often that you get a chance to fly solo."

As I climbed the stairs and turned to wave goodbye, Bryce shouted, "Don't worry about the salary. By the end of the year, he will bump you up to triple digits."

Triple digits! Wow! That's something I could only dream of. I gave him a thumbs up and boarded the plane.

Skyler gave me headphones to use with the plane's music system and told me to put my feet up and relax. It wasn't long all before we were in the air and Skyler announced we were at cruising altitude.

The colors outside my left window were a magnificent patch work of reds, yellows, orange and green leaves, dotted with blue water lakes, and an occasional Wisconsin small town water tower or grain elevator poking through the trees. It was so serine watching the kaleidoscope of colors that I felt myself wanting to doze off. But I couldn't go to sleep, there was so much beauty outside the jets window to absorb. I had to stay away and soak it all in.

I can't go to sleep. I have so much to think about. How do I tell Nettie L'Amour, Queen, the rest of the crew, and my cherished customers that I'm leaving?

Putting my headphones on and plugging them in, I flipped through the channels until I came upon a Broadway station that was playing "Climb Every Mountain." A fitting end to a magical trip.

Next on the channel was an instrumental version of "Somewhere Over the Rainbow," one of my favorite songs. I closed my eyes to think about "If happy little bluebirds fly beyond the rainbow, why oh why can't I...."

While listening to the soft music the ever-present whir of the jet's engines and the gentle vibration in the cabin seat finally got the best of me, and I soon found myself lulled into a deep, deep sleep.

Chapter 72

You Can't Make This $#!t Up

Monday, 6 p.m.

All of a sudden, I heard a loud snap and felt a gentle tapping on the toes of my shoes.

Not yet fully awake, I rubbed my eyes, slowly looked to my right and left, then asked, "Where am I?"

My eyes started to focus and all of a sudden, I recognized Leonard Jackson, the Von Oostrom shoeshine guy. What was he doing on my private jet?

"Listen buddy you had quite a snooze there. You've been asleep for almost an hour. You're lucky I didn't have any other customers the past sixty-minutes."

My head was still trying to figure out what was going on. I thought I was in an airplane contemplating my new job when in truth I was back at good old Von Oostrom's.

"I wish I didn't have to wake you up Mike, but I'm done with my shift."

What? I had been dreaming for the past hour and Leonard was just sitting there waiting for me to wake up? But it all seemed so real!

I fumbled around in my pocket, took out a ten, apologized for falling asleep on him while he was talking about his family heritage, and told him to keep the change.

Then who would show up at that exact moment but commandant Nettie L'Amour, and that douchebag Devin Krayfisch at her side. I knew immediately I was back at good old V. O.

"Mr. Triggs, security caught you on camera sleeping away the past hour in the shoeshine chair for every customer to see. We have it all on tape."

Krayfisch added, "You know the Von Oostrom policy about employees always presenting a good public face for the company. Even though you had finished your shift you should never be seen asleep on the sales floor!"

I didn't know what to say. I still thought I was going to be a personal assistant to a rich ambassador!

Nettie continued, "I want you to report to my office first thing tomorrow morning so I can write you up. This will certainly go in your file!"

Oh, no, not again.

'And tomorrow morning we can also discuss your apparent need to retake Mr. Krayfisch's orientation class. It's very apparent you need a refresher course in how we operate here at Von Oostrom."

You mean go right back to where I started? I don't think I could survive that again!

Then Krayfisch spoke up: "And tardiness will not be tolerated! Capisce?"

No, no, no! All this past year working I've been working my tail off and now they want me to be treated like a retail newbie!

As the two walked away, I thanked Leonard, shook my head, and quietly said to myself, "I've got to write a book about this...you can't make this $#!t up!"

* * *

If you enjoyed my book, please consider leaving a rating and/or review on Goodreads.com, Amazon or wherever you purchased this book.

You can follow me on my *Mike Triggs Author* pages on Facebook and Instagram or contact me at MikeTriggsAuthor@gmail.com.

Acknowledgements

You Can't Make This $#!+Up! has been a work in process since the day I took a retail job selling men's furnishings in 1994. As jaw-dropping events occurred over my time on the sales floor, I would jot down notes on index cards and file them away with the thought that one day I might write a book because I definitely had a story to tell.

When furloughed from my job during the Covid pandemic in 2020, I decided to use my time off doing something productive and forced myself to write for three hours a day. After hundreds of hours in front of the computer, I turned a dream of writing a book into a manuscript. And now it's being published.

All of the stories that appear between the covers are based on actual events, although I have taken the creative liberty of doing some embellishing along the way. With the exception of myself, my retail mentor and friend Kent Patet, and a few well-known names, the characters and institutions that appear in the book are purely fictional. Composite characteristics, altered timelines, and fabricated locations are used. Any resemblance to actual persons, living or dead, and locations is purely coincidental.

During my time in retail, I was blessed to have had some of the best managers imaginable. Unlike the fictitious Nettie L'Amour, who had it in for me from day one, Erik Nordstom, Brent Harris, James Bonner, Jim Mersnetser, David Bird, Carla Lohn, Sheryl McCormick, Mary Kelly, Laura Neubauer, Brooke White, Trisha Moeller, Traci McGowan, Lisa Vetter, Jamie Truhlsen and Jacky Chase all gave me the opportunity to be myself while growing my retail clientele.

I also love and appreciate the men and women whom I have worked on the sales floor. At times it must have been difficult to endure my mood swings, outbursts of laughter, quirky habits, and hearing me retell the same crazy stories over and over again.

Lamar Allen, Dee Apale, Maureen Sullivan Bauer, Roberta Bay, Jan Booher, Maryjo Brady, Terresa Chavez, Dan Burns, Mary Beth Carlson, Tracy Clemmons, Ruth Chrisler, Ann Gortmaker, Christine Davis, Christopher Dean, Stephanie Esping, Pamela Carter Gilbert, Michael Grey, Gail Mangold Gunderson, Abby Hakim, Christopher Hanson, Kate Kennedy Hartkemeyer, Betsy Hibbs, John Keibel, Dennis Kester, Skip Kilbourne, Michelle Kvasnik, Kim Lowry, Jill Lutgens, Marissa Magario, Cindy Mao, Kelly Mencel, Rebecca Noel, Dennis O'Borski, Christine Papadopoulos, Kent Patet, Leah Verrant Rahn, Laura Smith, Amanda Stahl, Beverly Boes Steffes, Jane and Gary Stephens, Nettie Stiles, Isaac Thompson, Kimberly Upshaw, Josh Ven Huizen, Logan Walsh and Sam Wright. You are all the best of the best!

If by chance I somehow forgot to include anyone on this expansive list cut me a break, I'll be 69 years old in a couple months and my memory isn't what it once was.

I must also say that I have been blessed to have some of the most wonderful customers who have shopped with me during my career in retail. I wish I could mention all of you by name. However, several definitely deserve a special "Thank You". Cathy and Paul Tieszen, Kimberly and Pierce Wittnebel and Molly and Charlie Adams have all brought a huge smile to my face each and every time they walked through my department. You are more than just customers you have truly become very special friends.

Steve Winzenburg, thanks for putting Tales from Trigsey on the air and for the countless hours you spent editing and collaborating on this book. It would not have been possible without you.

Thank you also to my editors and publishing specialists at Friesen Press who read my manuscript and guided this first-time author on a path to publication. Jamie Ollivier, whatever they are paying you, it's not enough. From our first call you gave me hope when over fifty other publishers and agents were not willing to give me a chance.

I'm also grateful for two special women from my childhood: Lula Cook, my local librarian and Sunday School Teacher who taught me to love reading and Helen Ducommun, my Junior High English teacher who helped me realize that I could be a better writer if I just exerted a little more effort.

Jahn Curren, Mary Kelly, Maryjo Brady, Suzanne Flaig, Susan Sernett Johnson, Sharon Pilmer, Kim Sunner, Tom Hillock, Kimberly Upshaw, Jill Vujovich-Laabs, Jeffrey Vaughn, Jacqueline Williams and Ralph Wilson thank you for reading my manuscript and offering your thoughts prior to publication.

I will forever be grateful to parents, Vince and Eileen Triggs, for lovingly supporting and encouraging me to follow my dreams, even when it often meant taking a less traveled path. I just regret that my dad did not live long enough to be able to hold my book in his hands.

And finally, I need to thank Rick Wade, my husband, partner, soul mate and best friend who has been at my side for the past 24 years. I love you sweetheart!

9 781039 154537